MW00643713

BURN
OUT

BOOKS BY JOSHUA HOOD

BURN OUT

JOSHUA HOOD

BLACK
STONE
PUBLISHING

Printed in the United States of America

First edition: 2024
ISBN 978-1-6651-0961-1
Fiction / Action & Adventure

Version 1

Blackstone Publishing
31 Mistletoe Rd.
Ashland, OR 97520

www.BlackstonePublishing.com

To my wife, Amy, who married a cop but believed in a dreamer.
I love you and am forever in your debt.

PROLOGUE

LAGUNA INN

Eureka, California

Mikey Boone drove into town at midnight, his gray eyes scouting the shadowed alleyways and darkened storefronts that clung to downtown Eureka like a shroud. The traffic light at the end of the block blinked red, and he slowed at the crosswalk, the Colt 1911 holstered beneath his faded flannel shirt digging into his hip.

Adjusting the pistol, he checked the map on his cell phone, and when the light turned green, he continued east on Second Street.

Nestled on California's famed Redwood Coast, five hours north of San Francisco, Eureka was a study in contrasts. By day it was a postcard-perfect beach town. A place where tourists spent their time out on the bay or snapping selfies in front of the stately Victorians that lined the streets of Old Town. But once darkness fell, Eureka's laid-back vibe turned sinister and the tourists retreated to the safety of their upscale B and Bs, leaving the streets for the thieves and drug dealers.

Boone could feel them watching him from the shadows. Unseen eyes taking his measure, trying to decide whether he was an easy mark, but after six years at Pelican Bay, Boone was anything but easy. Ignoring them, he thought about the text from Special Agent Keller that had pulled him out of bed and sent him speeding north on the 101.

> We need to talk. Meet me at Laguna Inn in
> one hour.

As a confidential informant, Boone had grown accustomed to his handler's texts at all hours and his proclivity for setting up late-night meetings at out-of-the-way shitholes. Sure, it was annoying, not to mention dangerous, but being at the special agent's beck and call was part of the deal that had kept him out of prison. If he'd been a younger man, Boone would have kept his fool mouth shut and taken the rap like a good soldier. But seeing as he was already sitting on two strikes when Keller booted in the door of his Garberville stash house and busted him with fifty pounds of Jalisco Cartel weed and an unregistered pistol, turning snitch seemed a hell of a lot better than spending the rest of his life locked in a six-by-eight-foot cell.

Or at least it had until Keller told him their target.

"I want you to get close to Daniel Cortez."

As the head of the Jalisco Cartel's illicit operations in Northern California, Cortez was as dangerous as he was cunning, and though Boone hadn't thought they had a chance in hell of getting close to the man, he'd done what Keller instructed. It had taken longer than expected, but he'd worn their wires and made their buys, turned ounces into pounds, and slowly worked his way up the ladder. Dutifully collecting the evidence his handler needed to put the man away. Now all that stood between Boone and his freedom was the testimony he was set to give the grand jury at the beginning of the next week.

It was almost over.

Then why the meeting?

Before he could come up with an answer, the phone alerted him that he was arriving at his destination, and Boone killed his headlights before pulling into the parking lot. He found a spot near the front and backed in. Leaving the engine running, Boone typed out a quick text, advising Keller that he'd arrived, then settled back into his seat to take in the scene.

As far as motels went, the Laguna Inn was a bona fide shithole, its boarded windows and patched doors the result of countless narcotics raids. Not the best place to stay the night, but on par with most of Keller's meeting spots. Still, something felt off, and sitting there with the red glow of the *No Vacancy* sign illuminating his truck like a giant bull's-eye, Boone felt suddenly exposed.

Vulnerable.

It was the same feeling he used to get before one of the yard fights at Pelican Bay, and the cold chill running up his spine prompted him to pull the Colt from its holster and shove it beneath his right thigh.

With the pistol now in easy reach, Boone thought of the number he'd call if he had to go to ground, wondering if the man on the other end would even pick up the phone. A decade ago he wouldn't have doubted it, but so much had changed since then, and now, sitting there in the truck, Boone wasn't so sure.

He'd help me out if I needed him—I know he would.

Tension mounting, Boone picked up his phone and fired off another text, this time in all caps.

> WHERE THE HELL ARE YOU?

He stared at the screen, waiting for a response, but all he got was three little dots telling him that his handler was typing.

Nervousness shifting to panic, Boone was about to give up on the texts and just call Keller when the scuff of a boot across pavement drew his attention to the parking lot. Looking up, he found two men hustling toward him, the shotguns in their hands leaving no doubt as to their intentions. He dropped the phone, and before it hit the floorboard, Boone had the pistol up and his finger around the trigger.

He fired through the windshield, the roar of the big .45 leaving him instantly deaf. Boone kept shooting until the first man went down and was transitioning to the second when he fired back.

The buckshot spiderwebbed the glass, the slam of the pellets into Boone's right arm instantly severing the nerve endings. Unable to hold on to the Colt, he let it fall. Blood spraying across the wheel, he yanked the transmission into drive with his left hand and stomped on the gas. The truck shot forward with a chirp of rubber, and Boone spun the wheel to the right, clipping his attacker with the steel bumper on his way across the lot.

By the time he hit the street, the speedometer was swinging past forty miles an hour. He yanked the wheel hard over, the sudden movement sending the back end sliding around. Boone let off the gas and managed to get it straightened out before pressing the accelerator to the floor. The wind hissed through the shattered windshield as he raced east for the mountains.

A glance at the rearview showed his back trail clear, and Boone used his knees to keep the truck steady before bending down to retrieve the phone. He swiped it across the floorboard, pinned it against the firewall long enough to pick it up, and called the only number saved to his phone, the one he had been thinking about just a few minutes before. The line connected, and as it trilled in his ear, Boone found himself holding his breath, praying that the man would actually answer.

C'mon . . . please!

But after five rings the call went to voicemail, and Boone felt the glimmer of hope dwindle as he left a frantic message.

"Slade, I'm in trouble, man. I really need you to call me back."

CHAPTER 1

The fire siren went off at dawn, its mournful wail echoing loud over the bushy pines and corrugated hangars that surrounded the Region 5 Smoke-jumper Base at Redding. Inside the barracks, Jake Slade was instantly awake and kicking free of his covers, his heart pounding when he rolled from his rack. As he was one of two rookies assigned to Redding, today's jump would be his first into an active blaze, and while he knew he didn't have to be the first man to the pack shed, Slade was damn sure he wasn't going to be last.

He bounded to his wall locker and dressed quickly in the green Nomex brush pants and yellow button-down fire shirt that were his uniform. Next came his boots and the dented Altoid tin that held the emergency survival kit Slade always carried with him, and he was ready to go. Shoving the tin into his cargo pocket, he snagged his cell phone from the charger and was heading to the door when the blink of the screen alerted him to a missed call.

He paused, hand on the knob, and glanced at the number. *Boone? What the hell does he want?* With no time to find out, Slade shoved the phone into his back pocket and rushed out into the hall. He paused to hammer a fist onto his jump partner's door. "Pitts, move your ass," he yelled, and then he was merging with the rush of bearded veterans already jogging toward the pack shed.

Once inside, Slade ran to his equipment cage and yanked his Kevlar jumpsuit from the rack. He pulled it on over his clothes and zipped it up, adjusting the stiff collar before retrieving his parachute harness from the speed rack. He shoved his arms through the straps and fumbled with the buckles, his dexterity nonexistent thanks to the double shot of adrenaline streaming through his veins.

Eight minutes. That was how much time he had to get geared up and into the back of the Dornier waiting on the tarmac. Anything under that time came with the chance of a window seat and maybe some extra legroom. Anything over and Slade knew his first jump would turn into a spectator sport.

C'mon, you can do this. Just take a breath.

By the time Slade got his leg straps buckled and tight, the digital clock on the wall was past the two-minute mark. A look around the pack shed showed most of the veterans already hustling to the door, but Pitts was still messing with his harness. Seeing his jump partner struggling, Slade stepped forward to help, but a rawboned man with a thick beard and angry eyes stomped in from the tarmac.

"Forget about him and get your ass on the bird."

The voice caused Slade's heart to jump in his chest, and for an instant he was back in smokejumper training getting his ass smoked on the grinder.

No, you're done with that shit. You made it. Then what the hell is Buck doing here?

Slade didn't know, but if there was *one* thing Buck had beaten into their heads during training, it was that a smokejumper *never* left his jump partner behind. Knowing he couldn't just walk out but afraid to stay much longer, Slade was trying to think of a way to stall when Pitts snapped his reserve into place and slapped him on the shoulder.

"I'm ready—let's roll."

Thank God.

Grabbing their helmets, they rushed out the door and into the sunlight, the exhaust from the waiting Dornier blowing hot in Slade's face. He ducked his head and grabbed onto the ladder, the hundred-plus pounds of gear strapped to his body threatening to send him tumbling to the ground.

Fighting against the weight, he managed to haul himself into the cargo hold and drop in an empty spot near the tail a split second before Pitts came crashing down beside him. As expected, his partner's first words were not about the jump but about the man in the pack shed.

"What the fuck is Buck doing here?" he shouted over the roar of the engines. "I thought they were putting him in ops for his last season."

"Guess not," Slade shot back.

He was doing his best to pretend that it didn't bother him, but deep down he was boiling. Prior to applying to the Redding smokejumpers, Slade had spent three seasons with the Sawtooth Hotshots—a hard-charging team from central Idaho—and during his tenure had battled some of the most intense wildfires of the last century.

From the 2020 North Complex Fire that devastated Northern California to the Cameron Peak in Colorado, Slade had put in the work and considered himself well prepared for the task at hand.

But that was before he met Buck.

As their lead instructor, the hard-nosed Texan was charged with thinning the herd. Or as he said, finding out who among the recruits *really* wanted to be there. It was a task he'd taken to with a religious zeal, and it had started the second they walked through the gate.

There had been nothing scientific about his methods. No skills to learn or techniques to master—just pain to endure and conquer. But while the rest of the instructors seemed content to stick to the edges of the scrum and spread the suffering equally among the recruits, Buck had eyes only for Slade, and no sooner had he hit the deck than the man was looming over him. His voice hard as an axe blade.

"You're that fucking *convict* I've been hearing about, aren't you?"

Convict. The word stung like a whip, and for an instant Slade wished he hadn't been so forthcoming on his application.

Why the hell didn't you just lie?

He knew the answer, just as he knew the glowing letters of recommendation his hotshot team leaders had put in his file would never outshine his criminal record. Not that it mattered. Slade had worked his ass off to get here and had no intention of taking the man's bait.

But that hadn't stopped his lead instructor from pouring it on.

"You might as well quit now because it will be a cold day in hell before I let a convict onto *my* team."

True to his word, Buck had hurried Slade on every run. Busted him on every infraction and punished him with every shit detail. Still, he refused to quit. Out of the ten recruits who'd started the course, he and Pitts were the only ones who'd made it to the last week. And when Buck was sent to operations three days before graduation, Slade knew there was nothing to stop him from getting his wings.

The fact he'd made it through came with the assumption that the hazing was over, but now that Buck was his team leader, Slade had the sinking feeling that it was only going to get worse.

Fucking asshole, he thought as the man climbed aboard and started toward them.

As if reading his mind, Pitts leaned in close. "Don't worry about that asshole. Training's over."

Pitts cracked a smile, then quickly turned away as Buck squeezed into the seat across from Slade. The older man glared at him as the Dornier bumped into position at the end of the runway, and while the pilot checked in with the tower and ran up the engines, he leaned forward, his eyes cold as ice behind the wire-mesh face shield that covered the front of his helmet.

"The next time I tell you to move, you *fucking* move. You hear me, rookie?"

Slade stared back, wanting nothing more than to punch the man in the throat but knowing that would get him kicked off the team before his first jump. He managed a nod. "Yeah, I hear ya."

Then the aircraft was hurtling down the runway like a greyhound slipped from its lead, and all Slade's anger vanished as the pilot pulled back on the yoke and the Dornier leaped skyward. They flew west, the scrubby foothills that marked their hasty departure giving way to the pine-carpeted peaks of the Six Rivers National Forest. Leaning forward in his seat, Slade looked into the cockpit, the distant thunderhead of gray smoke he saw stretched across the horizon turning his mouth instantly dry.

Prior to this moment he'd let himself believe that their twelve qualifying jumps had actually meant something, but looking at the smoke, he knew he'd been wrong. That was just a taste—this was the real thing. Feeling his heart rate rise, Slade closed his eyes and used the technique he'd learned as a hotshot to focus on his breathing.

He counted each inhalation, noting the tightening in his diaphragm and the rush of the air into his lungs and forcing his muscles to soften on the exhalation. Slowly the noise of the aircraft faded into the background, and with his mind clear, he opened his eyes, laser focused on the task at hand. Unfortunately, the same could not be said for Pitts, who was heaving like an asthmatic after a marathon.

"Jake . . . I don't think I can do—"

Seeing Buck watching them from across the bulkhead, Slade was quick to cut him off. "Just breathe, Pitts."

He nodded, but before he could follow Slade's advice, Buck was leaning forward, his eyes narrowed in disgust. "What the fuck is wrong with you, rookie?" he demanded in his sharp Texas twang.

"He's fine," Slade said.

"The hell he is. He's shaking like a cat trying to shit a peach pit."

"I'm . . . I'm just nervous, Buck."

If they'd been on any other crew, the admission *might* have earned Pitts a sliver of sympathy—maybe even a little understanding—but with this being Buck's last season as a smokejumper, all Pitts got from the salty veteran was his derision.

"You're nervous?" the man howled. "You hear that, boys? The rookie is *nervous*."

The laughter from the rest of the team seemed to drown out the roar of the prop, and now with an audience, Buck redoubled his efforts at ridiculing Pitts. Slade felt the blood rushing hot to his face. He took a deep breath, his hands curling into fists as he looked left, imploring their other crew boss to step in.

C'mon, Walt, you gonna do anything?

But the gray-haired man sitting at the rear of the aircraft was too busy listening to the radio, trying to make sense of the chaos unfolding below, to pay any attention to Buck's bullying.

Not that it would have mattered.

Since their inception in the 1940s, the smokejumpers had drawn hard men. Soot-stained adrenaline junkies who volunteered to jump into the path of a raging fire and beat it into submission. They were the tip of the spear. Proud of their lineage and determined to work harder, faster, and longer than any other crews on the line. As such, *weakness* was not a smokejumper word.

"I'm watching you, rookie," the older man said, jabbing a finger into Pitts's chest. "Both of you," he added with a glance at Slade.

While Pitts looked cowed, all the man's words did to Slade was piss him off. He hated a bully, and before he knew what was happening, Slade was reaching over and grabbing Buck by the wrist.

"Hey, asshole, do me a favor and lay off my jump partner."

Buck tried to pull away, but Slade held him tight.

"You sure you want to test me, rookie?" Buck demanded. "We might be out of training, but I can still make your life a living hell."

Before Slade could respond, the spotter came weaving through the cargo hold, his voice loud despite the roar of the props. "Save it for the fire."

It was time to jump.

CHAPTER 2

SIX RIVERS NATIONAL FOREST

Humboldt County, California

Slade let go of Buck's wrist, the shimmer in the man's eyes telling him that this wasn't over. *Well, bring it on.* He winked, wanting Buck to know that he wasn't the one to back down, and then turned his attention to the rear of the aircraft, where the spotter was unlocking the jump door.

He threw it open, and the slipstream roared into the cargo hold. The kerosene stench of burnt avgas and smoke from the charred timber caused Slade's eyes to water. He blinked the tears away, and when the air cleared a few seconds later, he could smell the subtle hints of vanilla in the wind that told him somewhere below, the fire was burning through a strand of junipers.

But it was the smoke that told the fire's story, and as the pilot banked east and brought the aircraft over the drop zone, Slade caught his first look at the blaze. The view was apocalyptic, the columns of jet-black smoke rising from the charred trees and blackened earth like something from a World War I documentary.

The spotter stepped into the door to toss out the streamers—the palm-sized bags of sand attached to twenty-foot lengths of scarlet crepe paper that the jumpers used to judge the wind. He sidearmed them out of the aircraft, and Slade watched them unfurl, their tails twisting and snapping in the air.

Noting the drift, the spotter yelled, "Left!" into his headset. The pilot responded, bringing the nose around to the east. Once the aircraft was steady again, the spotter threw out a second set and watched as they whirled and dipped in the slipstream before finally landing in the center of the jump spot.

"Get ready," the spotter shouted.

Slade was the third jumper in the stick, and after double-checking his equipment and snapping his chin strap, he gave Pitts a reassuring slap. "Hell of a day to be alive."

The engines roared as the pilot yanked the aircraft up to their jump altitude, and then it was time to go. As the jumper in command, Walt was the first out of the plane, followed by his jump partner, and then it was Slade's turn. He moved to the door and clipped the yellow static line that would deploy his chute into the static line cable while the spotter checked his equipment.

"Did you see the streamers?"

Slade nodded, and the spotter moved out of the way, motioning for Slade to take a seat on the floor. He assumed the position: hands on the jump handle mounted to the bulkhead, legs out, eyes locked on the horizon. He waited for the slap, body tight as a coiled spring, and when it came, Slade launched himself out of the aircraft.

Slade snapped into the position that had been drilled into his head a thousand times: legs together, chin on chest, hands protecting his reserve. The roar of the engine and the rush of the slipstream past his ears left him deaf, the wall of air kicking his legs over his head as he fell through the smoke.

Four seconds. That was how long it should take for the static line attached to the cable to jerk taut and pull his chute from the pack tray. Any longer and he'd have to pull his reserve. He started the slow count in his head, exactly like he had in practice. *Jump thousand. Two thousand. Three thousand. Four thousand.* But instead of the opening shock of his chute that Slade had been trained to expect, there was nothing but wind.

Falling at 120 miles an hour, he had less than three seconds to pull. Just as he was reaching for his reserve handle, the chute finally ripped free and jerked him to a painful halt. The sudden stop sent a whiplashing pain racing up his spine that knocked the breath from his lungs, but Slade shook it off and craned his neck to get a look up at the canopy.

A quick search showed it free of any rips or tears—anything that *might* keep him from being able to safely steer the ram-air parachute into the postage-stamp-sized landing zone hidden beneath the graphite haze. Finding it clean, Slade turned the chute into the wind and gave himself a moment to take in the scene unfurling around him.

At well over one million acres, the Six Rivers National Forest was the last of America's great wilderness. It was a primeval place. A rugged mosaic of saw-toothed peaks, skyscraping pines, and crystal-clear streams that were as picturesque as they were deadly. It was beautiful and uncaring, and damn, did it make Slade feel small, but even with the fire waiting for him below, he couldn't think of any place that he'd rather be.

Sensing the ground rushing up to meet him, he knew it was time to get his head in the game, and Slade pulled down on his right toggle until he felt the wind at his back. He could see the drop zone now over his left shoulder, but he held his course for another thirty seconds before pulling a left slip.

Almost there.

He was on the wire, tracking toward the center of the drop zone like a radar-guided missile. With the veterans on the ground watching him, Slade wanted to nail the landing, and he picked out a patch of bare earth in the center of the zone as his target. A final turn brought him back into the wind, and a tug of both toggles helped him shed his excess speed.

This is it.

He was there, so close that he could almost feel the ground beneath his boots, but just as he was about to touch down, an angry crosswind came gusting in from the east. The sudden updraft pulled him inexorably back into the smoke like an invisible hand. Cursing under his breath, Slade fought to get free, but he was too low and too slow to do anything but watch as the jagged rocks came rushing up fast to meet him.

This is going to hurt.

He hit hard, the slam of his body against the ground blasting the air from his lungs an instant before his helmet banged against a rock. The grate of plastic against stone and the spray of earth and grass through the wire-mesh face guard confirmed his worst fears.

He was being dragged.

Slade skittered across the ground, the wind hauling him fast toward the edge of a cliff ten feet ahead. Desperate to get free, he fumbled for his canopy-release system, and after popping the clasp, he hooked his thumb through the ring mounted to the top of the buckle and gave it a sharp tug. The riser snapped from his harness and the parachute deflated, and he came to a dusty halt two feet from the drop-off.

Slade let out a pained groan and rolled into a sitting position, a quick scan of the drop zone showing the rest of the team already on the ground. Now playing catch-up, he got to his feet and, after shoving his harness and chute into his gear bag, limped to the edge. A look down showed a fifty-foot drop with razor-sharp rocks and smoldering tree stumps waiting for him at the bottom.

Ho-ly shit.

"Dude, tell me you wore a GoPro," Pitts said, jogging over, "because *that* was awesome."

Before Slade could respond, Walt's booming voice came echoing through the trees. "Hey, rookies, are you gonna stand there sightseeing all day, or are you gonna help unpack this fuckin' gear?"

The question pushed Slade into action, and he charged up the slope, Pitts tight on his tail. The rest of the team already had the lid off the gear bundle the trail plane had kicked and was pulling out the gear. By the time Slade and Pitts arrived, the sawyers had their big twenty-eight-inch Stihl chain saws roaring and ready to go.

Not wanting to be left behind, Slade grabbed his Pulaski, the half axe / half hoe favored by wildland firefighters, and removed the protective cover. He checked the blade, its wicked edge a painful reminder that despite the innovations that had come along since the first smoke-jumpers threw themselves from a plane, their methods for combating an active blaze hadn't changed.

At its heart the job was to find the fire's head—its direction of travel—and get in front of it; then the sawyers would use their chain saws to clear out the large trees while the scrape came in behind them and hacked the duff down to its mineral soil.

Starving the fire of its fuel.

Gear in hand, Slade and Pitts fell in with the rest of the team in front of Walt, who laid out the plan of attack. "The fire is heading north toward these cabins," he said, pointing to the map. "The IC has already dispatched a hotshot crew and a pump truck to handle the evacuations. *Our* job is to dig a fire line around the cabins and hold until reinforcements arrive."

Briefing over, Buck turned to face Slade and Pitts. "All right, rookies, you made it here; now let's see if you can keep up." Then he was running.

CHAPTER 3

Stanford, California

Special Agent Pete Keller of the DEA stood outside the Stanford admissions office, his rumpled blazer and five-o'clock shadow in stark contrast to the well-heeled families he watched file in and out of the building. Having spent most of his career working undercover, Keller was used to blending in. Hiding in plain sight. But the askance glances of the passersby left him feeling exposed.

Paranoia slithered up his spine like a snake, its cold chill exacerbating the panic attack he felt crouched in the corner of his mind. Desperate to get out of his head, Keller dug his work phone from his pocket and opened Signal, the encrypted app he and the rest of the men assigned to the NorCal Anti-Drug/Corruption Task Force used to communicate with their CIs.

Though mandatory, the midday check-ins were standard operating procedure for the snitches working for the task force, and a quick scroll through the texts showed most of them had already checked in. But nearing the end of the texts, he realized one name was conspicuously absent.

Mikey Boone.

By itself, Boone missing his check-in didn't mean anything was wrong, but considering how much was riding on the man's upcoming grand jury testimony, Keller knew it warranted a call. Not wanting anyone standing outside the admin building to overhear the conversation, he started down the walkway that led to the street. Once out of ear-shot, he was about to make the call when a familiar voice stopped him in his tracks.

"Daddy—I knew you would come."

Emily.

At the sound of his daughter's voice, Keller stuffed the phone into his pocket and turned to see a fresh-faced teen loping gracefully up the sidewalk to his right. Smiling, he moved to meet her, and when she was close, he gathered her up in his arms. "Hey, kiddo, I told you I'd be here."

"Yeah," she said, beaming, "but I don't think Mom believed you."

Considering that it had been five years since their divorce, the comment hurt more than it should have. Still, Keller knew he'd earned it and managed to keep the smile when he released his daughter and turned to face the self-possessed brunette watching him from the sidewalk.

"Good to see you, Victoria. You look good."

"You too, Peter," she said, stepping in for a hug. "Is everything OK?"

"Yeah, why?"

"You look . . . worried," she said.

"I'm fine," he lied.

Eager to change the subject, Keller pulled away and turned back to Emily. "So, look at you, kid. You got into Stanford. That's a hell of an achievement."

"If it was up to me, she'd be going to Cal State," Victoria said, "but Brandon spoils her."

"And where is the good doctor?" Keller asked with a roguish grin. "Off saving lives?"

"In surgery," Emily said, taking his hand and pulling him back toward the doorway. "But we can talk about him later. Mom said that you were retiring. Is that true?"

"Yep. Two more weeks and I'm officially a civilian."

"I'll believe *that* when I see it," Victoria muttered.

Keller ignored the quip and hauled open the glass door that led into the admissions office. He held it until both women were through and then fell in beside his ex-wife.

"Are you sure you're ready to leave the Agency?" she asked. "I mean, what *are* you even going to do?"

"Maybe I'll go to a football game." He shrugged. "I hear Stanford's got a good team."

"Peter, I'm serious," she said, grabbing his arm. "Is this about what happened in Mexico?"

The question caught him off guard, and he stopped in the middle of the lobby, his mind filled with the rush of unwanted memories that always accompanied any mention of that fateful day in Veracruz.

When Keller first joined the DEA, he'd loved being on the streets and the adrenaline rush that came with working undercover. He was good at it, too, and soon developed a reputation as a solid investigator. But it was Keller's ability to recruit and run confidential informants that got him noticed by the brass back in Virginia.

In a world where most investigations were conducted on a computer, the ability to pluck a source from the street and then plant him or her inside a criminal enterprise was a valuable commodity. Which was how now *Senior* Special Agent Keller found himself in Mexico assisting the *federales* in their war against the Jalisco Cartel.

The posting came with the usual promises: another promotion and a corner office at DEA headquarters. But all that went to shit when one of Keller's sources was captured prior to a raid on a suspected safe house in Veracruz. Using torture, the cartel extracted everything it needed to know about the impending operation, and when Keller and the federales hit the house the next day, they walked right into an ambush.

Though the DEA investigations that followed cleared Keller of any malfeasance, there was nothing they could do for his conscience. Or his reputation. Unable to off-load the guilt or the nightmares that came with the deaths of the federales and him finding his source's mangled body, Keller turned to the bottle. He spent the next few years bouncing from one backwater posting to the next, and by the time he finally got to his current position as the DEA liaison for the NorCal Anti-Drug/Corruption Task Force, his marriage was over, along with his career.

"Peter?"

Victoria's voice pulled him from the past, and Keller looked up to find they were standing alone in the middle of the lobby. "Where's Emily?"

"Already upstairs," she said. Stepping closer, she asked, "Are you *sure* you're OK?"

Knowing he wasn't getting out of this without answering the question, Keller searched for a lie. Anything to steer the conversation from Mexico or his impending retirement, but in the end, it was the burr of his work phone that saved him.

Thank God.

Keller dug the phone from his pocket, his relief turning to dread when he saw the caller was Detective Robert Harris, a Humboldt County narcotics officer attached to the task force.

Dammit.

Conflicted, he looked up to tell Victoria that he needed to take the call, only to see her already moving to the elevator. "Hey, where are you going?"

She stepped into the car and turned to face him, her lips twisting into a wistful smile. "When you're ready to talk, let me know."

Then the doors slid closed, and she was gone.

Fuck.

A tiny voice in the back of his head warned him that this was his last chance. A final opportunity to be with his daughter before the world took her away forever. *Don't squander it.* Keller knew he should listen. But instead of following his gut, he did what he'd been trained to do and answered the phone.

"This *better* be important."

There was silence for a moment; then Harris's voice came over the speaker. "Hey, man, I'm sorry to bother you on your day off, but—"

"But what? Spit it out."

"Homicide has a couple of stiffs stretched out in the parking lot of the Laguna Inn."

"OK, what's any of that got to do with me?"

"They've got the shooter's plate from the CCTV. Look, there's no easy way to say this, but the truck belongs to Mikey Boone."

"Boone?" Keller demanded. "What the fuck are you talking about? Boone is in Fresno, laying low until the grand jury on Monday."

"Well, I've got two dead gangbangers and a couple of pissed-off homicide detectives who say otherwise."

Keller shoved through the door and stepped outside, the midday sun blinding after the gloom of the lobby. He cursed Boone under his breath, then took a second to rein in his rising anger and asked, "Has anyone told the boss?"

"Not yet. We all figured that since he's your CI, *you'd* want to make the call. Besides, you're the one pulling the pin. I've still got ten years left in this bitch."

Keller stifled a laugh, knowing bullshit when he heard it, and after thanking the detective for the heads-up, he ended the call. Still holding the phone, he cut across the grass, jogging toward the visitors' lot and the dusty government-issued Impala parked next to an ivy-draped wall.

He climbed inside and started the engine, his mind churning over how he was going to break the news to his boss, Director Richard Cole. He pulled out of the lot and drove south, the stately palms and coastal oaks that canopied the campus giving way to scrubby mesquite when he turned onto Junipero Serra Boulevard.

Traffic slowed as he passed the Stanford Golf Course, and he let off the gas and drummed his fingers on the steering wheel, Harris's parting words echoing in his mind. *You're the one pulling the pin.* There was a part of Keller that knew he should have gotten out earlier. Retired before ever agreeing to come and work the career killer that was the Forest Service–led joint task force, but his pride wouldn't let him go out on a loss.

The truth was, Keller harbored a glimmer of hope that he could still make it right. Somehow convince the DEA that they'd made a mistake pushing him to the side and maybe, just maybe, get one final shot at the brass ring. He knew it would never happen—not after this call from Harris—but still, Keller had given Boone his word that he would see him through the trial.

Fucking idiot.

Realizing there was no easy way to tell his boss that their star witness was now the primary suspect in a double homicide, Keller dialed the number from memory and steeled himself for the wrath he knew was to come.

Dammit, Boone, you really screwed me this time.

CHAPTER 4

Willow Creek, California

Director Richard Cole sat at his desk in the Trinity River ranger station, his eyes on the Excel spreadsheet displayed on his computer screen. The document was for the presentation he was scheduled to lead for the command staff this afternoon, and visually it was a work of art. A masterpiece of supervision.

It was all in there. Every report his rangers had submitted. Every citation they'd issued and arrest they'd made during the previous six months. While most of the other supervisors loved to inflate their achievements at the meets or brag about how they were running the best district, Cole didn't have to say a word because the numbers spoke for themselves.

Crime was down, while attendance in his corner of the massive Six Rivers National Forest was as high as it had been before the pandemic. But as he scrolled to the end of the document, it wasn't the glowing statistics submitted by his shift commanders that grabbed his attention but the smudge of red at the bottom of the overtime section.

Like a crimson cape being waved before a raging bull, the sight sent his heart hammering in his chest, and he scrolled left, looking for the commander who'd authorized the overtime. *Lewis, that son of a bitch.*

If Cole had worked for another government agency, the cost overrun would have barely been noticed, but he'd been at the Forest Service long enough to know that getting the next promotion had less to do with leadership and more to do with turning in a balanced sheet.

Fuming, he got to his feet and moved to the window, where he took a breath and let his gray eyes drift west toward the distant peaks of Three Creeks Summit. As usual, the sight brought a semblance of calm, and he felt himself relax.

Having already been promoted faster than most of his peers, Cole considered letting it go. After all, as a GS-11 he was making good money. The only problem was that with his wife's brand-new Yukon and his son needing braces and what seemed like an endless supply of electronic gadgets, Cole desperately *needed* that next pay bump.

While most rangers were drawn to the Forest Service because of their love of the outdoors or a desire to protect the environment, Cole had applied because of the job security. Out of all the people he'd talked to while filling out his application, not a single person had ever heard of anyone getting fired from the Forest Service.

Plus, the government insurance and retirement were hard to beat.

But it was only after he'd graduated from the Federal Law Enforcement Training Center in Glynco, Georgia, and took his first posting at the Six Rivers National Forest that he uncovered the dirty little secret no one had warned him about—the pay.

Cole had come from a well-to-do family, and with his measly paycheck barely keeping him above the poverty line, he'd known he needed to make a change. But where? After his first year, Cole had been thinking about leaving the Forest Service altogether when he had a chance encounter with one of the special agents assigned to the criminal-investigation division. The conversation started over one of Cole's field reports that had helped the agent arrest a poacher who had illegally hunted in Lower Trinity and ended with the man asking if Cole had ever thought of becoming an investigator.

Cole expressed little interest at first, but that changed when the agent casually mentioned that the job came with a higher pay grade and nearly limitless overtime. It was all Cole needed to hear. Still, getting moved over to the investigation's side of the house presented its own unique challenges, mainly less time in the office and more time out in the back-country, hunting poachers, illegal loggers, or anyone breaking the federal laws and regulations that governed the one million acres of forest.

It wasn't until he made the move to internal affairs—a job that fo-cused on protecting the forest not from outsider threats but from those within the department—that Cole found his niche. For most cops, having to investigate their own would be the ultimate punishment. A betrayal of their code and the vaunted thin blue line of silence that governed the chosen calling. Cole, on the other hand, saw nothing but opportunity and soon was feeling the power that came with digging up dirt on his coworkers.

He liked the work, but the best part of his job was the unfettered access to the transcripts of the budget and planning-commission meet-ings, where the brass talked about upcoming logging contracts and building proposals. Insider information that Cole could then turn around and sell to the highest bidder.

It was all illegal as hell, but for someone who knew how to cover his tracks, it was like stealing candy from a baby. At first he'd been making money hand over fist, but all that changed when the Forest Service inspector general tapped him to head up the NorCal Anti-Drug/Cor-ruption Task Force.

Cole had tried to beg off the assignment, but the brass in Eureka wasn't listening, and he'd been forced to accept. Which meant he'd also been forced to curtail his illicit side business. The first six months hadn't been bad, but he was now passing the year mark, and Cole was start-ing to feel the pinch.

Shoving his rapidly diminishing bank account from his mind, Cole turned his attention back to the problem at hand. He was considering whether he should write Lewis up or let him slide when his desk phone rang.

Annoyed by the interruption, Cole snatched the phone from the cradle and pressed it to his ear. "Yes?"

"Boss, we've got a problem."

Keller's tone put him instantly on guard, and Cole dropped into his chair, the dull pinch of a headache spreading across his forehead. "What *kind* of a problem?"

"It's Boone."

"Tell me."

Cole listened while Keller relayed the phone call from Detective Brown, and by the time he was through, it felt as if someone had taken a miniature jackhammer and turned it loose inside his skull.

"Sir, are you there?"

"Jesus, Keller, how could this happen? You had *one* fucking job, and that was to get Boone to the courthouse on Monday."

"I know, sir. This is on me. I'll find him. You have my word on that."

Cole thought about threatening him, telling him that he'd "better find Boone and clean up whatever mess he made," but the truth was Cole's days in the field were long gone. As were whatever investigative skills he'd once had. He was an administrator now—not a cop—and the truth was he needed Keller to find their CI or it would be his neck on the chopping block.

"Just do what you have to do and hurry," Cole finally snapped.

"Yes sir. Thank you—"

But Cole wasn't listening.

The call over, he slammed the phone down on the cradle hard enough to send a stack of reports sliding off the corner of his desk. "Shit." Cole was leaning forward to clean up the mess when there was a knock at the door, followed by his assistant stepping into his office.

"Everything OK in here, boss?"

"What the hell does it look like, McCoy?"

The man startled and moved to step back, then, remembering his purpose, held up a manila envelope. "This just came in for you. I think you're going to want to see it."

The gravity in McCoy's voice put Cole instantly on guard, and he glared at the envelope as if it were a snake. "What do you have?"

"More Freedom of Information requests from Hannah Fowler."

"That crackpot *again*? You've got to be shitting me."

"Hey, I'm just the messenger," McCoy said.

Out of all the problems that had come across his desk since taking the job, Hannah Fowler—the former Forest Service employee turned environmentalist commando—was by far the biggest pain in his ass. While most of the public affairs officers who'd dealt with Fowler in the past considered her relatively harmless, Cole had actually taken the time to read her blogs and listen to her antigovernment podcast. He'd followed her on social media and watched as her audience grew from a handful of granola-munching hippies to seventy-five thousand hard-core followers.

No, she was a threat to the status quo, and as soon as Cole accepted the job, he'd known it was only a matter of time before her constant probing and questioning about land-use policies would put him squarely in her crosshairs. His well-honed survival instincts screamed at him to tell McCoy to toss the folder in the trash, but Cole shoved them away.

I've never backed down from a fight, and I'm sure as hell not going to start now.

"Give it to me," he said, breaking the silence.

McCoy handed him the envelope, and Cole opened the flap and pulled out a file folder only to find a memo from the Office of Information Policy requiring his signature upon acceptance. Ignoring the cover sheet, he began flipping through the attached FOIA request.

A quick scan of the first three documents showed updated versions of requests Fowler had already filed—politely worded appeals that the Forest Service release the names and addresses of the timber companies they'd contracted to harvest a strand of fire-damaged timber in the Lower Trinity district. That Fowler wanted to know which logging firms had finally gotten their saws into the Six Rivers was nothing new, and if it had been up to him, Cole would have denied her on general principle. But seeing as the Forest Service lawyers had ruled they had no legal standing to deny her, he resentfully signed off on the request.

"Maybe she'll finally leave me the hell alone," he muttered.

Glad to be done with this issue, Cole was ready to hand the folder back when a quick scan of the final page stopped him dead in his tracks. Confused, he reread the heading. *Why does she want to know about the Red Cap closure, and why in the hell would she address the request to me?*

"Has anyone else seen this?" he asked.

"Just you, boss."

"Good, let's keep it that way," Cole said, taking the final sheet out of the folder and handing back everything else.

"Understood. What do you want me to do?"

"Send those up the chain," Cole said. "I'll handle this one personally."

McCoy nodded and headed for the door.

When he was gone, Cole studied the paper. His first thought was to destroy it, but then he remembered Johnny's braces and, sensing an opportunity for some easy money, pulled out his phone. He snapped a picture of the request and then fed it into the shredder, waiting until there was nothing left but a pile of confetti before typing out a quick text.

> Got some information for you.
> Usual rate if interested.

CHAPTER 5

Buck pushed them hard, ignoring the slide of the shale beneath their feet and the gut-churning drop to their left as he raced down the trail. Slade had to give it to his crew boss—the man could move for an old guy, and while Slade wouldn't have had an issue keeping up on flat ground, the treacherous terrain combined with the weight of his gear soon left him winded.

Then there was the fire—the intense heat of the flames and the oppressive choke of the smoke—as it stalked them through the timber. At first, Slade could only see her flanks, the nonthreatening surface burns that seemed content to feast on the half-charred scrub left in her wake, but as they continued north, the rapidly rising heat and the deepening smoke told him they were getting close.

Slade could hear it before he saw it—the predatory roar of the head as it galloped somewhere off to his left. He wanted to stop and get a look, size up the enemy he'd come here to hunt, but Buck was there to keep him moving.

"Pick up the pace, rookie. Let's go!"

Slade did as he was told, and they ran for another two hundred yards, dodging the ankle-breaking roots and fist-sized stones that littered their path. Finally, they reached the top of the rise and were just starting down the back side of the slope when the flame front came bursting from the trees.

It was moving fast, the scream of the flames and sizzling hiss of the sap-filled trees giving it a bestial sound. There was something primeval in its destructive beauty—a mesmerizing shimmer that was both terrible and fascinating at the same time—and Slade couldn't stop staring. He could feel the heat now, hear the pop of the pine cones and the squeal of unseen animals as they raced for safety.

God, she's beautiful.

The sight took him back to the Cameron Peak Fire and the first time he saw a smokejumper in action. At the time he was the "lead saw" with the Sawtooth Hotshots, a hard-charging twenty-four-year-old who *thought* he knew a thing or two about fire. They'd been cocky and convinced they were going to kick the "bitch's" ass, but after two days of throwing everything they had at the blaze, it was still burning.

No matter what they tried, she came howling back, snapping like a crimson serpent. Beating them down until they were exhausted. Trapped in the black, cut off, and running out of water, Slade was convinced they were going to be overrun when a Forest Service Sherpa came racing low over the trees. At first he thought it was an air tanker, but instead of the rust-red fire retardant he expected to see, it was a load of smokejumpers that came tumbling out of the aircraft.

Watching them slice through the gray haze was like watching a gift from God—soot-stained angels come to snatch him and his crew from certain death. But once they hit the ground, they turned into demons, attacking the fire with a skill and savagery Slade hadn't even realized was possible. Together, they all worked the next eighteen hours straight, beating the fire into submission. By the time they were done, Slade and the rest of his crew were dead on their feet.

The smokejumpers, on the other hand, were just hitting their stride, and after thanking the hotshots for the "warm-up," they were formed up and moving out. Off to help another crew caught deeper in the fire. For Slade it was a pivotal moment, and though at the time he could barely hold on to his Pulaski, he knew that whatever it took, one day *he* was going to become a smokejumper.

Pitts shouting at him to get "his head out of his ass" snapped him back to the now, and Slade turned to find the team gathered around a large boulder at the edge of a willow thicket.

"Anchor point," Walt shouted.

After that, there were no more words, only sounds: the roar of the 70 cc engines of the chain saws as the sawyers sliced through the stumps and limbs that lined their path, followed by the grunts of the swampers grabbing the downed limbs and flinging them into the edge of the encroaching flames. Once they'd cut a line, Slade and the rest of the scrape got to work, the sallow sunlight glinting off the blades and edges of their hand tools as they attacked the earth.

With the fire closing in, all sense of time vanished, giving way to heat, sweat, and the relentless pounding of picks and shovels against dirt and roots. And yet the fire continued its relentless advance, the updraft from its heat sending a swarm of embers into the pines.

The dried branches provided ready fuel, and soon the trees were burning like roman candles, the sudden crack of the sap-filled limbs sending embers spattering into the canopy and onto the smokejumpers.

Slade cursed as a spark found its way down the back of his yellow shirt, felt his skin sizzle as he slapped it out. *Fucker.* A flicker of movement from his left caught his attention, and Slade turned his head to see a small fire dancing in the pine brush behind him.

"We've got spots."

He stepped off the line long enough to deal with the spot fire, but no sooner had he stomped it out than another one popped up. Hacking a branch off a juniper, he used it to beat out the flames, then the next, all while Walt pushed the scrape to keep digging. "Faster, let's go. My grandmother can cut line quicker than that."

While Slade battled the spot fires, Pitts and the rest of the men picked up their pace, flinging dirt and roots as the inferno crept closer. For the next hour they continued hacking their way north, until they finally linked up with the hotshots who were using the road as a firebreak.

Between swings of his Pulaski, Slade paused to scan the perimeter, noticing the burnt-out cars and the distant outlines of cabins through the haze. "Has that area been cleared?" he shouted to one of the hotshots.

"What?"

Before Slade could repeat the question, Buck came storming down the line. "First six, go link up with Walt," he said, pointing back the way he'd come. "The rest of you, dig in." He paused to take a pull of water and then turned his attention to Slade. "Why are you standing there? Get to work."

"Shouldn't we go check the cabins?"

"Your job is to dig, not think. Now get to work," Buck ordered as he turned away.

Slade bit down on the anger and glanced back over his shoulder, eyes stinging from the smoke as he studied the cabins. Buck was an asshole, but the man knew what he was doing, and if his team leader wasn't worried about the cabins, he shouldn't be either. But Slade just couldn't let it go.

"What's going on?" Pitts asked as he continued digging.

"What if there is someone inside? I mean, shouldn't *someone* check?"

"Are you crazy?" Pitts demanded. "You can't leave the line. Buck will have your ass."

With the flame front rapidly approaching their position, Slade knew Pitts was right—knew that even *if* there was someone up in the cabins, breaking the line now could be fatal.

Where the hell is that pumper?

As the flame wall approached, the probing orange fingers it sent out ahead found nothing but stripped earth. With no fuel to feed its advance, the head finally slowed. The heat was the first to subside, followed by the smoke and then finally a yell from one of the sawyers. "She's laying down."

"We've still got spots," Buck shouted.

Stepping off the line and guzzling water from his CamelBak, Slade started stomping out the spot fires around him. A quick glance at his watch showed that it had been almost three hours since they'd hit the ground. The hollow rumble in his stomach and the sudden weakness in his arms and back were quick to remind him that he needed to eat to keep up his strength.

Leaning his Pulaski against the nearest unburnt tree, he reached into his personal gear bag and pulled out an energy bar. The gloopy mass of peanut butter and nuts he found inside looked nothing like the picture on the label; still, the rush of sugar and carbs into his system had an immediate effect. Taking a deep breath of satisfaction, he was reaching for another when he heard a woman's scream echoing through the trees.

CHAPTER 6

SIX RIVERS NATIONAL FOREST

Humboldt County, California

Slade spun and peered through the smoke, searching for the source of the cry, but before he could find it, the wind came slashing through the trees, the sudden blast of fresh air breathing life into the dying burn. The flames reignited with a defiant roar, and the smokejumpers leaped back into action, Buck shouting for everyone to "get back on the line."

Slade ignored the heat on the back of his neck and stepped forward. "Pitts, tell me you heard that?"

"I didn't hear shit. Keep digging."

"No, man, there's somebody up there."

The fire all but forgotten, Slade hefted his Pulaski and started up the hill, toward the darkened outlines of the cabins, but he hadn't managed more than a few steps when Buck cut him off.

"Where the hell are you going?"

"I heard a scream. There's somebody up there."

"Are you sure that's what you heard, or was it the heat?" Buck demanded. "Your first fire will do all types of crazy stuff to your mind."

Slade knew what he'd heard, but staring at Buck, he felt the first hint of indecision creeping into his mind. Maybe he was right; maybe it was the heat.

"Well?"

Before Slade could respond, the wind came gusting through the trees, and in an instant the flames were soaring skyward, the heat and intensity of the flare-up shoving them both back on their heels.

Buck was the first to move. "Get on the fire line, now!"

Slade was reaching for his Pulaski, ready to get back in the fight, when the white beam of a flashlight came sparkling from the window of one of the cabins. "Look, right there," he shouted, pointing at the light.

"Shit! *Go*—I'll handle this," Buck yelled.

Slade didn't need to be told twice, and he grabbed his Pulaski and charged up the hill. It was less than twenty-five yards to the cabin, but after spending the last eight hours on the line, Slade was exhausted. But he kept moving, hacking his way through the flaming undergrowth that blocked his path.

By the time he made it up the stairs and onto the porch, he was running on fumes, his lungs burning from inhaling the superheated air.

His body screamed at him to stop. His mind begged for him to turn around and head back to the safety of the fire line, but Slade refused. Someone inside needed help, and he was the only one who could provide it. Summoning the last of his strength, he dragged himself to the door, forgetting to check the knob before flinging it open.

Fueled by the fresh flow of oxygen, the flames that had been smoldering inside came back to life with a vengeance, and they broiled out onto the porch. Slade rolled to the right but wasn't quick enough to avoid the fireball that ignited the sleeve of his Nomex shirt.

Face singed by the heat, Slade stepped back and beat his flaming arm against the side of the cabin. He got it out, but the momentary lapse in judgment left him shaken. Pissed off that he'd made such a rookie mistake.

C'mon. You know better than that.

Thankful Buck hadn't been there to witness his screwup, Slade took a deep breath, and properly refocused, he moved back toward the door. *No more mistakes*, he told himself. Then he ducked inside. The interior of the cabin was dark, the only source of light the flames chewing on the furniture. Slade kicked a blackened wing chair out of his path and started toward the hall, the off-gassing from the smoldering wallpaper leaving a chemical taste in the back of his throat. Hacking against the smoke, he moved along the wall and into the living room and called out, "Is anyone in here?"

His voice sounded weak amid the shattering glass, and the heat sent the room spinning before his eyes. He waited for a response, wondering if he'd made a mistake, until he heard a choked reply drift down from above.

"Up . . ."

As he moved to the stairs, the ceiling buckled and a section of burning masonry the size of a dining room table came crashing down in front of him. Slade raised a hand to protect himself from the shower of sparks and embers that puffed toward his face, and hurdled the obstacle. He stuck the landing, but the shudder he felt beneath his feet told him that the flames had found the subfloor.

Realizing it wouldn't be long before the cabin came collapsing down around him, Slade redoubled his efforts and took the stairs two at a time. From the outside the cabin had looked small and quaint, but the line of closed doors he found at the top of the stairs seemed to stretch on forever. Not sure where to go, Slade yelled, "Where are you?"

"Down here," someone shouted.

Coughing hard, he continued along the hall, feeling the shake of the floor as the stairwell collapsed behind him. A second shout brought him to a room halfway down the hall, and he threw the door open to find a woman with a wet towel wrapped around her face crouched in the corner.

"We've got to go," he said.

She nodded her head and got to her feet while Slade grabbed a desk chair from the corner of the room and flung it through the window, the incoming rush of fresh air soothing his ragged lungs. "C'mon," he said.

She followed him out onto the roof, the beam from the flashlight in her hand slicing through the smoke. "Where to?" she asked.

"Shit . . . I'm thinking."

"Well, you better hurry up," she said as the lick of flames came creeping out of the window.

Moving to the edge of the roof, Slade looked down. Seeing the glimmer of the swimming pool below, he turned back to the woman. "We're going to have to jump," he said, pointing to the sliver of water.

He expected her to balk, but instead she gave him a determined nod and moved to the edge. Not giving her a chance to second-guess the decision, Slade grabbed her by the waist and heaved her over the side, offering a silent prayer as she sailed through the air. At first, he thought he'd shorted the throw, but then he heard a splash and saw a geyser of water spraying over the concrete porch.

Then it was his turn.

Flinging the Pulaski downward into the grass, Slade stepped back, not seeing the buckled shingles until it was too late. Unable to hold his weight, the section of roof gave way and his foot crashed through the hole. Realizing he had only seconds left before the entire roof collapsed, he quickly jerked his foot free, the jagged edges tearing at his skin. Ignoring the pain, he dashed forward and launched himself over the edge, praying the pool was deep enough as the water rushed up to meet him.

CHAPTER 7

Eureka, California

The Cessna Citation Mustang banked low over Arcata Bay, the aircraft's landing lights glinting off the blue-gray water like sun off steel. The pilot brought the jet in for a gentle landing, the chirp of the tires and roar of the engine brakes followed by a smooth taxi to the dilapidated hangar on the far side of the field, where a blacked-out Chevy Tahoe sat waiting.

In the main cabin, Tito Zavalia rubbed a hand over his tired eyes and slipped on a pair of aviators before getting to his feet. He grabbed his single carry-on and started toward the airstair, replaying in his mind the phone call from the American lawyer a few hours ago that had brought him to the United States.

As usual the man was short and to the point. "There's a problem with Daniel Cortez. We tried to handle it *internally*, but—"

"But the men you hired fucked it up?"

"That's right," Hale said after a pause. "I was told that you specialize in dealing with time-sensitive matters and that you are familiar with Mr. Cortez."

Tito knew all about Cortez's situation because *he* was the one his boss had originally sent to establish the Jalisco Cartel's position in the illegal marijuana-grow business. The one who had shot, stabbed, and beaten the rest of the cartels out of Northern California before setting up

Jalisco's own supergrow in the Six Rivers National Forest. What he *didn't* know was how that *pendejo* Daniel had fucked everything up. Wasted the millions of dollars in bribes the cartel had paid to the state and local authorities by allowing a DEA informant to infiltrate the operation.

However, it was clear that Tito's boss cared less about the money or the time than about keeping his sister's favorite son from spending the rest of his life in a prison cell, which left Tito no choice but to accept whatever task he was being given.

"How long do I have?"

"Mr. Cortez's case is scheduled to go before the grand jury on Monday. I was led to believe that you were familiar with the situation."

"Seventy-two hours. That's not a lot of time," Tito mused.

"Can you do it?"

This time it was Tito's turn to be silent. "How many targets?"

"Two," Hale answered, "and we have a man on the inside who will provide you with everything you need."

"Then I am on my way."

Returning to the present, Tito grabbed his backpack and buttoned his sports coat on the way to the exit, where the steward stood waiting. "Are we good?" he asked in Spanish.

"Yes, your uncle made a call, so there is no need to deal with immigration," the attendant said. "I hope you had a pleasant flight."

He nodded and headed down the stairs to where a stone-faced man with wide shoulders stood next to the Tahoe. He opened the back door and Tito climbed inside before dropping his pack on the seat next to him and studying the black duffel resting on the floorboard. Leaning down, he unzipped the flap and pulled a Glock 17 out of the bag.

He expertly dropped the magazine and checked the chamber. Finding it empty, he ran the slide and dry-fired the pistol to get a feel for the trigger before checking the Trijicon SRO mounted to the slide. He adjusted the brightness and, once satisfied, slapped the magazine into the pistol and racked a hollow point into the chamber.

Shoving the Glock into his holster, Tito leaned back in his seat.

Prior to joining the cartel, Tito had been a member of the Fuerza

Especial de Reacción, the Mexican special forces units that were his president's weapon of choice in his half-hearted war on the cartels. It was a dangerous job. One that required a cold heart and a steady hand, but most importantly it required a man who was able to spend hours observing his targets through the rifle scope. Watching, waiting, until it was time to make that one perfect shot.

Being patient was easy when you were waiting to kill a man, but the same could not be said when you were waiting to hear from a source, and the fact that the lawyer's "inside man" had yet to reach out was beginning to piss him off.

Tito's mood darkened at the delay, and he was beginning to lose his sense of humor when his cell phone vibrated in his pocket. *About damn time*, he thought, pressing a Bluetooth into his ear.

"You're late," he said.

His greeting caught the man on the other end off guard, and he stuttered a nervous apology. "I-I'm sorry, it's been a busy morning, and I've got to be careful."

Tito wasn't interested in the man's excuses and was quick to cut him off. "I don't care about your problems. Do you have the information or not?"

"Yes."

"Then give it to me."

"The first target is Hannah Fowler. I have her address, picture, and phone number in the file I'm sending you."

"And what about Boone?"

With the first target, the man had sounded confident about his information, but at the mention of the informant's name, Tito heard hesitation in the man's voice.

"He hasn't made contact with his handler or anyone at the task force since the failed hit at the motel. But I'm tracking every development, and *when* they find him . . ."

This wasn't Tito's first time dealing with what the cartel referred to as an "outside consultant," and while most were professionals—men and women who stood behind the information they trafficked—he'd run into his share of amateurs. Sources who wrongly considered themselves somehow removed from the overall results of the operation.

It was a dangerous mindset. One that could jeopardize what was already a time-sensitive operation, and Tito knew it was time to put the man in his place.

"Stop talking and listen!" he snapped.

The man did as he was told, and Tito let the silence drag until he could almost feel his source squirming on the other end of the line. Then he continued, his voice cold as a cemetery wind. "I was *told* that you knew the informant's location. *If* I've been misinformed, please let me know; otherwise I will be adding *your* wife and children's names to the list."

"There is no need to threaten my family," the man assured him. "I've already told you that I can find him."

"How?"

"The task force put a tracker on Boone's truck. Once everyone leaves this office, I can use one of the office computers to access his location," the man insisted.

"Fine. What about the crime scene?"

"T-the crime scene?"

The man was flustered now. Off balance. Which was exactly how Tito wanted him. "There was a murder, correct? Which means there were bodies, and bodies attract cops. Do you have someone on-site tracking their progress?"

"No . . . I mean yes," his source stammered.

"Well? Which one is it?"

The man paused to take a breath, and when he continued, his voice was steady. "Yes, I've got a man on the scene, a DEA agent named—"

"A DEA agent? Are you out of your fucking mind!"

"No, wait. He's a burnout. A loser who is about to retire," the man assured him. "He's nothing."

Tito wasn't convinced and said so.

"Look, I will handle Keller if he becomes a problem," the man said. "You've got my word on that."

Having a DEA agent in the mix was a good way to complicate what was supposed to be a simple kill mission. And Tito hated complicated. Still, here he was, and with his bosses back in Mexico expecting results, he had no choice but to play the hand he'd been dealt.

"Fine, but I want regular reports."

"Yes, of course," the man said.

"Good, now send everything you have to my email," Tito said, unzipping his pack and pulling out his tablet.

"I'm sending it now."

There was a flurry of keystrokes on the other end of the line, followed a moment later by the ding from the tablet. Tito typed in his passcode and, after confirming that he'd received the target packet, came back on the line. "I've got it."

"Is there anything else?"

"Yes," Tito said. "I need you to listen *very* carefully. We don't have time for mistakes. After you find Boone's location, you will disable the tracker and wipe the computer clean so no one else can use it. Do you understand?"

"I understand."

"Good. I will be in touch," Tito said.

He hung up without waiting for the man's response and, after a quick scan of the target packet, leaned forward in his seat. "Our first stop is Willow Creek. Do you know it?"

"Yes sir."

"Then let's go—we've got people to kill."

CHAPTER 8

SIX RIVERS NATIONAL FOREST

Humboldt County, California

Mikey Boone drove north on State Route 96, his frazzled mind still trying to make sense of the gunfight at the Laguna Inn. He'd replayed the scene a hundred times, starting with the secure text from Keller that had brought him to Eureka and ending with the ambush in the parking lot.

He'd looked at it from every conceivable angle—run it forward, backward, and sideways—and each time he came up with the same answer. Someone in the DEA task force had sold him out. That the text sending him to the Laguna Inn had come from Keller put his handler at the top of his list. After all, he was the agent in charge, which meant he had the means, and if selling Boone out to the cartel provided the cash needed to send Keller's daughter to Stanford, then the agent damn sure had the motive.

However, as much as Boone wanted the pieces to fit, needed them to, he couldn't get there. The truth was, he'd been shaken down by enough dirty cops to be able to smell one from a mile away, and since becoming an informant, he'd yet to see Keller break a single rule. No, the man could be a jerk, but he wasn't corrupt, or incompetent for that matter, and the hit at the Inn had reeked of amateur hour.

Though Boone wished he could take credit for his survival, he knew

the only reason he was breathing was because whoever had placed the
hit had used local talent instead of a professional. For the cartel it was a
minor setback, but for Boone it was a reprieve, a chance to get the hell
out of the area before they sent someone who wouldn't miss.

A *sicario*.

The thought made him shudder, and he shook it away, trying to
remember how far it was to the turn. It had been years since he'd been
this far north, and his memory was hazy. The details and distances not
quite as sharp as they'd once been. He was certain that he was close,
but how close? Boone didn't know, but not wanting to miss the turn,
he took his foot off the gas, allowing the truck to slow as he scanned
the wall of pines that lined the narrow two-track. He tapped the brakes,
bringing the truck to a crawl, but even then, Boone nearly missed the
rusted *No Trespassing* sign peeking out from the thick brush that hung
over the mouth of the old logging road.

Throwing the truck into reverse, he backed up and then cut the
wheel hard to the left, the low-hanging limbs scraping against the metal
like wooden talons. Any other time the sound would have made him
wince, but with his attention divided between the throbbing pain of his
hastily dressed bullet wound and the axle-breaking potholes that lined
the roadway, it barely registered.

The road, like the land itself, was harsh and unyielding. A proving
ground that separated the men from the boys.

March or die. It was the motto retired Special Forces major Thomas
Grant had stenciled over the door of the bunkhouse Boone and Slade
had shared during their time at New Horizons. The mantra Grant had
screamed during the agonizing hikes through the mountains and the
punishing obstacle course he'd used to instill confidence in the troubled
teens the state had sent him to reform. By today's standards, Grant's un-
orthodox methods would have landed him in jail—or at the very least
brought up on child abuse charges—but back then there was still a large
segment of the country that believed in the now-archaic concepts of
self-control and personal responsibility.

But like the country itself, Grant had changed with the times, and when the state revoked his social work license in 2014, he shuttered New Horizons. Now instead of helping kids, Grant was using his skills to teach survivalists and preppers how to live off the grid. Together with a group of like-minded individuals, he'd helped establish the Citadel: a network of abandoned timber camps, mines, and old forestry cabins hidden in the mountains.

Like the name implied, the Citadel was a refuge, an insurance policy for a hardened few who felt the rule of law was on the verge of total collapse. For Boone it was the perfect place to lie low and hopefully steal enough supplies to get the hell out of California—if he didn't run out of gas first.

He managed to coax another mile out of the pickup before the engine finally stalled on the downslope of a hill. Using the truck's forward momentum, he coasted it into a thicket of willow trees and then grabbed his pack. Using the map he always kept in his glove box and an old compass, he determined his current position to be five hundred yards short of the game trail that would take him up to an old logging cabin. As much as he didn't want to make the hike, Boone knew he didn't have a choice.

Shouldering his pack, he crossed the road and trudged north, counting his steps the way he'd been taught at New Horizons. When he reached the appropriate pace count, he ducked into the trees and paused at the mouth of the trail that would take him up into the mountains. He pulled out his phone and stared at the screen, wanting to call Slade again but knowing he couldn't risk it—not without the DEA or the cartel tracking the call.

Shoving the phone back into his pocket and tightening his shoulder strap, Boone started up the trail.

———

An hour later he was inside the old forestry cabin, the afternoon light seeping around the edge of the wool blanket tacked over the cabin window. He dropped his pack in the living room and scanned the interior. At first glance the cabin was spartan to the point of being abandoned, the old couch and coffee table in front of the fireplace the only furnishings in the front room. But Boone knew better, and after shoving the coffee table to the side, he pulled out his old Case pocket-knife and dropped to his knees.

A quick search of the area showed a tiny notch cut into one of the boards, and he eased the blade into the slit and pushed down. At first nothing happened, but then the hidden latch gave way with an audible click, and Boone was able to pry the board from the floor, revealing a hidden compartment loaded with food, medical supplies, and an old lever action .30-30.

Man, I love preppers.

Leaving the rifle for the moment, he grabbed some food and the medical kit and carried it all into the kitchen. He set the cans on the counter and turned on the tap, drinking greedily from the water. After taking his fill, Boone re-dressed his wound and went back to the den, where he checked to make sure the rifle was loaded before leaning it against the arm of the couch. Then Boone took a seat, the stress and fatigue that had marked the day crashing down on his shoulders like a lead weight.

Boone hadn't wanted to come to the Citadel, and he sure as hell hadn't wanted to call Slade, but he didn't have a choice. The cartel just had too much influence, too many people who wouldn't hesi-tate to drop a dime if they saw him in town. Even way up here in the mountains, Boone knew that he was just prolonging the inevitable. No, the *only* way he was going to make it out alive was to find some-one he could trust—someone who knew the mountains well enough to guide him to Oregon—and Slade was the only person he knew who fit the bill.

Well, not the only one, he thought. There was always Grant.

The thought came and went with a sardonic smile. Grant would never help him, not after everything *he'd* done, but Slade was a different story. Slade had never been able to tell Boone no, and even though they hadn't parted under the best of circumstances, Boone was confident if he could just get his old friend on the phone, he could convince Slade to help him out.

Slade was going to call. He had to. Otherwise, Boone knew he was a dead man.

CHAPTER 9

Humboldt County, California

Slade jogged down the firebreak, the woman he'd pulled from the pool clinging weakly to his neck. A patchwork of burns covered her arms, and her breathing came in short, ragged gasps. While the burns looked bad, it was the smoke inhalation that had Slade worried, and knowing that she needed medical attention as soon as possible, he increased his pace.

Feet sloshing in his waterlogged boots, Slade continued down the firebreak, his bloodshot eyes locked on the Forest Service pumper parked on the side of the road. He trotted past the truck, but instead of the ambulance he knew Pitts had requested for him after he radioed ahead, all he found was the weary pump crew spooling hose from the reel mounted to the back of the truck.

Whirling back the way he'd come, Slade found the truck's supervisor. "Hey, where the hell is the bus?"

"Someone at the command center said it was still too hot to send it up. It's staged at the bottom of the hill."

Slade shifted the woman in his arms, his already exhausted back muscles straining under her weight. "At the *bottom* of the hill?"

"You know how it is with those asshats." The man shrugged. "It's all about liability. I'd offer one of my guys to take her for you, but we're a little busy."

"Forget it."

Slade pushed his tired legs into a jog and followed the trail down the slope. *Liability, my ass.* By the time he made it to the bottom, word of his exploits had spread, and a knot of onlookers was gathered around the ambulance. The crowd was made up of support staff and members of the fire crews who'd shown up late and had yet to be given a job. Men with clean faces and unsullied uniforms who cheered him on as Slade stumbled the final ten yards to the waiting ambulance.

There was a news team too, one of the local stations, and when the reporter saw him coming, he grabbed his cameraman and rushed over. All Slade had time to do was duck his head before the man was firing questions. "We heard about the rescue on the scanner—are you the one who pulled her out? What's your name?"

Keeping his head down, Slade bulled past him. "Keep that camera out of my face," he insisted.

"Just tell me your name."

Alerted by the noise, the paramedics pulled a gurney from the back of the ambulance and kicked down the wheels. "Make a hole," one of them shouted as Slade pushed through the crowd. They arrived just as he was nearing the end of his strength, and he gratefully let the lead paramedic take the woman from his arms.

"I've got her."

Slade nodded his thanks and turned to one of the newly arrived crewmen. "Hey, can you keep them back?"

"What, you don't want to be on TV?" The man grinned. "I thought smokejumpers loved the limelight."

"Not this one."

"First time for everything," the man said before turning to block the reporter. "You heard the man—*no* interviews."

While the reporter grumbled, Slade followed the gurney to the back of the ambulance and helped the paramedics lift it into the back. Still sensing the focus of the camera on his back, Slade moved past the doors and slumped against the far side of the bus. It was the first time he'd fully stopped moving since hitting the drop zone eight hours prior, and with the adrenaline rush that had come from pulling the woman out of the fire ebbing, Slade felt wrung out as an old dishrag.

He took a long drink from the CamelBak strapped to his back and lowered himself to the ground, wondering how long the news crew would stick around. The last thing he needed was to draw more attention to himself. That would get Buck riled for sure.

The slam of the ambulance door followed by the sight of the paramedics walking around the bus snapped him back to the present, and Slade forced himself upright. "How is she?" he asked.

"The burns look worse than they are, but she's got a serious case of smoke inhalation, so we're transporting her to Saint Joseph for observation and fluids."

Slade nodded, feeling instantly at ease. "Thanks for letting me know."

"Things could have gone a hell of a lot different if you hadn't gone in to get her," the paramedic said.

"Just doing my job." Slade shrugged.

The medic stepped closer and lowered his voice. "That's not what I heard."

Slade frowned at the man, not sure what to make of the comment. "What are you talking about?"

"Those guys over there work in the operations tent, and I heard them saying that someone from your crew had already called those cabins clear when you went in. Could be bullshit or—"

"Or what?"

"Or could be someone screwed up." The man shrugged. "Either way, that makes you a hero."

A hero?

Slade rolled the word around in his mind, the feel of it leaving him instantly uncomfortable. "No, I was just doing my job."

The medic nodded and was about to reply when his partner started beating his hand against the side of the ambulance.

"Hey, we need to roll."

"Duty calls," the paramedic said, shooting Slade a wink before climbing behind the wheel. "Stay safe."

"Yeah, you too," Slade muttered.

By the time the ambulance pulled away, the sun had buried itself low behind the mountains and the shadows were stretching long over the charred landscape. For the hand crews out on the line, fighting fire was dangerous enough in the daylight. With the approaching dusk most were already on the move, their minds on the plates of hot chow and well-earned night's sleep waiting for them back at the fire camp.

The smokejumpers, on the other hand, would be staying out, eating tasteless MREs, and the only chance at sleep would come after they spent most of the night cold trailing: checking the ash for any hidden coals that could cause a restart. Considering what was waiting for him back at the camp, Slade was in no rush to get going, but standing there looking up at the darkening sky, he realized it wasn't the work but having to deal with Buck that had him stalling.

It wasn't that Slade was afraid of his team leader as much as he was just tired of fighting, tired of having to prove that he had what it took to fight fire with the best of the best. He'd done enough of that back when he was with the Trinity River Conservation Camp, when he and the rest of the inmates had to wear county-correction orange instead of the wildland yellow.

Not that he was complaining. No, the truth was, fire camp had saved his life. Taken a punk kid from Garberville with a bad attitude and zero prospects of a future that didn't involve a cell and given him a purpose. Meaning. An opportunity to prove that he was more than the sum of the parts of his screwed-up life. It was this search that had drawn him to fire camp in the first place, and the camaraderie and shared adversity he found while fighting fire was something he couldn't let go.

Wouldn't let go.

Slade had known going into the job that there was a tribalism to wildland firefighting. A hierarchy that differentiated the ground pounders from the elites like the hotshots and smokejumpers, and he'd busted his ass to make sure that he was the best. However, despite all his hard work, Buck had made it clear that no matter how hard Slade worked, he'd always be an outsider.

"Not anymore," he promised himself.

Taking a deep breath, Slade turned and started the long, lonely trek up the hill. As he walked, he repeated those two words in his mind, determined that no matter what Buck threw at him, *this* time he wasn't backing down.

CHAPTER 10

Slade reached the apex in time to see a Forest Service Sherpa come in low over the trees, the blink of its nav lights shimmering through the smoke coiling up from the spot fires that surrounded the still-smoldering cabins. The pilot held it steady long enough for the loadmaster to kick the supply bundle from the cargo ramp, and then the aircraft was banking east, the drone of its engines swallowed by the immensity of the forest.

Slade found himself counting in his head as the bundle tumbled through the air. *One thousand, two thousand, three thousand.* Exactly four seconds after being kicked into the slipstream, the cargo chute snapped open and the bundle slowed, the slight breeze carrying it over the clearing where the rest of the team stood waiting.

The loadmaster had been on the money with his wind call, and the bundle thumped down in the center of the clearing, the rest of the team clapping while Pitts trotted out to retrieve it. Like all of the shit jobs on the team, unloading the bundles and hauling the food and equipment back to the fire line was a job for the rookies. Slade knew all he had to do was stay put to avoid the grunt work, but his conscience wouldn't let him. Not when it meant that Pitts would have to pick up his slack.

Wondering when he'd become such a softy, Slade followed the fire-break down the hill and then cut across the open ground to help his jump partner. He was at the edge of the clearing, close enough to hear Pitts cursing while he struggled to unhook the chute, but before he could clear the last line of trees, the flash of a headlamp in his face stopped him dead in his tracks.

"I wondered if you were coming back," Buck said.

"Why wouldn't I come back?" Slade asked, lifting a hand to shield his eyes.

"Well, I figured you'd be too busy cheesing it up for the TV cameras to remember that you actually had a job to do."

Slade took a step forward, his rage getting the better of his exhaustion. "Is that what you think of me? That I'm in this for the glory?"

"I'm not really sure *what* to think about you right now."

"Well, let me help you figure it out," Slade said, moving in close. "I might have a record, but I've earned my spot on this team. And I'm not going anywhere."

"Is that a fact?" Buck asked.

"It is, so either we can work together, or I can have Walt transfer me to another team. Either way, I'm done taking your shit. From now on, you treat me *exactly* like you treat the rest of the guys. No more hazing, no more bullshit—just let me do my job."

"And if I don't?"

"Then I'm going to show you what other skills I learned in prison."

"Are you threatening me?" Buck asked.

"No, I'm just trying to save you from a trip to the hospital," Slade said. "It's your call."

Buck stared at him for a moment, the look in his eyes half anger, half respect. Finally, he nodded. "You've got balls, kid, I'll give you that. But we are going to see if you've got what it takes to run with the big boys."

Slade was about to respond when Walt's tired voice came through the radio. "Hey, Buck, where you at?"

"I'm near the bundle," he said. "Slade just got back, and he's giving me an update on the woman he pulled from the cabin."

"How is she?"

"She's going to make it, thanks to Slade."

"That was good work," Walt said, then immediately shifted back to the reason he'd reached out. "Listen, we've got some spot fires up near my end, and with Johnson busting his knee on the jump, I'm a little shorthanded."

"You need one of the rookies?" Buck asked.

"Roger that."

Eager to get out of the cold trailing he knew was waiting for the team after unloading the bundle, Slade was all too happy to volunteer. "I'll go," he said.

Buck nodded and keyed up on the radio. "That's not a problem, boss. I'll send you Pitts."

Send Pitts, what the hell?

The thought of having to spend the rest of the night cold trailing with Buck when there were active fires still burning was too much to bear, and when his team leader signed off, Slade rounded on the man. "You're sending Pitts? What's up with that bullshit? I've got twice the experience he does."

"Maybe so," Buck said, grinning, "but you're the one who wanted to be treated just like another one of the guys."

"Anyone ever tell you that you're an asshole?"

"I might have heard it once or twice, but never from a rookie," Buck said. "Now, stop crying and go change out of those wet boots. We've got work to do."

CHAPTER 11

Keller raced south, the Impala's emergency equipment echoing loudly over the highway. In most places the moan of the siren and the frantic blink of the lights were enough to send the safety-conscious citizenry drifting to the emergency lane, but not on the West Coast. No, in California the motorists seemed to take it as a fascist's display of government power. A direct attack on their personal liberty that they combated by swinging into his lane and hitting the brakes.

Thanks to the evasive-driving class Keller had taken at Quantico, he easily dodged the first two cars, but after nearly plowing into the back of a Prius a few miles outside Santa Rosa, he cut the lights and sirens. Staying in the emergency lane, he stomped down on the gas, and the Impala's big V-8 howled like a scalded dog as he rocketed forward.

Traffic petered out around Fair Oaks, and once on the other side of the city, Keller had the road to himself. He set the cruise control and settled back in his seat, giving in to the meditative moan of the tires on the asphalt. As he zoned out, Keller's thoughts drifted to Emily and the shame of leaving Stanford for a job that no longer wanted him.

He'd wanted to be there for her, but old habits died hard. The guilt, on the other hand, was as fresh as ever, and it came as it always did. The cold knot in the pit of his stomach followed by the acidic burn of self-loathing that crawled up the back of his throat like bile after one too many cigarettes.

Keller shoved it away and turned his focus to Boone, wondering what in the hell the man had been doing at the Laguna Inn. He didn't know, but the flash of the road sign alerting him that he was twenty miles from Eureka steeled his resolve.

He could see the crime scene from the highway. The red and blue strobes from the police and fire department vehicles packed into the parking lot combined with the white glare from the halogen lights attached to the news van were like something from a circus.

"These hicks could fuck up a wet dream," he muttered to himself.

With his anger nearing its boiling point and wishing desperately for a cigarette, Keller swung the Impala off the street and stopped short of the bored deputy leaning against the Humboldt County Sheriff's Office sawhorse pulled across the drive. The man stared at him with the vacant look of someone who'd rather be doing anything but his job, then pushed off the horse and came sauntering over.

"You can't park here," the deputy said. "You are going to have to—"

"Just shut the fuck up and move the damn sawhorse," Keller snapped, flashing his badge.

At the sight of his shield, the man snapped to, suddenly all spit and polish. "Yes sir. Of course, sir."

He moved the barrier, allowing Keller to pull through and park behind an unmarked Tahoe. Hauling himself from the vehicle, he took a moment to stretch his back before popping the trunk with the fob, where he traded his sports coat and tie for the navy-blue DEA windbreaker.

Reaching back inside the trunk, he opened the lid of the small Pelican case he kept under the tire. Inside he found his emergency stash of Marlboro Reds and a book of matches.

Keller ripped the cellophane free and rapped the pack against the flat of his hand before fishing out a cigarette. He lit it and took a deep drag. After three months of not smoking, the lungful of nicotine hit his bloodstream like a shot of morphine.

God, has anything ever tasted so good?

As he smoked, Detective Harris came ambling over, his greased-back hair and the biker rings favored by the narco detectives shimmering in the light. "I thought you quit."

"And I thought these idiots knew how to run a fucking crime scene," Keller snapped back.

"Not my circus, not my monkeys." The man shrugged. "I'm just here to back you up."

"Thanks," Keller grunted.

"How did things go with Emily?"

"Fine until *you* called," Keller snapped back. Immediately regretting his outburst, he rubbed a hand across his face and muttered an apology. "How about we just focus on the scene?"

"No problemo," Harris said. "The CCTV from the hotel shows Boone pulling into the lot around midnight and parking over there. He cut his lights but kept the engine running like he was waiting for someone."

Keller nodded and took in the scene, noting the fluorescent yellow markers the evidence techs had laid out on the grimy pavement before shifting his gaze to the boxy security cameras perched beneath the eaves of the hotel. "And you're sure it was Boone?"

"The camera is a piece of shit, but we got a good shot of the plate."

"I'm going to need a copy."

"Already done," Harris said, handing over a plastic case with a freshly burned DVD inside. "You talk to Cole?"

"Yeah," Keller said, shoving the case into his jacket pocket.

"And?"

"I owned it. Told him I fucked up and I'd find Boone."

"I'm all about being noble, but does it ever get lonely up there on your cross?" Harris asked. "I mean, did it ever occur to you that if Cole wasn't so cheap with the overtime, maybe we could have kept Boone in town and watched him ourselves instead of letting Fresno PD babysit him?"

"What's done is done." Keller shrugged. "Now, walk me through it again."

"It's like I said: Boone backed in, and thirty seconds after he cut the lights, those two shitheads came running out of the motel with a couple of hand cannons," Harris said, pantomiming a man holding a rifle. "Boone dropped the first one—"

"Forget the gun—what was he doing here?" Keller interrupted.

Harris shrugged. "Maybe he was trying to score?"

"No, Boone was clean."

"Pete, I know he was your CI and all," Harris said, "but Boone was a criminal, and he was using us just as sure as we were using him."

Keller nodded and surveyed the area around him, the unanswered question stuck in the back of his mind like a splinter. *What the hell were you doing here, Boone?*

"Please tell me we've got something on the two stiffs," he finally said.

"According to the homicide detectives," Harris replied, nodding to the two men in ill-fitting suits hovering around the bodies, "they're just a couple of low-level bangers. But I went ahead and snapped a few pictures of their ink."

"Let me see them."

Harris pulled out his phone and handed it over. "Fair warning, my wife says I'm the world's worst photographer."

"She's not wrong," Keller said as he studied the screen.

The first picture was dim and slightly out of focus, and he swiped past it, focusing all his attention on the second image. This one was better, and when he zoomed in, Keller could clearly see the bolded *JNIC* inked on the man's forearm.

"Shit, it's the Jalisco Cartel."

"First it's pot and now it's attempted murder," Harris said. "You weren't lying about these guys."

"Yeah, and I've got a bad feeling that *this*," Keller said, pointing at the bodies, "is just the beginning."

"Why do you say that?"

"Because when the Jalisco Cartel wants someone dead, they don't stop until you are in the ground," he said, looking up and casting an eye over the onlookers lingering around the edge of the crime scene.

"Considering all the eyes on us, I'd wager that someone in Mexico has already gotten the call that Boone is still breathing, which means we've got about eighteen hours to find him and get him into protective custody. Because after that we'll be looking for a corpse."

CHAPTER 12

Willow Creek, California

While Enrique negotiated the sprinkling of late-afternoon traffic, Tito sat in the back of the Tahoe, scrolling through the information on Hannah Fowler his source had sent him. The attached picture showed a blond woman with a tanned face and cheery eyes.

According to her bio, Fowler was a former forest ranger—a crackpot who'd spent more of her time accusing her bosses of mismanagement and cronyism than she had patrolling the forest. After a few years on the job and a half-dozen write-ups, she'd resigned her posting to wage a one-woman war on anyone who dared threaten her beloved forest. And since leaving, Fowler had fearlessly targeted everyone from the Six Rivers superintendent to the heads of the local timber companies.

In his work as a sicario, Tito's targets were usually pieces of shit. Rival gang members who'd dared to encroach on the cartel's turf or the occasional thief stupid enough to try and jack one of their loads. Not environmental crusaders and certainly *not* women.

In fact, the only reason Fowler was a blip on this particular radar was because she'd started asking questions about a piece of land she had no business knowing about. Sitting there, Tito found himself wondering if her decision to go after the grow sites was a publicity stunt or just plain stupidity.

Tito didn't know and honestly didn't care. He had his orders, and they were to put Boone and Fowler in the ground, so that was exactly what he intended to do.

He spent the rest of the drive poring over the attached satellite map, absorbing everything he could about the target location. According to the imagery, Fowler lived in a trailer on a small parcel sandwiched between Forest Service land and a large cornfield that separated her from the newly built housing community to the north. It was isolated and rough country with the only way in or out a lone gravel drive.

Tactically it was a nightmare, and if Tito had been going against professionals or a quarry that knew he was coming, he would have needed more time. At least a day to do a proper recon and establish a pattern of life on the target. Once that was done, he would have mapped his primary ingress and egress route.

Then there were the contingencies: how he would get out if he came under fire, the name of a local doctor if he was hit, and the myriad of other details that were part and parcel of his lethal trade.

Luckily, Fowler didn't know he was coming, which gave Tito the element of surprise, and that, plus the array of law enforcement badges and credentials he'd seen in the duffel, gave him an idea.

"How do you want to play this?" Enrique asked.

"We go in through the front door," Tito said, tugging a Humboldt County Sheriff's badge with a metal chain around it from the bag and looping it over his head.

"Are you serious?"

"It will be dark by the time we get there, and with this truck and the badge, she'll think we're cops," Tito said.

"So you are just going to walk up there and knock?"

"I've done it before." Tito shrugged.

"What if she doesn't open it?"

"That's why I've got this," Tito said, holding up a suppressor.

"Man, you are one ballsy son of a bitch."

"Sometimes that's all you need."

An hour later Enrique pulled the Tahoe off the highway and followed an unnamed road into the foothills of Baldwin Peak. The sun went down early in the mountains, and even with the onboard GPS alerting them to "turn right in one hundred yards," they almost missed the mouth of the gravel trail that snaked east through the timber.

"Right there," Tito said, pointing to the sliver of gray barely visible beneath the shadow-draped pines. Enrique made the turn and killed the running lights while Tito pulled on a pair of latex gloves and screwed the suppressor to the end of the Glock. He could see the trailer now, the sallow glow of the porch light illuminating neatly trimmed hedges and a sky-blue Jeep parked at the end of the gravel drive.

Enrique pulled in behind the Jeep, and Tito climbed out. He shoved the pistol into his waistband and followed the gravel walk to the porch, making sure the badge around his neck was visible before knocking. At first there was nothing, but after a second, louder knock, he saw the shadowed outline of a woman through the fogged pane of glass in the center of the door.

"Who is it?" she asked.

"Sheriff's office, ma'am," Tito said, flashing a reassuring smile. "Would you mind opening your door?"

There was the rattle of locks being thrown, and then Hannah Fowler stood in the open doorway, her face twisted into a concerned frown. "Is there something wrong, Officer?"

"We had a report of a gas leak in the area, and they sent me to check it out," he said.

"A gas leak?" she asked, sniffing at the air. "I don't smell anything."

"Neither do I," Tito said, still wearing the smile, "but I've got to check. Do you mind if I come inside?"

"Not at all," Fowler said, motioning him forward.

Tito stepped through the doorway and found himself in a tastefully decorated entryway that smelled of freshly cut flowers. He glanced into the living room, where the TV was playing a nature documentary, and then back at Fowler. She was prettier in person, and her blue eyes conveyed an innocence that her picture failed to capture.

A shame I've got to kill her.

"Who called in the leak?" she asked.

Tito ignored the question and stepped forward, trying and failing to see into the kitchen. "Is there anyone else inside the house?"

"No, I live alone," she answered. "Now, do you mind telling me who called in the leak?"

When he turned to face her, the frown was back, and the convergence of the worry lines at the corners of Fowler's eyes sent his hand sliding for the butt of the Glock hidden at the back of his waistband.

Might as well get this over with.

Tito had the pistol out fast as a snake, and before Fowler could respond, his finger had curled tight around the trigger. The Glock bucked in his hand, and the 9 mm it sent punching through Fowler's forehead dropped her in place.

Tito holstered the pistol and bent to retrieve the empty shell casing from the floor. Tucking it into his pocket, he turned his attention to the body splayed across the floor, his instincts telling him to carry it to the truck, drive it into the mountains, and leave it for the predators. But before he'd boarded the jet that brought him to the States, Tito had received a call from Gabriel Cortez, the head of the Jalisco Cartel, and the man had wasted no time making his expectations clear.

"This is not just about saving my nephew," the man said. "It's about sending a message to anyone stupid enough to interfere in our affairs."

A message.

Knowing that if the boss had wanted subtlety, he would have sent another shooter, Tito grabbed Fowler by the leg and dragged her lifeless body into the den. Ignoring the crimson smear left across the cream-colored carpet, he dumped her unceremoniously beside the gas fireplace and continued into the kitchen, where he pulled the stove away from the wall and ripped the gas line free.

Tito waited for the hiss and the sulfury smell of natural gas, and when he was sure it was flowing, he went back into the living room and turned on the fireplace.

You want ash, I'll give you ash.

CHAPTER 13

Willow Creek, California

Jake Slade trudged south through the blackened timber with the rest of the mixed crew of smokejumpers and hotshots tasked with cold trailing the now-dormant fire. Compared to the head-on attack of fighting an active blaze, cold trailing was tedious business. All the digging, flipping, and scraping required to locate and extinguish the live burns simmering beneath the fire-blackened deadfall left Slade feeling like he was playing some masochist version of Whac-A-Mole. Still, it was part of the job, and Slade knew the sooner they got it done, the sooner he and the rest of the line could get some much-needed rest.

Pausing to pull down the filthy bandanna tied over his mouth, Slade took a drink from the CamelBak strapped to his back. The first swallow came out of the hose warm as bathwater, and Slade swished it around to clear the grit from his mouth. Spitting it out, he took a longer, cooler drink, savoring the feel of the water over his parched throat while he gazed at the smoldering wasteland before him.

Might as well get this over with.

Leaning into the fatigue, he hefted his Pulaski and stepped to the jagged section of a fallen tree lying across his path. He swung the tool high and brought it thudding home, feeling the blade twist when he hit his mark. It was a solid blow, but Slade knew the moment he felt the impact reverberate up his tired forearms that he hadn't hit it hard enough.

On cue, Buck emerged from the shadows to his left, his own Pulaski resting comfortably on his shoulder. "Gonna need more ass than that to split *that* sucker."

Annoyed, Slade ripped the blade free and spit on his gloves in preparation for another swing. "Don't you have anything better to do than watch me work?"

"I'm not watching you. I'm supervising."

Slade rolled his eyes and gripped the handle tight as he wound up for another swing. He hit harder this time, giving it everything he had, but still the stubborn log refused to split. *What the hell is this thing made of?*

Buck shook his head and stepped forward, a wry smile creasing his soot-stained face. "Here, let me show you a trick."

Slade stepped back and eyed the man. "A trick? What, are we friends now?"

"You really are a pain in the ass, you know that?"

Slade was sweating, hot despite the rapidly cooling forest, and as much as he wanted to tell Buck to fuck off, he was too tired not to take the man up on his offer. "Fine, knock yourself out."

"When I first came to the smokejumpers, I was all gas, no brake, just like you."

"Is that a fact?"

"Yep. Thought I could power my way through whatever I found on the ground, even a hard-ass piece of oak like this," Buck said, giving the log a rap. "It took me a while, but finally I came to realize that the only way to get ahead was to work smarter, *not* harder."

"I don't understand."

Instead of answering, Buck used the toe of his boot to flip the log over, exposing its ash-gray belly. He gave it a kick to check for sparks and then, with one swing, chopped through the fire-softened underside.

Slade shook his head in disbelief. "Well, shit."

"Stick with me, kid, and you might just learn something."

They cleared for another hour, and by the time they finally reached the fire line that marked the southern edge of the burn, it was almost seven thirty. While Buck checked in with Walt over the radio, the crew found a cleared spot on the edge of the unburnt pines and collapsed.

Slade dropped next to a large boulder and shrugged out of his pack. The relief was instantaneous, and he let out a contented sigh, the rumble of his stomach reminding him that he had yet to eat dinner. Slade dug into his cargo pocket and pulled out the MRE he'd been carrying with him since leaving the drop zone.

After slicing open the bag, Slade dug in. He ate fast, making short work of the entrée and the accompanying pound cake and following it up with a liter of water from his Nalgene bottle. He could have eaten more but decided to rest instead, and after packing up all his trash, he leaned back against his pack, the brush of his hand against the hard outline of his phone stuffed into his pocket reminding him of the call from Boone.

Slade pulled the phone from his pocket and stared at the screen. There was a part of him that wanted to call the man back, or at the very least listen to his message, but Slade knew he wouldn't. Not after what Boone had done. There was a time when they'd been at New Horizons when Slade had thought of Boone as the brother he'd never had. Boone had protected Slade from the older kids when he first arrived, taught him how to make the hospital corners Grant required when they made their beds, and even carried some of his gear during the first couple of long hikes.

Back then, Boone had been everything Slade wanted to be: strong, funny, and quick to learn no matter how hard the task. But there was a darkness beneath his easygoing exterior—a selfishness that allowed Boone to manipulate those he called friends without any visible conscience.

The first time he got Slade to lie for him was after Boone had smuggled in a carton of cigarettes to sell to the other kids. When Grant found the contraband, Boone convinced Slade to blame it on Silas, one of the older boys set to graduate at the end of the month. It had seemed like a small thing at the time, but Slade had trouble sleeping that night, and his guilt only got worse when he woke up the next day to learn that Grant had kicked Silas out of the camp.

"Who gives a shit?" Boone had laughed. "He was an asshole anyway."

Yet worse than the guilt was the fact that having lied for Boone once, Slade was now under his thumb, and before he knew it, his complicity had stretched from cigarettes to beer and finally weed.

How Boone had ever gotten plugged in with the outlaw marijuana growers who proliferated in the backwoods of Humboldt County, Slade never knew, but toward the tail end of their "tour" at New Horizons, Boone had given the illegal growers the locations of a handful of hunters' shacks and cabins Grant and some of his survivalist buddies had built in the mountains. When the former Green Beret learned that some of the local growers were using the structures to hide their pot from the cops, he went ballistic.

For once, Slade had nothing to do with Boone's schemes. In fact, the first time he found out what Boone was up to was when Grant confronted them with the evidence. Having always seen Grant listen to both sides, Slade had thought the older man would give him a chance to prove his innocence, but Grant hadn't even given him a chance to speak.

"Your word is no good here, Jake," he said. "I want you gone by morning."

The hell with them both, Slade thought, pulled to the present as the light from Buck's headlamp came bouncing down the trail. Shoving the phone back into his pocket, Slade got to his feet and dusted off his pants. "What's the word?"

"Good news is that it looks like we've got some weather coming in. High winds and a forty percent chance of rain."

"And the bad?" one of the hotshots asked.

"Still no time for when we are heading back, so I hope everyone brought their umbrellas."

On cue there was a flash of light followed by a low rumble from the far side of the trees.

"Looks like that thunderstorm is here," someone observed aloud.

Slade glanced up at the sky, wondering if he needed to get his poncho out, but instead of clouds, he saw stars through the haze of smoke that hung over the canopy. Frowning, he turned his attention east and focused on a yellow glow filtering through the gaps in the trees.

"I don't think that was thunder," he said.

"Oh yeah?" Buck drawled. "You a meteorologist now?"

Slade ignored him and began walking toward the distant light. "I'm going to take a piss."

He pushed deeper into the trees and stepped behind a large pine. While he answered nature's call, he watched light flickering through the timber, convinced that it was growing in intensity.

Might as well check it out.

Zipping up, Slade pushed through the now-thinning trees. He walked for another five yards and into a clearing overlooking the valley, then stopped in his tracks, the sight of flames spewing from the burning trailer below turning night into day.

"Fire!" he yelled.

CHAPTER 14

Willow Creek, California

Slade rushed back to the makeshift camp, his voice echoing loudly through the trees. "Willow Creek is on fire."

"What the hell are you talking about? There's no fire," Buck replied.

The words had just left his lips when his radio chirped to life and the voice of the dispatcher came hissing across the net. "Dispatch to Pumper One and all available units. We've got a reported explosion and possible structure fire in the vicinity of—"

In an instant everyone was on their feet and grabbing their gear. "Every damn time," one of the hotshots moaned.

"Welcome to the smokejumpers," Buck said.

With no time for more rest, Slade dug out a pack of freeze-dried coffee and poured it into his mouth. He chased it with a gulp of water and winced, praying it would give him the boost he needed for the battle to come. Shouldering his pack and hefting his Pulaski, Slade got ready to move while Buck made contact with dispatch.

The conversation was short and quick to confirm what everyone already knew—besides the responding pumper, they were the only crew in the area. A look at the map showed it to be two miles to Willow Creek, and with Buck in the lead, they started down the hill at a steady jog.

After a day digging line, a cross-country run with a heavy pack and gear introduced Slade to a different dimension of pain. Besides his already sore legs, his lungs were now burning, and the Pulaski hanging over his shoulder felt like it had been filled with lead.

Still, Buck held his pace, and with the older man showing no signs of slowing down, Slade was determined to push himself until he dropped. Once on flat ground they veered east, leaving the hotshots who couldn't keep up in their wake.

"C-can we get a tanker in here?" Slade panted.

Buck shook his head. "Not when it's dark."

Deciding to save both his questions and his breath, Slade ran in silence, his eyes on the flames spreading through the darkness ahead. He could smell the fire now. Not the earthy scent of trees and brush, but the noxious stench of upholstery and rubber. As they closed in on the last four hundred yards, Slade could feel the heat and hear the crash of shattering glass and the boom of the gas lines that crisscrossed the property.

The fire was spreading, the half light of the flames illuminating the sparks drifting over the cornfield that separated the trailer from the community of smaller homes on the east side. *Shit, it's going to jump.*

While keeping the flames away from the other homes was paramount, the first thing on Slade's mind was seeing if anyone was actually inside the burning trailer. While Buck laid out the fire line, Slade pulled away and headed for the rear of the structure.

"Get your ass back here," Buck yelled.

Slade ignored him and, pulling his mask over his face, ran toward the sliding glass door. Holding his hand up to ward off the heat, Slade made it to the porch and got a quick glance inside before the heat and smoke sent him stumbling back. For an instant he thought he saw the huddled shape of a person on the far side of the kitchen, but with his eyes watering he couldn't be sure.

"I—I can't see if there's anyone . . ." he got out after pulling back to stand near Buck.

"Stop playing the fucking hero and do your damn job," Buck barked.

For once, Slade was too tired to argue, and he joined the hastily assembled team of hotshots and hand crew men as they began digging line. They hacked at the earth and tried to create a hasty perimeter, but the head was moving too fast.

Shit, this isn't going to work.

The bellow of a horn through the smoke announced the arrival of the pump truck, and as soon as it bumped into view, Buck was screaming at Slade to get the hose. Slapping one of the hotshots who'd been pulled into their makeshift work crew on the back to let him know he was stepping off the line, Slade rushed back to the vehicle.

"Damn, son, every time I see you, things are going to shit," one of the men said from the back of the truck. Slade looked up to find the supervisor he'd seen on the firebreak grinning down at him.

"I'm just lucky that way," he responded, reaching up for the hose.

The man handed it down, and while the rest of the pump crew set about regulating the pressure, Slade dragged the hose toward the fire line. He was almost there when one of the men hit the fill switch and water came coursing through the hose. In an instant the line went taut, the weight of the water nearly ripping the hose from Slade's hand. Struggling to hold on, he muscled it toward the cornfield, his legs and back shaking from the effort.

Chest heaving and vision spinning, Slade knew he was reaching the end of his strength. But no sooner had the thought crossed his mind than he heard one of the hotshots yell out, "She's turning on us."

Slade looked up to see the head circling back, the cavernous yaw of its flaming mouth like a dragon trying to swallow its own tail. With nothing but fresh timber between it and the fire line, it quickly picked up speed, closing the distance as it charged up the hill.

As a younger man Slade had looked at fire the same way the first cave dweller did when he rubbed two sticks together and created a spark. It was an ally: a friend that cooked his food, shielded him from both the dark and cold. It wasn't until he became a wildland firefighter that he saw its true nature. Realized that it was a wolf in sheep's clothing. A predator that hunted, fed, and killed without conscience. An enemy to be engaged and destroyed with extreme prejudice.

To Slade and the men around him, fighting fire was not a battle; it was a war. A zero-sum game between man and nature, which was why smokejumper and hotshot crews were innately militaristic.

But damn, was it beautiful.

His tired muscles forgotten, Slade hoisted the hose over his shoulder and dragged it the last of the way, shouting for the men to make a hole before passing it off to one of the hotshots. With Buck directing the flow, the hotshot opened the nozzle and sprayed the flames. But Slade knew it wasn't enough.

"We need something else."

"If you've got a plan, I'm all ears," Buck said.

A quick glance around the area showed a tractor sitting at the edge of the field, its rear blade glinting in the firelight. "What about that?" Slade asked, pointing toward it.

"If you can find the keys . . ."

Keys, my ass.

Leaving Buck to direct the hand crew, Slade hustled over to the tractor and turned on his headlamp. Not finding the keys in the ignition, he pulled out his pocketknife and ducked under the steering wheel to pry out the wires. It had been a long time since Slade had hot-wired a car—or anything for that matter—but after a few seconds of slicing and splicing, he had the John Deere running. Another thirty seconds spent fumbling with the blade got it extended and to its lowest setting. Slade jumped into the seat, threw it into gear, and stomped on the gas.

He swung the wheel wide of the encroaching flames and came in at a right angle, cutting across the fire's path. The tractor moved slower than he expected, but the blade was sharp and cut the corn down to the earth. However, it took multiple passes, and despite each strip he cut, the flames continued their relentless advance.

By the time Slade lined up for his final pass, the flames had closed to within five feet, and their radiant heat left him feeling like he was trying to suck air from a blast furnace. Starved for oxygen, the engine stuttered and the tractor slowed. Slade kept his foot on the gas, trying to finish the cut before the flames overwhelmed him.

"Get out of there," Buck shouted.

Realizing he wasn't going to make it, Slade reached down and fumbled with the throttle lock. He gave it a hard pull, aware of the flames coiling to envelop him. The instant he felt the engine lock into position, Slade threw himself from the stricken tractor and, praying the gas tank didn't explode, ran for his life.

CHAPTER 15

After leaving the crime scene, Special Agent Keller headed back to the office he shared with the task force at the Humboldt County Sheriff's Office. With the night shift already out on the streets, he had the place to himself. He grabbed a laptop from the darkened squad room, then headed into the kitchenette to scrounge up a lukewarm cup of coffee.

Not wanting to be disturbed if anyone came back to the office, he carried the laptop and the coffee to one of the interrogation rooms. He closed the door behind him, took a seat at the table, and loaded the DVD into the player.

The footage was from the entire day, and Keller hit the fast-forward button while sipping the coffee. Like Harris said, the camera was a piece of crap, and the analog footage zipping by on the screen reminded Keller of the old patrol cameras they used to show on *Cops*.

Slowly day turned to night, and Keller pulled out his pad to scan the notes he'd taken at the crime scene. According to Harris, Boone had arrived at around midnight, and while the exactitude of the time wouldn't have been a big issue for most civilians, as an investigator Keller had learned the hard way that cases often hinged on the most minute details. With that thought in mind, he waited until the time stamp at the bottom hit midnight before pressing play.

Leaning back in his chair, Keller popped a stick of gum into his mouth and clicked the ballpoint pen, his eyes locked on the screen. Ten minutes later, he watched Boone's pickup roll into the lot, his headlights already off. After pausing to note the *exact* time of arrival, Keller hit the play button, his eyes locked on the screen in anticipation of the shooters rushing into the frame.

They came in fast and hard, but before they could get their shotguns into action, Boone beat them to the punch. The flashes inside the cab were followed by the puffs of safety glass as the bullets blasted out through the windshield and then back in the form of the return fire from the lone survivor's shotgun.

Having now seen the entire video, Keller started it over, studying it frame by frame from the moment Boone arrived in the parking lot. When he found one that gave him a clear view inside the cab, he hit the pause button and zoomed in.

Magnified, the already pixelated image blurred into a fuzzy gray wash of shadows and light. Even so, Keller had seen his daughter use the same move a hundred times and had no problem identifying the source of the light shining up from Boone's lap.

He's texting. The question was, *who* was he texting?

If Boone had been any of the other thirty-nine million people who lived in California, Keller would have had to wait for a warrant to find out. But Boone was a convicted felon, and part of the "snitch jacket" that he'd signed to become a confidential informant gave the DEA the right to tap into his phone.

Exiting the video, Keller opened another window, logged into the man's Google account, and began downloading his phone history. Compared to the fiber broadband they had at the federal building in Sacramento, the sheriff's office's outdated cable felt slow as dial-up. As the minutes stretched by with nothing but the spinning wheel on the screen, he was beginning to think that his request had timed out when the monitor finally blinked white and the results appeared.

About damn time.

According to the phone log, Boone had texted the same number three times before the men came rushing out of the motel. Usually, the realization would have sent Keller scrambling for a pen and scrap of paper so he could copy it down and run it through one of the Agency's reverse directories to find the owner, but this time there was no need.

Staring at the screen, looking at his *own* number, Keller found himself wondering if someone was screwing with him. *How is this possible?* Then he remembered who he was dealing with. Besides being one of the most violent and ruthless cartels, the Jalisco Cartel was also one of the most profitable, and thanks to its control of oil, cocaine, and meth production, it was able to afford the best cryptology and counterintelligence platforms on the market—tools that made spoofing a cell number ridiculously easy.

But while they were able to fool the caller ID on both Boone's phone and the computer, Keller knew they weren't advanced enough to trick the actual provider. Opening a second window, he brought up the AT&T website, and after entering the credentials he'd used to set up Boone's account, he logged in.

Keller leaned forward, scrolling through the list of numbers AT&T had tracked that day, until he found what he was looking for.

Got you.

Using the mouse, he dragged the phone number into a reverse phone directory and hit the Enter key, the shot of adrenaline that came with being on the hunt coursing through his bloodstream like an electric charge as he waited for a hit. But the high was short lived, and instead of the name he'd been hoping for, the *No Results Found* that popped up a moment later sent him crashing back to earth.

Well, damn.

Slamming a fist on the table, Keller leaned back in his chair and stared up at the ceiling, searching his mind for his next move. *C'mon, c'mon, think.* But he had nothing. Tired from the long day and already fiending for another smoke, he was about to take a break when he noticed a solitary phone number at the bottom of Boone's phone history.

Keller ran the number through the reverse database, and this time he got a name.

Jake Slade.

When a quick Google search failed to bring up any information, Keller decided to play a hunch and logged into the National Crime Information Center, or NCIC.

Created by the FBI in 1967, NCIC was the justice system's central database—a searchable repository of criminal records, fugitive information, stolen property, and missing persons. That it contained the personal information of not only those who'd committed crimes but also the suspects, victims, and persons of interest involved in millions of cases made it one of the largest collections of phone numbers on the planet, and this time when Keller submitted his query, he found himself looking at a California Corrections mug shot of a man with hard eyes and short hair. However, his record showed none of the charges Keller was used to seeing—no felony drug possession, aggravated assaults, or anything more significant than the grand theft auto charge that had landed the man in jail.

There was a handful of disciplinary records for the fights he'd gotten into during his first few months behind bars—fights that according to the prison guards Slade hadn't started but had no problems finishing—but still, he didn't have half the record that Boone did.

Then why the hell did he call this man?

Keller's confusion only deepened as he read through Slade's request to join the Trinity River Conservation Camp and the glowing status reports from Cal Fire that followed. By the time he reached the end of the official record, he had more questions than answers.

Confronted with another roadblock, Keller got to his feet, grabbed his cup, and headed out into the hall. The coffeepot was empty, and he scrounged around in the cupboard for the filters and canister of Folgers to make another pot. He found what he was looking for, and a few minutes later the coffee maker was gurgling contentedly.

The carafe had just begun to fill when Keller remembered the tracker they'd put on Boone's truck when he first came to work for them. *How could I have forgotten that?* Leaving the break room, he was on his way back to his computer when he noticed a sliver of light leaking from one of the offices in the squad room.

Too amped up to bother seeing who'd come in, Keller went back to his computer and logged into the tracking site. For once, the internet was up to the task and the site came up immediately. Taking it as a good sign, Keller typed in the case number, but his optimism evaporated the moment he saw the message on the screen.

Live track terminated per hosting agency.

"What? No!" Keller shouted, his stomach tightening into a knot.

Thinking it a glitch, he reentered the search, only to get the same result. He kicked the side of the desk hard enough to leave a dent and then dug his phone from his pocket and punched in a number from memory. "C'mon, answer."

The phone trilled in his ear, and Keller thought it was going to voicemail until the line finally connected and a tired voice said, "Pete, do you have any idea what time it is?"

"Yeah, Robby, and I wouldn't be calling you if it wasn't urgent," he replied. "I just need to ask you one question."

"Fine, what is it?"

"Do you remember that tracker we put on Boone's truck when he first came to work for us?"

"I remember . . ." There was a pause as the man yawned loudly. "What about it?"

"Someone turned it off and removed all the data."

"That's impossible. You must have—"

"Robby, I'm looking at the screen now, and I'm telling you it's not there. Is there any way you can check it on your end?"

There was an exaggerated sigh, followed by the creak of springs as the man got out of bed. "Fifty bucks says it's a glitch."

Keller hoped the man was right, but something in his gut told him he wasn't. Speculation was a cop's worst enemy, which was why it was so important to stay focused on the facts of a case. Still, listening to the flurry of keystrokes coming across the line, Keller had a sense that there were unseen forces working against him.

But who, and more importantly, why?

Before he could come up with an answer, Robby was back on the line.

"Damn, you're right."

Keller asked, "Is there any way to tell who erased it?"

"No, they wiped the logs."

"What does that mean?"

"It means," Robby said, "that whoever did this knew what they were doing."

Keller's shoulders slumped. "Well, thanks for—"

"Hold on," Robby said, "I think they forgot to clear the IP address. Yeah, they did."

"Where?" Keller asked.

"Looks like it was from one of the supervisors' computers at the sheriff's—"

Remembering the light from the squad room, Keller leaped to his feet and raced across the hall. He threw open the door, ready to confront whoever was inside, but it was empty. The only sign of life was the bounce of the screen saver across the monitor.

Still, someone *had* been there. Keller was sure of it.

On a hunch, he pulled out the chair and touched the seat. The feel of residual heat against the palm of his hand confirmed that whoever they were, Keller had just missed them.

CHAPTER 16

Eureka, California

Two blocks away, Richard Cole slowed his Forest Service pickup at the light and took a deep breath. He let it out slowly and tried to still his shaking hands, all too aware of the bullet he'd dodged back at the sheriff's office. He'd thought using their computer instead of the one at his office was a good idea. Clever even. But it had nearly turned into a disaster when Keller showed up.

The thought of what could have happened if Keller had seen him sent his stomach twisting into knots. Cole shook it off and typed out a quick message to Tito.

> It's done.

Fifteen minutes later he was standing in his darkened kitchen, picking at the reheated plate of meat loaf that should have been his dinner. With his wife and son already asleep, the silence of the house was unnerving, and as much as he didn't want to think about the litany of federal laws and state statutes he'd broken by canceling the tracker on Boone's truck, it was hard to think about anything else.

Accessing the system had been easy enough, but the digital cleanup that followed had taken much longer than Cole had planned. If the tracker had been solely under the Forest Service purview, he wouldn't have bothered, but since everyone on the task force had access, including Keller and the Humboldt County detectives, he knew he couldn't afford to leave any trace.

Cole spent the drive home going over in his mind every directory he'd scrubbed and file he deleted, and by the time he pulled into the drive, he'd been confident in his work. But standing there in his kitchen, he found himself suddenly unsure.

What if I missed something.

The doubt slipped unbidden into his mind, and the thought of Keller finding out that he'd tampered with his investigation sent icy fingers of dread curling around his stomach. The fear robbed Cole of his appetite, and he knew that he was done eating. Giving up on the meat loaf, he carried his plate to the trash can, scraped it clean, and then loaded it into the dishwasher before heading upstairs.

Forgoing a shower, he slipped into bed, careful not to awaken his wife next to him. He was tired, and his eyes were heavy from the two hours spent staring at the computer screen, but instead of sleep, Cole found himself staring up at the darkened ceiling. His mind drifted back to the first time he'd been approached by the cartel.

The first meeting came with a $50,000 advance and the understanding that Cole would keep Red Cap closed until the cartel harvested its illegal marijuana crop. It was an easy ask, one Cole had accomplished with the stroke of a pen, but in retrospect he should have known it was going to take more than a closure notice to keep someone like Fowler from sticking her nose where it didn't belong.

That bitch.

A better man might have felt guilty about what he'd done, but not Cole. No, he'd tried everything in his power to keep Fowler out of the area, but she just wouldn't listen. Wouldn't leave it alone. As far as he was concerned, both Fowler and Boone had gotten what they deserved for screwing around with the cartel. Still, Cole knew that Keller would have questions. After all, Boone was his CI, which made the man *his* responsibility.

However, it wasn't the DEA special agent's digging that had Cole unnerved but the sicario he'd spoken to on the phone. There was something about the man—something about the coldness in his voice—that had him worried.

Realizing there was nothing more he could do, Cole was just drifting off to sleep when his phone began vibrating on the bedside table. Quick to silence it before it woke up his wife, he slipped out of bed and padded into the bathroom. Closing the door behind him, he squinted against the glare of the light and looked at the caller ID.

McCoy.

Here we go.

"McCoy . . . what's going on?"

"Boss, I'm sorry to wake you, but we've got a problem. Hannah Fowler is dead."

Cole let the statement hang in the air for a moment as he went over the performance he'd been practicing since leaving the office. "Dead . . . What happened?"

He was expecting McCoy to tell him that she'd been killed in an accident. Something tragic but explainable, like that Fowler had broken her neck trail running. A clean death with no need to investigate.

Instead, he got, "Someone shot her in the head and then blew up her trailer."

"Wait, *what?*"

"Yes sir," McCoy continued, "the whole valley is on fire."

Fowler's dead and *Willow Creek is on fire? What the hell has that psycho done?*

The news left Cole weak in the knees, and he stumbled over to the tub and took a shaky seat on the edge. A sudden queasiness gripped his stomach, but he shoved it away and forced himself to listen to what his assistant was telling him.

"The county is requesting all available assets, both fire and law enforcement personnel, but so far Keller is the only one to respond."

"Keller? Why the hell is Keller responding to a Forest Service call?"

"No idea."

Shit.

Cole wanted to tell McCoy to call Keller back. Order him if he had to, but knowing that it would only draw unnecessary attention, he decided against it. Then again, he couldn't afford to have Keller anywhere close to Tito's trail.

If you can't beat 'em—join 'em.

The thought came out of nowhere, but it hit home, and Cole knew what he had to do. "I want you to get Keller on the radio and tell him I'm getting dressed and will meet him at Trinity River."

"You're going in? But why?"

"Because it's in *my* district and someone has to be there to set up an operations center before the state turns this into a fucking goat rope."

"I'm on it."

Ending the call, Cole headed back into the bedroom and pulled on his forest greens. Once dressed, he headed downstairs, and after stuffing his feet in his field boots, he was about to head outside when he remembered his promise to Tito.

"I will handle Keller if he becomes a problem."

That thought in mind, Cole stepped into the garage and crossed to a shelf lined with old paint cans. Standing on tiptoe, he grabbed an old primer can from the back and pulled it down. He carried it over to his workbench and popped the lid with a flathead screwdriver, revealing an unregistered Glock he'd once confiscated from a poacher. Though Cole had never actually thought he might need the pistol, he hadn't booked it into evidence just in case. Still, he found himself hesitant to take it.

While it was far from an ideal end, Hannah Fowler was dead, and barring any unforeseen circumstances, Cole was sure that Boone was soon to follow. Still, there were too many variables—too many unknowns—and with that crazy fucking sicario still on the loose, he knew it was better to have the Glock and not need it than the other way around.

His mind made up, Cole pulled the pistol from the can and dropped the magazine. Finding it loaded, he headed for his truck, praying he could make it through the next day without having to kill anyone.

CHAPTER 17

Willow Creek, California

Slade sat alone in the shade of an unburnt fir tree, his eyes on the twisted remains of the still-smoldering trailer. As he watched, a pair of crime scene techs in white Tyvek suits hefted a black body bag from the ashes and carried it to the van waiting at the edge of the yellow tape.

The realization that someone had actually been inside cut him like a knife, but the guilt was tempered by the understanding that he'd done everything he could. Slade took a breath and let his eyes play over the scene: the smoke coiling toward the rising sun, the flash of lights from the police and rescue equipment packed around the shell of the trailer, and the detectives interviewing the cluster of neighbors standing on the other side of the now-charred cornfield.

Off to his right, Buck finished his phone call to Walt and came loping over. "You did a good job with that tractor," he said.

"Thanks. Too bad it didn't help."

Buck studied him for a second, then with a shake of his head lowered himself to the dirt. "Look, kid," he said, pulling a rugged hip flask from his breast pocket and unscrewing the top. He took a long pull before handing it over. "Before you go beating yourself up about not being able to save the world again, Hannah Fowler was already dead. There was nothing you could have done. OK?"

Slade just shook his head.

"Everyone agrees that if you hadn't used the tractor to cut line, things would have been a hell of a lot worse."

"I can't help but wonder what would have happened if we'd gotten here sooner. Maybe if I'd run faster, she would have—"

Buck took another drink and sucked his teeth as he stared at Slade. "You keep thinking like that and you are going to drive yourself crazy. All you can control is what's in front of you."

"That's not good enough," Slade said.

"When I first came to this job, I thought I could save everyone and everything. But the truth is, we're just polishing the brass on the Titanic, and the sooner you learn that, the better off you will be."

"How can you say that?"

"Because it's the truth. Fire is nature's way of taking out the trash, keeping the ecosystem in balance. I mean, take a look around," Buck said, lifting the flask in an encompassing sweep of his arm. "Five years ago nobody was building houses this close to forest land. Now we've got developers demanding the Forest Service update their boundaries so they can clear-cut disputed land and build more neighborhoods. And up in the mountains they're diverting streams and cutting down trees so rich pricks from out east can have a summer house with a nice view. Used to be you could just let a fire burn itself out, but you try that now and the insurance companies will have your ass."

"But these are people's homes. Their lives are at stake. They need us."

Buck took a slug and grinned at Slade. "You come talk to me after you've been doing this for ten years and your back and knees are so jacked up you can hardly walk. When you're all used up but still have to run a mile and a half in eleven minutes to keep your job, I promise that you will have an entirely different outlook."

Slade studied the man, wondering how he could do the job when he was obviously so jaded. "If you hate it so much, then why did you leave ops to come back to the line? Why not pull the pin and retire when you had a chance?"

"Because I can't afford to retire—not yet anyway," Buck said, taking one final drink before capping the flask. "Now, regarding our current situation, Walt said they're going to take us off the line to get some rest after the Forest Service cops come up here and take our statement."

"Another statement?" Slade asked. "What else could they possibly want to know?"

"They probably want to know where you learned to hot-wire a damn tractor," Buck replied. "I know I do."

Slade looked at him, not sure if Buck was serious or back to screwing with him, but either way he knew that he was on dangerous ground. It was one thing for Buck to be aware that he'd been to prison; it was another thing for them to actually talk about it, and both made him uncomfortable. Determined not to go down that particular rabbit hole right now, Slade placated the man with a half truth.

"My old man was a mechanic. He used to have a bunch of beaters sitting around the yard, and I just kind of messed around with them until I figured it out."

"My old man was a drunk who used to beat the hell out of me and tell me I wasn't ever going to amount to shit," Buck said. "Getting away from him was the reason I joined the army as soon as I could sign the papers."

"The army, huh? Well, that explains why you were such a dickhead during training." Slade meant it as a joke, but instead of a smile Buck hit him with a hard glare.

"Let me tell you something, kid—those wings you got at graduation might make you a smokejumper, but they don't make you part of this team," he said, his voice matter of fact. "I run the show here, and if you can't handle what I dish out, then maybe *you* need to start looking for another crew."

Slade looked at the other man and nodded. He was right and they both knew it. The question wasn't whether Slade could stick it out. He'd proved he could. The bigger issue was whether he'd ever find the acceptance that he had been looking for, because without it, this job was just like all the others: a dead end.

CHAPTER 18

Willow Creek, California

Finished with their conversation, Buck shoved the flask back into his breast pocket and got to his feet. "I better go let the rest of the crew know we'll be pulling out soon," he said, dusting himself off.

Slade nodded and watched the man leave, Buck's comment about not being part of the team stinging more than he was willing to admit. Pretending not to give a shit was a full-time job, one he'd been forced to master early, when his old man walked out when he was ten and his mom turned to the bottle, leaving him to fend for himself.

Left to his own devices, Slade gravitated to the streets, and after falling in with the wrong crowd, he was quickly swept up in the outlaw culture that pervaded Northern California's notorious Emerald Triangle. For most of the kids he ran with, crime was a rite of passage, and they wore their rap sheets like badges of honor. Slade, on the other hand, just wanted to fit in.

Most of his crimes were petty, like stealing shoes to replace the ones rotting off his feet or shoplifting beer for the older kids, but a month after turning eighteen, Slade made the mistake that would change everything. He'd been drunk and thinking about his old man when he stumbled across the Camaro idling on the curb, and to Slade's drunken mind the car had seemed like a sign.

The cops had other ideas, and after he led them on a three-hour car chase through the mountains, his dream ended with the set of spike strips they pulled across the road. The chase landed him in the hospital—but it was the grand theft auto and reckless endangerment charges that sent him to Folsom.

Slade could hear it now: the clang of the bars slamming shut, the incessant noise of the cellblock. The pervading stench of fear, rage, and unwashed bodies that told him he'd come to hell on earth. The first days and weeks were all about survival, but after the initial shock wore off, his mind turned to how he was going to get the hell out of Folsom. Prior to being locked up Slade knew nothing about California's dependency on prison labor, but like all inmates he was given the opportunity to pick a job or trade to help him on the outside, and that was when he first heard about the conservation program.

At first his decision to sign up was just another scam, a chance to get outside and away from the shitty food and mind-numbing boredom that came with being locked up. But he quickly found upon his arrival at Trinity River Conservation Camp #3 that fire camp was anything but a vacation. During that first week, Slade ran more than he had in his entire life, and every night all he could think about was quitting. But knowing what was waiting for him if he did bail, Slade held on.

Slowly, his determination and fortitude began bearing fruit, and with his muscles growing stronger and run times shorter, he began to find a camaraderie in the suffering he shared with his fellow inmates that filled something inside of him that he hadn't known was missing. Still, it wasn't until Slade found himself standing toe to toe with his first fire that he knew that he'd finally discovered his purpose. And he'd be damned if Buck or anyone else was going to take it away.

Slade was pulled back to the present by the sight of a rising dust cloud kicked up by the US Forest Service truck racing toward them on the gravel service road. Seeing Buck approach, he got to his feet. "Looks like the rangers are here."

"Shit," Buck groaned.

Slade tracked the USFS vehicle as it came up the drive. It stopped behind the ambulance and two men climbed out. "Who's in charge of this crew?" the driver asked loudly, the badge on his Forest Service greens flashing in the light.

Like the rest of them, Buck was tired and eager to head back to camp for some much-needed rest. His voice was tight when he spoke. "I am. Who the hell are you?"

"Richard Cole," the man said. "I'm *assistant* director of the Trinity Forest district."

Buck wasn't impressed with the man or his title and was quick to let him know. "We've been out here all night, and my men are tired. So if you want to know what happened, I *suggest* you go ask one of the cops who just took our statements."

Slade could have kissed Buck for what he said, but he knew from the look on the director's face that he wasn't the type to take a brush-off.

"I'm not asking them. I'm asking *you*," he snapped back.

While Buck and the director went back and forth, Slade turned his attention to his partner. Though the man wasn't wearing a uniform, Slade had seen enough cops to know what he was looking at, and when he started to approach, Slade's first instinct was to get out of there as quick as possible. But before he had a chance to move, the man was turning in his direction, scanning the faces of the smokejumpers and hotshots gathered in the corner of the clearing.

Slade knew to walk away now was only to invite attention, so he kept his head down and slipped behind one of the taller hotshots. From his new vantage point, he watched the man remove a sheet of paper from his pocket and study it before carefully observing the faces of everyone gathered near him.

Apparently not finding who he was looking for, the cop exchanged the picture for a cell phone, and Slade watched as he tapped out a number. But instead of holding the phone to his ear, he held it in his hand and kept moving, his eyes scanning the men in front of him.

What the hell is he doing?

The answer came a second later, when Slade felt the buzz of the phone in his pocket, then heard the opening chime of the ring. Without thinking, he reached down to silence it, and when he looked up, he found the man staring right at him.

"Jake Slade? I'm Special Agent Pete Keller with the DEA," he said, pulling out his badge wallet. "I've got a few questions to ask you, if you don't mind."

CHAPTER 19

Willow Creek, California

Except for the eyes, the soot-stained man standing before him looked nothing like the mug shot. If it hadn't been for the trick with the phone, Keller would have walked right past him.

"What is it you want to talk about?" Slade asked.

"Better if we speak in private," he said.

"Not too much of that out here. Or hadn't you noticed."

"Then walk with me," Keller said.

"Lead the way."

Keller turned to his right and started toward the tree line, the burnt grass brittle under his feet. He stopped beneath a box elder, its leaves curled by the heat of the fire, and fished a pack of cigarettes from his pocket. Keller pressed one between his lips and sparked the lighter. He studied Slade's face through the flame, wondering what kind of a man he was dealing with.

Usually, just the sight of the badge and the DEA stamp across his ID card was enough to get the most hardened criminal sweating, but Slade was cool as ice. His face unreadable beneath its filthy mask.

What little Keller knew of smokejumpers came from what he and Cole had talked about during their early-morning drive from the Trinity Rivers station. It had been a bare-bones briefing. Just the facts. Still,

Keller was fascinated to learn more about a man who would willingly throw himself from a perfectly good aircraft.

"First thing you've got to understand about these guys is that all the wildland firefighters are nuts. I mean, you've got to have a screw loose to chase a fire when everyone else is running the other way. But these smokejumpers . . . man, they're a whole different breed of crazy."

"Oh, that's *real* helpful," Keller said, rolling his eyes. "You know, I think you missed your calling—you should have joined the FBI and become one of those profilers."

"Funny," Cole said. He tried a different track. "When I was in IA, we had some biker rally coming through. The day before it was supposed to happen, I got a call from the patrol commander telling me that there were going to be some Hells Angels, and he wanted me to go scout things out and make sure there wasn't any trouble."

Keller snorted. "Trouble? What did he think they were going to do, start making meth in the middle of the forest?"

"Do you want to hear my story or not?"

Keller would have loved to keep ribbing his boss but knew better than to push it. And that, plus his genuine curiosity about the smoke-jumpers, made him back off. "My fault. Please continue."

"So I head down to the gas station he said they were going to use to fill up, and I see all these bikes coming down the road. There had to be at least fifty of them, and they've all got the beards and leather vests, the whole *Sons of Anarchy* thing. They pull in, and I'm wondering how I'm going to be able to tell the Hells Angels from the rest of them."

Sensing his partner wanted him to ask how he'd pulled it off, Keller went ahead and obliged him. "You used their cuts, the patches they wear on the backs of their vests, to ID them?"

"Didn't have to," Cole said.

"Then how?"

"They were just a different breed." He shrugged. "I mean, when you go to the zoo, you see the tigers, the cheetahs, and the leopards—all the jungle predators—right?"

"Yeah."

"But then you go see the lions, and after you've seen the king . . . well . . . after that, the rest of them are just cats. That's how the Hells Angels were compared to the other bikers, and it's the same with the smokejumpers. They're just built differently. Have to be to do what they do."

At the time it had seemed a strange analogy, but standing there looking at Slade, Keller got it. "Tell me something. What made you want to be a smokejumper? Fighting fire the regular way just *not* dangerous enough for you?"

"Is that what you want to ask me about?" Slade replied, dismissing the offered cigarette.

Keller took a drag, wondering how he should play this.

He'd learned early in his career that the key to a successful field interview was all about the prep work. Taking the time to study the suspect's profile. Learning his history. Getting to know what made him tick. It was a subtle art—a carefully choreographed dance—but this time Keller was going in cold.

"Well?" Slade asked.

Might as well put it all out there.

"No, I'm not here to ask you about smokejumping. I'm here to ask you about Mikey Boone and why he called you last night."

"Who said he called me?"

"Your phone records," Keller replied.

He watched the smokejumper, searching his face for any microexpressions that would signal the lie to come. But besides the slight tightening around the eyes, Slade took the question in stride.

"You got a warrant for that?"

"Don't need one. Boone was my CI; that's confidential—"

"I know what it means." Slade cut him off. "I've known Boone for a while but never figured him for a rat."

"Just goes to show you never really know anyone." Keller shrugged. Then, deciding it was time to get down to business, he crushed out the cigarette and stepped closer to Slade. "So, about that phone call."

"He left me a message, and before you ask, no, I haven't listened to it and don't plan on doing so."

"You mind if I listen to it?" Keller asked.

"Knock yourself out." Slade opened up his voicemail and handed the phone to Keller.

He took it with a grateful nod. "I'll play it on speaker so we can both hear it."

The voice was definitely Boone's, and muted as it was from the wind noise in the background, Keller could hear the pain in his voice. The fear. ". . . I'm in trouble, man . . . I really need you to call me back." Keller played it again, hoping to appeal to Slade's sense of duty or the altruism that seemed to reside in the hearts of most first responders. "He sounds like he's in bad shape," he said, handing back the phone.

"Whatever trouble Boone has gotten himself into this time, I can promise you that it has nothing to do with me," Slade replied.

"But he's your friend, right?"

Keller was fishing now, and from the look he got after his first cast, it was obvious that he was using the wrong bait. But this wasn't his first time around the dance floor, and he was quick to change the axis of his attack.

"Does the rest of your crew know about your record? Know who you were before you became a smokejumper?"

"Why the fuck does everyone keep bringing up my past?" Slade demanded. "Who the hell do you think you are?"

Keller was surprised at Slade's response, but having finally gotten a reaction from the other man, he went all in. "If you help me out, I can make it all go away."

"Help you how?"

Keller was flying by the seat of his pants now, way out on the edge, but he knew he had to keep going. Reel Slade in while he had him on the hook or risk losing his only chance of finding Boone. "How well do you know these mountains?"

"Better than most. Why?"

"Our last position on Boone was north of here, about twenty miles away from that old halfway house called New Horizons," Keller said. "You ever heard of it?"

"I might have," Slade said.

"According to your juvie records, you spent some time in that area."

"I thought those records were sealed."

"What can I say," Keller replied with a smile. "I'm good at my job. Now, do you know it or not?"

"Yeah. I know it."

"If I get you up there, do you think you could find Boone and bring him out?"

"That's wild country, lots of places to hide," Slade responded. "It would be like looking for a needle in a stack of needles."

"But could you do it?" Keller pressed him.

"Do I have a choice?"

"We've all got a choice. You just have to make yours now. Because you can do it with my offer on the table, or in about ten seconds my boss is going to take over, and then it's all out of my hands."

Slade was silent, his eyes hot enough to cut steel, and then finally he nodded. "I can do it, but my boss is never going to go for it."

"You let me worry about that."

CHAPTER 20

Humboldt County, California

Tito Zavalia leaned against the hood of the Tahoe, savoring the early-morning sun against his face and the cup of coffee he'd picked up from the Golden Rush Espresso. Straight-line distance, it was only forty-five miles from where he'd killed Hannah Fowler to his current perch on the southern edge of the forest, but due to the plunging valleys and ragged peaks that surrounded the area, they'd been forced to take the long way around.

Besides their circuitous drive through the mountains, the only other complication had been the complete lack of lodgings near their target area—an inconvenience that had forced an additional hour's drive north to Yreka. But Tito wasn't complaining, because besides the great night's sleep he'd had at the Best Western, they'd also scored a complimentary breakfast before leaving town.

Finishing his coffee, he pulled a small spotting scope from the pocket of his woodland BDUs. Lifting it to his eye, he was in time to see an old Ford Bronco hauling a trailer loaded with four dirt bikes swing into view. As a rule, Tito liked to work alone, but considering the unfamiliar terrain and the fact that the target knew they were coming, he'd decided to make the call for more men. Plus, his boss had been very clear that failure was *not* an option.

In Mexico, finding a team of capable shooters was never more than a phone call away. Fortunately, it turned out the Jalisco Cartel had plenty of trigger pullers in the North American stables too.

"I need guys who can take orders, preferably former military," he'd told his driver. "And they need to know the area."

The men Enrique found for the task were former Marines. Grunts who'd seen combat in Iraq and Afghanistan before coming home and using their hard-won skills working for the cartel to make triple what they earned overseas. While his driver had never worked with the men directly, he'd assured Tito that they were "switched on." But more importantly, one of them had grown up hunting in the area and knew it well.

The truck came barreling up the rise and swung into a tight circle before parking next to the Tahoe. There were four men inside and three got out, all armed and wearing faded plate carriers. Tito pegged the broad-shouldered man with the thick brown beard as the leader and wasn't surprised when he motioned the other two to take up a security position around the truck before starting over.

"Mr. Zavalia?" he asked.

"That's right."

"My name is Johnny. I was told you need our services," he said, his right hand never straying from the grip of the Staccato P in its thigh holster.

"Take off your sunglasses," Tito ordered.

Johnny did as he was told, not flinching a muscle when Tito stepped in close. While some people would have you believe that the measure of a man was in the company he kept or the clothes that he wore, Tito knew that was bullshit. The truth was in the eyes, and he looked deep, reading the former Marine's soul the way most people would read a book.

"You'll do," he said.

With a whistle Johnny called the other men over. "This is Matt and Ringo. The ugly fucker behind the wheel is Nash."

Introductions made, Tito tugged the map from his cargo pocket and spread it on the hood of the Tahoe. "Our target is in a cabin at the top of this ridge," he said, pointing to the hand-drawn X on the map. "I understand one of you is familiar with this area."

"I know it like the back of my hand," Johnny said.

"Good, then what's our best route?"

The burly Marine took a moment to get his bearings, then pointed to a spot on the map. "If it were me, I'd leave the trucks here and use this logging road to travel north."

"And how do we get to the top?"

"This wood line is full of game trails. I know a few of them that will take us up the ridge and get us into the high ground here," he said, pointing to a spot just west of the *X*. "From there we should have perfect overwatch on the target."

"How many men are we looking at?" Ringo asked.

"Just one," Tito replied.

"And the ROE?" Matt asked, using the military abbreviation for *rules of engagement*.

As much as Tito wished he could just kill Boone and be done with it, there were questions that needed to be asked, mainly who else knew about the grow site and if the DEA had any other informants in their organization.

"I need him alive."

"We can handle that," Johnny said. "All we need are our tools and we're ready to rock and roll."

"Follow me," Tito said, leading them to the rear of the Tahoe.

He double-clicked the key fob and the liftgate yawned open, the hiss of the hydraulics followed by an appreciative whistle from Matt when he beheld the small arsenal waiting in the cargo area.

"Daaaamn," he said, plucking an M67 fragmentation grenade from its foam crating and holding it up for inspection. "Who you got waiting for us in that cabin—Bigfoot?"

"He's a target, nothing more," Tito said.

"Too bad we can't smoke this guy," Nash added, hefting a belt-fed M249 SAW. "I haven't shot one of these in a hot minute."

"Cut the shit and get geared up," Johnny said, passing flash-bangs to the men. "We move out in five mikes. And don't worry," he said to Tito, "we'll get him alive."

CHAPTER 21

Willow Creek, California

While Buck arranged transportation for the rest of the Willow Creek crew, Slade climbed into the Forest Service pickup for the ride back to the operations center. He'd hoped to use the drive to get some answers, mainly why the DEA needed a smokejumper to do its job for it, but he never had the chance because the moment the engine started, both men were on their phones—Cole behind the wheel on his Bluetooth, Keller in the passenger seat talking on his cell the old-fashioned way.

Slade's attempts to eavesdrop on the dual conversations unfolding in the front of the truck only served to muddy the waters, so he quit listening and settled back in his seat. Mentally and physically exhausted after twenty-four hours of near-continuous motion, Slade struggled to keep his eyes open. But lulled by the whine of the tires and the cool blow of the AC across his face, Slade realized he was fighting a losing battle.

I'm just going to close my eyes.

Sleep was quick to come, but while his body rested, his mind worked overtime to process the emotional and sensory overload that had come with the fire. Slade found himself back in the forest, the woman he'd rescued from the pool clinging to his neck.

His only thought was to get her down the hill and into the hands of the waiting paramedics, but as he ran, she shifted in his arms, and suddenly he was carrying the body bag from the mangled trailer. The shock of the sudden transformation stopped him in his tracks, his confusion eclipsed by his horror at the screams emanating from the now-moving bag.

She's alive.

Slade lowered the bag to the ground and tried to get it open, but the zipper was stuck, and her thrashing made it impossible to get a grip. She was crying, "I can't breathe. Please get me out!"

He thought about using his knife, but afraid he might cut her, Slade continued to yank on the zipper until his fingers were bleeding. Finally, it popped free, and he got the bag open. But when he looked inside, it wasn't the woman he'd pulled out of the pool. Instead, Boone was staring back at him.

He looked at Slade with accusing eyes. "You were going to let me die, weren't you?"

Slade shook his head from side to side, trying to speak, but before he could form the words, Boone had him by the throat.

"Liar!"

Back in the truck, Slade jerked awake, his heart hammering a mile a minute. Instinctively he reached up to his throat, expecting to feel blood, but there was nothing. *Thank God, it was just a dream.* Sweating now, he wiped his face against the sleeve of his shirt and was working to slow his racing heart when they pulled up to the operations center and Keller jumped out of the vehicle.

Slade threw open the door and climbed out of the truck, taking a deep gulp of air before grabbing his bag and moving to the hood, where Keller stood talking. Seeing him coming, the special agent turned to face him. "Man, you were out like a light."

"Not much sleep on the fire line," Slade replied. "So, now that we are here, what happens next?"

Keller nodded to Cole. "Just waiting to see if the boss can get the brass to give us the green light, and then we go get Boone."

"And here I was thinking you were the one calling the shots."

"Boone is my CI, which puts me in charge of the case, but Director

Cole runs the task force, and we need his approval to use Forest Service personnel on Forest Service land."

"So you don't even have permission yet?" Slade demanded. "Then why did you come at me so hard back at the trailer?"

"Take it easy."

"Take it easy?" Federal agent or not, it took every ounce of Slade's self-control not to punch the man in the face. "Let me tell you something. This might just be another day in the office for you, but this is *my* life on the line. I worked my ass off to get here, and for you to show up and threaten to fuck it all up—"

Aware that he was shouting now, Slade forced himself to stop talking and took a step back. "You fucking cops are all the same."

"Look, I'm sorry if I came on too strong, but this *is* going to happen. Now, if you do your part—"

"No more talk. I want it in writing, or I walk," Slade snapped.

Keller's eyes went flat, and he took a step forward. "I don't appreciate being threatened. What if I say no?"

Slade heard the warning in the agent's voice and knew he was dancing dangerously close to the edge, but he was too pissed off to care. "Then I suggest you find someone else to get Boone." Not waiting for Keller's response, he turned and started for the shower trailers on the far side of the camp.

"Where are you going?" Keller called after him.

"To get a shower. Let me know when you've figured out what you want to do."

Five minutes later Slade was sitting on the bench outside one of the tiny shower stalls in the trailer, pulling off his filthy clothes. Dropping them on the floor, he grabbed a bar of soap from his pack and turned on the shower. He stepped in without waiting for it to warm up, the rush of cold water over his skin igniting the symphony of bruises and cuts that covered his body.

The pain was sharp as a razor blade, but it paled in comparison to the emotion he'd felt when Keller had brought up his criminal past.

All Slade ever wanted was a place to belong—a purpose—and that was exactly what he'd found in the camaraderie and shared adversity of the fire line. Slade had gotten his first taste at fire camp, and by the end of his first season as a hotshot, it was in his blood. It was a part of him now and the reason he'd agreed to help Keller, to keep his place on the crew. But standing there under that water, Slade realized he had another problem.

Mainly, there was no way in hell Buck was easily going to let him do this.

No, the grizzled smokejumper would be pissed at Slade for leaving, even temporarily, which meant he needed to get back to the operations center before Buck arrived and hammer out his deal with Keller. Turning off the water, Slade used an extra T-shirt to towel off. Once dry, he dressed in the spare uniform he'd kept inside his pack, and after lacing up his boots, he headed for the door.

CHAPTER 22

Slade was on his way back to the operations tent when a mud-spattered hotshot crew buggy came rolling into camp, the deep-throated rumble of its 6.0 L diesel putting the rest of the all-terrain vehicles parked around the area to shame. To the uninitiated, the big brush truck looked like an ambulance on steroids, but to Slade and anyone who'd spent any time on a hotshot crew, it looked like home.

Thinking it was heading to the other side of camp, he paused to let it pass, overcome by an unexpected nostalgia. His time with the Sawtooth 'shots had been simple and free from ego and the big personalities that came with being a smokejumper. In the hotshots, no one gave a shit about who he'd been or what he'd done in the past. No, all that had mattered was Slade's ability to fight fire, and standing there, he found himself wondering if he'd made a mistake leaving the team.

Six months ago, the thought would have barely registered, much less taken hold, but after everything that had happened at Willow Creek, he wasn't so sure. Besides his empathy, his ability to leave the past *in* the past had always been his greatest strength, but as much as he hated to admit it, the conversation with Buck had left him rattled. The uncertainty that followed was something new, but before he could follow the thread to its natural conclusion, the driver brought the crew carrier to a halt, and Buck swung down from the passenger seat.

"Well, don't you look clean. Must be nice to get a shower while your team leader is out in the field."

"Yeah, it feels good," Slade agreed. "You should try it sometime."

The cocky smile Buck had been wearing fell from his lips, and he took a step closer. "I should have known that little talk we had would have fallen on deaf ears."

"Oh, I heard ya," Slade said, moving to meet him, "but I've never been one to let an asshole run me off."

Before Buck could respond, Keller stepped out of the tent. "The operation is a go. We've got a briefing in five minutes."

"Operation? What operation?" Buck demanded. "What's going on?"

Slade opened his mouth to speak, but seeing the anger couched in his team leader's eyes, he thought better of it. "Ask him," he said, nodding to Keller.

Buck turned to face the special agent. "Well?"

"All I can tell you is that Slade has volunteered to help us with a sensitive rescue mission," Keller said. "Director Cole has already cleared it with your boss. Now, if you will excuse us, *we've* got a briefing to attend."

It was the first time Slade had seen anyone put Buck in his place, and it was a struggle *not* to smile. Still, he'd been around the man long enough to know that his Texas-sized ego couldn't allow Keller to steamroll him. Not with a subordinate bearing witness.

Buck was silent for a moment, then nodded as if he'd made some internal decision. "Fine, but I'm still his team leader, which makes Slade *my* responsibility. So if he goes—I go."

Wait. What?

Slade hadn't expected Buck to volunteer, but the tug of a smile at the corner of the special agent's lips told him that Keller had. *Sneaky bastard.*

"Well, now that we've got *that* cleared up," he said, reaching for the door handle, "let's get moving. We're burning daylight."

Keller pulled the door open and stepped inside, and Slade moved to follow. But before he made it across the threshold, Buck grabbed his arm and pulled him close. "Just to be clear, if *any* of this comes back on me, it's *your* ass."

"Good to know," Slade said.

Once inside the tent, Keller led them to a table in the corner where Cole was busy typing on his phone while another man in Crye Precision multicam stood looking at a large topographic map. "Buck, Slade, this is Captain Dyer, the team leader of the Forest Service SWAT team."

"A SWAT team. Well, this just keeps getting better and better," Buck moaned.

"Don't let Captain Dyer's presence alarm you," Keller said. "Bringing him into the mix was the only way Cole could get approval for the operation. But even with his team coming along for the ride, we expect this to go nice and quiet."

If the comment was meant to assuage Buck's anxiety, one look at his face told Slade that it wasn't working, but to his credit he took a seat at the table.

"Tell me what you need us to do."

"Director Cole and I," Keller said, "are part of a Justice Department task force that has been targeting Jalisco Cartel activity on Forest Service land during the past six months. We've been working to locate an illegal grow site believed to be run by Daniel Cortez, and we managed to get a confidential informant into the cartel's operation and were preparing to indict Cortez before the grand jury on Monday when we ran into unforeseen circumstances. We've got a leak," Keller said sheepishly.

"A leak? What the hell does that mean?" Buck asked, looking to Cole for clarification.

But the man was still glued to his phone.

Slade wondered who he was texting and what was so important that it couldn't wait until after the briefing, but a second later he realized Buck was staring at him.

"Well?"

"Boone cut off contact with the DEA and took off for the mountains," Slade said, "and since I know the area, they want me to help locate him."

"They want *you* to locate him? Hold on. Time out. Would you gentlemen give us a moment?" Buck asked, grabbing Slade by the arm and pulling him away from the table.

"Don't take too long," Keller said. "I need you geared up and ready to go in thirty minutes."

The second they were out of earshot, Buck demanded, "You want to tell me what's going on here, or do I have to beat it out of you?"

"It's complicated," Slade said.

"Well, then I suggest you get to talking."

"There's a cabin," Slade blurted. "Well, there's a bunch of them, actually. A network up in the mountains guys around here call the Citadel."

"And how do you know all this?"

"I, uh . . . got into some trouble when I was younger. Nothing *serious*," Slade explained, "but—"

"But what?" Buck asked, the sudden interest Slade saw in his eyes making him uncomfortable.

"Never mind. The point is that the last ping Keller got from Boone's phone indicated he wasn't far from one of those cabins. That's what we are going to check out."

"O-K," Buck said. "But you still haven't told me why Keller came to *you.*"

"Because I grew up with Boone. He trusts me, and when Keller found out that I knew the area, he came out to see if I would help find him."

He could sense Buck's next question. Knew he was about to ask what *he* was getting out of helping the DEA, but before the man could ask, Slade saw Cole shove his phone back into his pocket and step up to the table.

"If you two wouldn't mind, we've got a briefing to finish," he said.

"It's going to be fine," Slade said. "Trust me."

"You'd better be right."

Their sidebar ended, they headed back to the table, Buck as tense as Slade had ever seen him.

"You get everything sorted out?" Keller asked.

Buck ignored him, his eyes on Cole. "So let's say Slade can find this guy—then what happens?"

"We drop you two in, and you bring him out."

"You realize we're smokejumpers, right? Not cops. We aren't exactly trained for this kind of thing."

"If my guys could handle it, we would," Captain Dyer said. "Unfortunately, besides Air Force PJs, smokejumpers are the most suited for high-altitude rescue operations."

"I still don't like it," Buck muttered.

Keller let the comment slide and turned the briefing over to Captain Dyer, who pointed to the small laminated maps on the table. "If everyone will look at their maps, you will notice the large black square in the center. That is our search area, and it's based on Boone's last known location. Now, usually we'd go in nice and quiet, but considering the time constraints and the sheer size of the area, we are going to use a helicopter."

While he spoke, Slade studied the map, searching for a familiar landmark or terrain feature—anything that might help him picture the area in his mind. But it had been a long time since he'd last been in the mountains, and he was soon lost amid the spiderweb of contour lines that marked the map.

Frustrated, he traced the river, following it up the valley before moving his finger north to the one place forever burnt into his mind: Grant's cabin.

He marked the spot with a black *X*, then turned his attention to the grayed-out section next to it.

What in the hell is that?

Captain Dyer must have noticed the puzzled look because he paused the briefing and asked, "You got a question, Slade?"

"Yeah, what is this gray section and why is it not in our search perimeter?"

"That's the Red Cap zone," Cole said. "It's closed because of fire damage."

Slade knew it was common for the Forest Service to close sections of land after a fire so they could clear the burnt timber and repair the trails. He also knew *if* Boone was trying to get to Grant's cabin, cutting through the restricted area would be his shortest route, and he told Cole as much.

"The ping Keller got on Boone's phone showed him to be a good two days' hike from the Red Cap," Cole replied. "Which makes staying within the allotted search grid our best chance of finding him."

"But what if the ping is wrong?"

"It's not," Cole said. "Now, if there are no more questions, I've just been advised that the helicopter is on its way, and I've been told the pilots are not equipped to fly in the dark. We need to get a move on."

CHAPTER 23

While the former Marines unloaded the dirt bikes, Tito Zavalia checked the batteries of the drone packed in its Pelican case. Seeing that it was fully charged, he latched the case and stuffed it into his assault pack along with an extra set of flex cuffs and two magazines of .308 for his Accuracy International AT.

Tito shouldered the pack and grabbed his rifle, cinching the sling tight across the front of his chest before climbing onto the scuffed Yamaha TT-R. He stomped down on the kick-starter, the burble of the bike's 125 cc engine echoing low beneath the cathedral of trees where they'd parked the trucks, and snapped his Garmin GPS into the mount secured to the handlebars. He hit the power button, and while he waited for the satellite to sync, he took a moment to refamiliarize himself with the bike's controls.

During his time in the Mexican special forces, Tito's primary means of infiltration was via helicopter. However, due to the geographic extremes of his country—the towering mountains, sweeping deserts, and impenetrable jungles where the cartels liked to hide their operations—he and the rest of the men assigned to the FER were trained to use trucks, ATVs, and even horses to close in on and destroy their enemies. Still, it had been years since he'd actually ridden a dirt bike, and considering what was at stake, he would have preferred to walk. The only problem was that according to the latest call from his source, they weren't the *only* ones looking for Boone.

While the man had been unwilling to go into specifics over an unsecured line, he'd made it clear that the DEA were planning to send a team into the mountains to recover Boone. Tito had asked him how long he had, but the man couldn't give him anything more than, "They are on their way."

Time. It was the one enemy he couldn't defeat with a bullet. Not that it mattered. They weren't far, and Tito knew that if they moved fast enough, all that would be left of Boone was ash and bone.

Once the rest of the men were mounted up, he gave Johnny the sign to move out, and the former Marine responded by goosing the throttle. "Try to keep up."

Then he was gone—rocketing north like the devil himself was on his tail.

Never one to back down from a challenge, Tito gave the throttle a hard twist that sent the Yamaha's back tire spinning on the trail. At first nothing happened; then the rubber cleats that dotted the tire caught hold, and the bike shot forward, the sudden acceleration threatening to jerk his arms from their sockets.

The first quarter mile was all about survival, and he just held on, trying to keep the front tire out of the potholes and away from the razor-sharp stones that lined his path. He was muscling the bike, trying to impose his will on the machine, and it wasn't long before his hands and forearms began to cramp from the death grip he had on the handlebars.

Forcing himself to relax, Tito peeled his right hand from the throttle and shook it out. He was about to repeat the motion with the left when Johnny came to a stop ahead. Squeezing the hand brake, Tito slowed the bike and brought it to a rolling stop beside the former Marine. He was about to ask what Johnny was looking at when he saw the matted grass at the edge of the road and tire tracks leading to the hastily hidden pickup. The sight of the truck sent adrenaline coursing through his blood. They were close; he could feel it. Now all they needed to do was find the trail that would take them into the mountains.

It took a few minutes, but then, out of all the experienced people on the team, it was Enrique, his stoic driver, who finally found the trail. "I *almost* missed it," he said, pointing to the scratch of bare earth hidden beneath the tangle of overgrowth. Needing to make sure it was the correct one to follow, Tito ducked beneath the trees, his eyes sweeping the ground, searching for any sign of Boone's passing.

The ground was hard as a rock from lack of rain, and while there were plenty of signs—broken twigs and matted pine needles—that confirmed *something* had come this way, a cursory look showed nothing but animal scat. He was about to key up on the radio and tell Johnny and Matt to keep searching when he saw the hint of a boot print pressed into a moss-covered stone. Tito unslung his rifle and leaned it against a tree before lowering himself flat.

From his stomach the world took on an entirely different appearance, and after a few seconds he was able to make out a second track, then a third. Now confident that they were on the right path, Tito grabbed his rifle and returned to his bike.

"This is it."

Johnny nodded and once again took point, the trail leading them east through the trees and out across a wildflower-dotted meadow. The ground stayed flat and smooth for the first two hundred yards, but at the edge of the clearing it made a hard left turn before charging toward the mountains. Where the crushed grass and matted flora had made it easy for Tito to follow Boone's path, now with the dirt giving way to rock, it was all up to Johnny. Luckily, he was up for the task, and besides calling the occasional halt to dismount and take a closer look, he kept them moving higher into the mountains.

The track narrowed as it followed the spine of the ridge skyward, the sudden drop-off along the side of the trail leaving Tito feeling like he was riding a tightrope.

Fighting the push of the wind and desperate not to look down, it was all he could do to keep his eyes on Johnny and trust the man didn't make a mistake that would send them all plunging to their deaths.

It took ten minutes of slow, careful riding and an elevation gain of three thousand feet to make it up to the plateau Johnny had picked out on the map. By the time Tito killed the engine, his nerves were stretched thin and the back of his camo shirt was soaked with sweat.

"Holy shit," Matt said, kicking free of his bike and glancing back the way they'd come. "How the hell did that guy get up here on foot?"

Tito didn't know, and honestly, he didn't care. All that mattered to him was finishing the job and hopefully finding an easier way back down when it was done. With that thought in mind, he dropped his pack and removed the book-sized quadcopter from the Pelican case. After snapping the rotors into place, he flipped the power switch, then pulled on a pair of gray first-person-view goggles. He grabbed the controller and ran the tiny engines to full power, waiting for the FPV goggles to sync with the digital camera mounted to the body of the drone, then launched it upward.

The quadcopter leaped to the sky, and Tito guided it over the shelf of rocks to his right, dodging the scrub and wispy branches of the mountain dogwoods that littered the peak. Once clear, he held it in a hover and slowly panned the camera across the clearing he found on the other side.

While they were in full sun, the clearing was still bathed in shade, and even with the HD camera it took him a moment to pierce the shadows and locate the tiny cabin hidden beneath the trees on the other side.

Got you.

With his target located, Tito spent the next minute surveying the area, noting the pair of boulders and the large tree stump they could use for cover when approaching from the front. Even though the drone was quiet, he didn't dare venture too close to the target and kept it high in the trees as he approached the cabin. He zipped it over the porch and then south around the corner, inspecting the battleship-gray propane tank that sat on a concrete pad ten feet from a shuttered window, then moving around back, where he found a second door.

Reconnaissance complete, Tito recalled the drone, and after stripping off the goggles, he walked the men through the plan. "We are going to do a simultaneous breach. Johnny, Ringo, and Enrique, you take the back while me, Matt, and Nash hit the front. We use flash-bangs to take him down hard and fast, but I need him alive—got me?"

The men nodded, and Tito gave them a second to check their weapons while he slung his rifle and pulled out his Glock. Then it was time to move.

CHAPTER 24

THE CITADEL
SIX RIVERS NATIONAL FOREST
Humboldt County, California

Mikey Boone lay on the couch, feeling a slight breeze through the window he'd cracked open before lying down. With his mind and body exhausted from the previous twenty-four hours, Boone had fallen asleep the moment he closed his eyes.

Going to sleep had never been an issue for him. Staying asleep, well, that was a different story.

During their time at New Horizons, Slade had joked that Boone could sleep through an earthquake, but all that changed his first week at Pelican Bay. The truth was, prison wasn't the place for hard sleepers, a fact Boone had learned the hard way when his white supremacist cellmate had gotten hopped up on some bad crystal meth his old lady had smuggled in and tried to strangle Boone in his rack. Since then, even the slightest noise would pull him from a deep slumber, which was why Boone wasn't surprised when he suddenly found himself wide awake and looking around the cabin.

He lay there for a second, senses straining for whatever it was that had woken him up. But besides the blowing of the wind through the half-opened window, there was nothing. Still tired, Boone closed his eyes and tried to drift back to sleep, but his mind wouldn't let him.

Something was wrong. But what?

Then it hit him. *Where did the birds go?*

Instantly on guard, he grabbed the rifle propped against the arm of the couch and got to his feet. He moved to the window and peeled back the edge of the blanket he'd tacked over the frame in time to see three heavily armed men rushing toward the cabin.

The sight of them sent a finger of ice tracing up his spine, the sudden chill freezing him in place. Vapor locked, all he could do was stare while his sleep-fogged brain struggled to understand how they'd found him. His first thought was to run and hide, but seeing their guns, he knew it wouldn't matter.

They'd come here to kill him, and Boone knew if he didn't get a grip on his emotions, that was exactly what they were going to do.

His survival instincts kicked in hard. The fear and confusion that had held him rooted to the spot suddenly morphed into a white-hot rage.

You want my blood, then come and get it.

Boone lifted the .30-30 to his shoulder to fire, the bang of his heart echoing like the beat of a war drum. He focused on the sights, ready to fire, but as the men moved closer to the porch, he saw that they were wearing plate carriers.

Damn, who are these guys?

While the .30-30 was good for small game, Boone knew it wouldn't put a dent in the men's body armor, and even if it did, he didn't have the ammo for a firefight. Which left him with no choice but to run.

Turning on his heel, Boone slipped away from the window, leaving the rifle on the floor, and grabbed his backpack and the Colt on his way to the kitchen. He rounded the corner and was reaching for the knob when the back door came flying open. Stopping short, he lifted the pistol, expecting a man to follow, but instead of a target all Boone saw over the sights was the silver cylinder that came cartwheeling through the open doorway.

Time slowed as he watched the flash-bang hit the ground, the metallic clatter as it skittered across the floor taking Boone back to that fateful night when the DEA had raided his house. Instinct took over, and he kicked the flash-bang back the way it had come, the toe of his hiking boot sending it spinning past the armed man standing just outside the door.

The canister landed in the trees and detonated with a thunderous roar. The rush of the concussion and the crackling flame that spread hungrily across the dry pine needles diverted the assaulter's attention from the task at hand.

Seeing the man standing there, Boone disengaged the 1911's thumb safety and fired, the two shots from the big .45 blowing the attacker off the back step. He followed him to the ground over the pistol sights, and when he saw that he wasn't getting back up, Boone stepped out onto the stoop, not seeing the second man until it was too late.

He tried to get the pistol up and onto target, but before he had a chance, his attacker butt-stroked him hard across the face. Boone's nose exploded in a spray of blood and his knees buckled, but somehow he managed to stay on his feet. Staggering forward, he launched himself at the man and bowled him off the porch.

They landed in the grass and rolled across the dirt. Blood pouring from Boone's shattered nose, he fought like a wildcat, ignoring the tear of his skin and the rush of blood from his reopened wound.

When his attacker grabbed the barrel of the 1911 and tried to rip it away, Boone let him have it. The man's triumph turned to pain when Boone slammed a fist into his face, followed by a sharp knee to the groin.

You fucker.

The man grunted and went limp, and Boone scrambled to his feet. Then he was running, his legs pumping beneath him as he sprinted for the tree line. A look to the left showed the flames from the flash-bang spreading across the pine straw, so Boone ran right. His only thought was getting to the river.

He ran hard and was almost there when a flicker of movement off to his left caught his attention. Boone glanced over his shoulder in time to see a lone man with a rifle lining up for the shot. *Shit.* He tried to change course and veer out of the line of fire, but before he had a chance, there was a spit of flame from the muzzle, quickly followed by the sledgehammer blow of a bullet slamming into his leg.

The impact sent him spinning to the ground, and the pain that followed would have kept him there if it hadn't been for the sight of the man stalking toward him. Even at a distance, all it took was one look at those dark eyes, and Boone knew he was facing a long and painful death.

"No. *No!*" he screamed.

Desperate to get away, he rolled onto his stomach and tried to crawl for the trees, but his damaged leg refused to comply. The man was on him in an instant and stomped a boot down hard on the back of his wounded leg.

Boone screamed, the pain radiating through his body a living thing. He tried to wiggle free, but the man held him pinned to the ground, his voice a snake's hiss when he spoke.

"I've been looking for you."

"No, please, I'll do anything, just don't . . ."

"You should have thought about that before you turned on the cartel," the man sneered as rough hands lifted Boone from the ground and dragged him toward the cabin.

CHAPTER 25

Thirty minutes later Slade was geared up and standing on the landing pad, his eyes on the UH-60 Black Hawk that came thundering in from the east. The pilot flared for a landing, the rush of the downdraft nearly shoving Slade off balance.

He stumbled and would have gone down if Buck hadn't grabbed him by the arm and held him upright.

"Steady, rook."

Slade muttered his thanks and followed Buck when the crew chief emerged from the dust storm and waved them forward. "Watch your head," he shouted, pointing toward the rotors.

With the weight of the gear strapped to his body, it was hard enough to move, much less duck, but not wanting to get his head chopped off by the whirring blades, Slade made it happen. He climbed into the open cargo hold and looked around, searching for a place to sit.

"You ever flown in one of these?" Buck asked, taking a seat by the open door and kicking his legs out of the aircraft. "Best seat in the house."

Slade had flown in plenty of helicopters—the Bell Rangers and old Hueys the army had gifted the Forest Service—but the Black Hawk was an entirely different animal, one that oozed raw power. From his point of view, sitting *anywhere* near the open door seemed like a recipe for disaster.

"If you're scared, take a seat on the bench. I won't tell anybody," Buck taunted.

Sure, you won't.

Swallowing his trepidation, Slade took a spot beside the other man and kicked his legs beneath the military-issue rachet strap the crew chief had pulled across the open door. According to their preflight brief, the strap was more than strong enough to keep them inside the helicopter, but one look at its rusted buckle and weathered polyester webbing left Slade feeling less than secure.

The hell with that, he thought, reaching for the personal retention lanyard secured to his harness. While Slade fumbled to clip into one of the ring tie-downs that dotted the metal floor, Keller and the SWAT team climbed in and got situated.

The crew chief waited for everyone to don the tactical headsets hanging from the hooks and then keyed up on the radio. "You guys ready?"

Keller nodded and flashed him a half-hearted thumbs-up, his grayish pallor telling Slade that he shared his discomfort. The members of the SWAT team, on the other hand, looked perfectly at ease and didn't so much as bat an eyelid when the pilot twisted the throttle wide open.

The big turbine roared from the sudden rush of power, and the torque from the rotors squatted the helo on its wheels. It held the crouch, the airframe vibrating so hard that Slade was sure the rivets inside the cargo were going to shake themselves loose. But before that could happen, the pilot pulled back on the stick and the Black Hawk leaped skyward.

Slade resisted the urge to grab onto the strut and forced a calm he didn't feel. Keller, meanwhile, had no qualms, and he held on tight while the pilot yanked the bird west and sent it rocketing low over the trees.

"Man, I hate these damn things," he said over the internal net.

You ain't the only one.

Compared to the smooth forward flight of a fixed-wing aircraft, the Black Hawk felt like a washing machine on the verge of shaking itself to pieces, and for the first few seconds, Slade was confident the damn thing was going to vibrate itself out of the sky. But after a few minutes of level flight, his body grew acclimated to the feel of the bird and the constant noise that was a helicopter in flight.

"So let me get this straight," Buck said. "We're just supposed to fly around here and *hope* we find this guy?"

Slade looked over at Keller and then back to his team leader. "Yeah, that pretty much sums it up."

"Damn, no wonder this country is broke as shit."

It was a fifteen-minute flight to the search area, and once on station, Keller keyed up on the radio. "All right, Slade, it's on you."

Where he'd been unable to get his bearings on the map, now that he was actually over the terrain, things began to look familiar. The first feature to jog his memory was a rugged cleft dug out of one of the peaks, followed by a saddle that looked like an inverted nose. And then he saw the sun-bleached hilltop where Boone and Slade had once made camp during one of Grant's exercises.

OK, I can do this.

Turning his attention back to the map, Slade keyed up on the radio and guided the pilot north. "The first cabin should be over the ridge, in a depression flanked by some funky-looking pines."

The pilot made the turn, and a few seconds later they were hovering low over the structure. Unfortunately, all it took was one passing glance to realize that it was empty.

"Well, that's a bust," the pilot said. "Next."

They repeated the pattern for the next twenty minutes, the helo's flight pattern and Slade's dodgy memory taking them back and forth across the mountains. All of the spots he could remember were dry holes, and with the pilots beginning to complain about their fuel, Slade was beginning to think that this entire operation had been one big waste of time.

"We've got smoke at our nine o'clock," the pilot advised.

In an instant Slade forgot all about the mission and began scanning the sky. "You see it?" he asked Buck.

"Yeah," Buck said, pointing to the tendril of black seeping from the green expanse of pines that carpeted the mountainside.

"Look, guys, this is not why we're here," Keller said, trying to keep them on point.

"That's where you're wrong," Buck snapped back, already checking his chute. "This is *exactly* why *we* are here."

Keller looked at Slade for help, but all he could do was shrug. "He's right. As dry as it is down there, that blaze can easily get out of control and burn half the mountain before they could send in another crew. Besides, if you look at the imagery," he said, holding up the satellite printout of the area, "you'll see there's a cabin on square D-23."

"Where?"

"Right here," he said, pointing to the edge of a wooden roof poking out from beneath a wall of trees on the south side of a rectangular clearing.

"Is it one of Grant's?"

"It's not one that I've ever been to, but it's been years since the last time I was—"

"It doesn't matter; we're jumping," Buck interrupted.

A look at his face showed Slade that he was in full team-leader mode, and there was no use arguing with him. Keller must have realized it too, because he backed off and threw his hands in the air in mock submission.

"Fine, go fight your fire, but just for argument's sake, what happens if Boone *is* down there?"

"What are the odds of that?" Buck demanded.

"About the same as finding a fire this close to our search area," Keller snapped back, "if you catch my drift."

The pilot bringing the helo in low and slow over a clearing near the fire killed the conversation, and he gave both the jumpers thirty seconds to get the lay of the land before climbing back to jump altitude. With no spotter on board, Buck handled the streamers, and after both of his throws revealed a gentle wind blowing in from the south, he gave a satisfied nod and turned to Slade.

"This one is by the books, so there shouldn't be any of the crazy shit you pulled on the first jump."

"Yeah, I got it."

While Slade got ready, Buck turned to Keller. "And *you*—make sure you keep that bird clear until I call for it. The last thing we need is the rotor wash turning that little flare into a fire wall."

Seeing the agent was already annoyed with Buck over his insistence to jump the fire, Slade thought Keller was about to lose his cool, but instead he dug another piece of wintergreen from his pocket and added it to the wad of gum he'd been chewing since lifting off. "Go put your fire out, sparky."

Slade suppressed a laugh and turned to the door. He'd had his doubts about Keller when they first met, but the man was growing on him. That he had an unnatural talent for pissing Buck off sure didn't hurt.

"Quit grinning and get ready to jump," Buck ordered.

Wiping the smile from his lips, Slade assumed the position, and then with a slap from Buck, he scooted himself out of the helicopter. Unlike the mule kick of wind and throat-burning exhaust that came with jumping from a Dornier, the downward shove of the Black Hawk's rotor wash was almost gentle, and four seconds after he'd pushed free of the cargo door, his parachute fluttered open.

I could get used to this.

After checking his canopy for holes, Slade grabbed his toggles and steered into the wind, the blow of the breeze bringing him the familiar scent of woodsmoke and pine sap. However, for once it wasn't the fire burning below but the splendor of the view—the granite majesty of the mountains and the leaden shimmer of the river—that confirmed what Slade already knew. Jumping fire was in his blood, and short of selling his soul to the devil, he'd do whatever it took to keep doing it.

What a job.

Turning his attention to the landing, Slade trimmed his chute to bleed off airspeed and carefully corkscrewed to the ground. He nailed a textbook landing and popped his risers. With the fire burning merrily through the trees at the top of the slope, there was no time for congratulations. Slade ripped his Pulaski free and glanced back to find Buck struggling to remove his harness. "While we're still young," he urged.

"Shut the hell up and wait."

"Wait, my ass," Slade muttered.

He knew Buck was right, but the fire was calling him, the dry crackle of the flames and the whoosh of the erupting spots as irresistible as any siren's song. Though weak, the blaze was spreading fast, growing in both size and strength as it moved from the duff to the trees. "C'mon, I can handle this."

"No, you fucking wait."

Standing there, watching the fire spread instead of doing something about it, took everything Slade had. Finally, Buck got himself untangled and came up to join him. "Damn, I can't believe you actually listened."

Slade was already moving as he said, "Now that you're finally here, how about we get to work before she burns us off this mountain."

"Lead the way, sweetheart."

In the time it took them to climb the slope, the fire had begun to attack the trunk of a stunted fir. Slade was first to the tree and got to work hacking at the lower branches. The Pulaski's razor edge made for quick work, and as soon as one limb was free, he tossed it back to Buck, who stomped out the fire and threw it into the charred circle the fire had already consumed.

Working in tandem they hacked, stomped, and smothered the fire back up the slope and then got to work digging a fire line around the perimeter. They worked in silence, scraping the duff down to the bare earth. Their only communication was the thud of their hand tools into the dry ground and the scrape of the blades against the rocks and stones hidden beneath.

Separated from any additional fuel source, the fire finally folded in on itself, its flames waning before their eyes. "We'll cold trail that later," Buck said, moving toward the cabin nestled on the edge of the clearing.

A glance at his watch told Slade that they'd only been on the ground for fifteen minutes, but his Nomex shirt was soaked with sweat and his muscles burned from the frantic effort of putting out the fire. His body begged him to take a second to catch his breath, but Slade would be damned if he showed any weakness in front of Buck.

If he's still moving, then so am I.

Shoving the discomfort from his mind, Slade double-timed it up the hill and attacked the remaining flames flickering around the front porch of the building. By the time Buck called it cold, Slade's legs were Jell-O and his hand was cramped around the handle of his Pulaski. He wanted to drop the damn thing, stagger down to the river he could hear just out of sight, and throw himself in, but he could feel Buck watching, and that was all it took to keep him standing.

"That was fun," he said.

"Fun, my ass," Buck panted as he tugged out his Nalgene bottle. "That was a bitch, but you did good."

"For a rookie, you mean."

"No," Buck said, unscrewing the top and handing the water over. "You did a hell of a job."

Slade mulled over the compliment, searching for any unseen hooks or barbs, and finding it clean, he gave the man a nod and took the water. Though thirsty enough to drain the entire bottle, he held himself to a solitary drink and then handed it back. While Buck shoved the bottle back into its pouch, Slade scanned the area, searching the blackened ashes for the fire's source.

A glint of silver from a pile of charred pine straw drew his attention to a blackened metal canister the shape of a tiny Coke can. Slade walked over and bent down to pick it up. "Smells like gunpowder," he said, tossing it to Buck.

"It's a flash-bang," he replied. "We used them when I was in the army. The question is, what's it doing here?"

Slade didn't know, but with his skin crawling from what felt like unseen eyes all around him, he had an unexplainable urge to get off the mountain. "If he was here, don't you think he would have come out when he heard the helicopter?"

"Well, there's only one way to find out," Buck said, nodding toward the cabin.

"Wait, you want me to go up there and check it out by myself?"

"He's your friend and this is your fucking mission, so hell yeah, I want you to go check it out," Buck snapped. "Besides, someone has to stay out here and handle these spot fires. That said, I'd suggest you get a move on before we lose the light."

"This is because of what I said back at the tent, isn't it?" Slade asked.

"You're damn right it is," Buck sneered back. "And since *you* got us into this mess, I'd suggest you hurry and check that cabin, before I'm tempted to throw your ass off the mountain."

"You just stay out here and watch my back," Slade snapped, then turned and headed toward the cabin.

CHAPTER 26

THE CITADEL

SIX RIVERS NATIONAL FOREST

Humboldt County, California

Leaving Buck on the perimeter, Slade approached the porch, the combination of the flash-bang-induced fire and the feeling that he was being watched putting him on edge. With the fire out and the sound of the helicopter long gone, an eerie silence had fallen over the clearing, and the squeak of the steps beneath his feet sent a shiver rushing up his spine.

Boone, your ass better be in here.

Cautiously, Slade crossed the porch and pushed open the door, the squeak of the hinges impossibly loud in his ears. He was tempted to call out to the man, but instead, he looked inside and took stock of the scene.

Despite the absence of any flames, the interior of the cabin was shrouded with smoke, and the particulate-laden air caught in the back of his throat. Slade coughed and spat a wad of phlegm out the open door, then stepped inside.

The den was small, and with the bay window shaded, the only light was a trickle of sun from the doorway. Unable to see any details, Slade moved to the window, only to realize someone had tacked a blanket over the window frame.

Boone was definitely here, but where is he now?

He ripped the blanket free and opened the window wide, the current of air that came rushing inside sending the smoke retreating to the rear of the cabin. He went to the kitchen and, after propping open the back door and turning off the gas to the stove, turned to study the room, his eyes drawn to the fresh bullet casing on the ground.

First a flash-bang and now this. Damn, Boone, where the hell are you?

That the man had stayed inside the cabin while a fire was spreading outside was unlikely; still, Slade had to check. He called Boone's name. Getting no response, he continued down the hall, a quick check of the bedroom and a look behind the bathroom curtain showing the cabin was indeed empty. Confident that Boone wasn't lying inside passed out from carbon monoxide poisoning, he threw the bathroom window open and leaned out to find Buck stomping out the last of the spot fires.

"You find him yet?"

"He was here, but so far no sign of him," Slade said.

"Well, keep looking before Keller—"

Before Buck could finish his thought, the agent was on the radio, his voice sounding tinny beneath the whine of the turbines.

"Any sign of Boone?"

"I'm about to start my back clear, but so far there's no sign of him," Slade replied.

"OK," Keller said, the defeat in his voice unmistakable. "Knock it out and then get back to the drop zone. The pilots are starting to bitch about fuel."

"Good copy."

Transmission ended, Slade headed back the way he'd come and was crossing toward the front door when he saw the old lever action on the ground. While the rifle put him instantly on guard, it was the wet gasp from the body crumpled in the far corner that grabbed his attention.

"Boone!"

Flipping the coffee table out of his way, Slade yanked the jump knife from its sheath and cut the zip ties securing his old friend to the chair. The mangled face he found staring back at him when he rolled Boone onto his back was barely recognizable.

"Jake . . . I . . . I knew you'd—"

Slade stared at him, his mind trying to process the man's wounds and, more importantly, figure out how he was still alive. "Oh God, Boone . . ." He pressed his left hand hard against the bullet wound on the other man's leg in a vain attempt to slow the bleeding. "Just hold on, man, I'm going to get you out of here," he said, and turning toward the open window, he shouted for Buck.

"Boone's hurt—we need the medical kit."

There was a scuffle of boots outside, and then his team leader appeared at the window. One look at the bleeding man in his arms, and Buck was turning and running down the hill to the medical bags they'd dumped with their chutes.

Remembering the medic in the helo and realizing Boone was going to need more medical care than they could give, Slade was about to key up on the radio and alert Keller when Boone grabbed his hand. "Th-there's no time for that," he said, pulling him close. The effort left him breathless, and when he spoke, his voice was barely a whisper. "You have to go see—" He stopped to suck in a shaky breath, the momentary pause and the failing voice drawing Slade in closer.

"See who?"

"G-Grant."

The name jarred Slade like a hard landing, and he sank back on his heels, his mind overcome by the torrent of unwanted memories that followed. "I can't, not after—" He broke off and tried to pull his hand free from Boone's, but the dying man held him fast, his grip suddenly strong as iron.

Boone was begging now, his one good eye burning with the feverish intensity of a man who knew his end was near. "Please."

Slade closed his own eyes, wanting to refuse, even needing to, but the words wouldn't come. The thought of facing the grizzled Green Beret who'd once been closer to him than a father was too much to bear. Too painful even after all the time that had passed. Still, Slade knew he couldn't deny Boone his dying wish.

"P-promise me," Boone begged.

Slade nodded and opened his eyes. "I promise, but first we are going to get you out of here."

Pulling his hand free, he pressed the talk button and called Keller, alerting him to the need for an immediate evac, before pulling a tourniquet out of his medical kit. "Buck, where's that kit?" he shouted, cinching the tourniquet tight over Boone's injured leg, already knowing that he'd lost too much blood for it to matter.

Boone was shaking now, one of the first signs of shock, and remembering the mangy quilt he'd seen in the bedroom, Slade hustled down the hall to retrieve it. He yanked it off the bed and brought it back, tucking it tight around the now-unresponsive man's shoulders.

Why does it have to be Grant?

Slade flashed back to his arrival at New Horizons and the first time he'd met the cantankerous Green Beret. Slade had been half-feral when he arrived, more beast than boy thanks to his recent stint in juvie, and as such had a natural mistrust of authority. But he'd held his tongue until Grant started in on the whole "discipline equals freedom" spiel.

While some of the less streetwise kids in the group were quick to buy in on the idea that hard work and dedication were all they needed to pull their shitty lives from the gutter, to Slade it sounded like the punch line to a bad joke, and he was quick to let Grant know.

"You think those plaques make you some kind of an expert in suffering?" he'd asked, nodding to the military memorabilia that lined the wall of the man's office.

"What do you think?" Grant asked.

"I think you're full of it."

That they'd butted heads during the first month was a massive understatement, but while Grant was tough on him, he was also fair, and slowly they reached a common ground. It was during his time at New Horizons that Slade first learned to shoot a rifle, hunt, fish, and live off the land. He became self-reliant and strong, and for the first time in his life, he began to understand that respect wasn't just given but had to be earned.

Grant took him to Las Alamitos, where he introduced Slade to some of his buddies in the 19th Special Forces Group. They'd hung out and let him run through the shoot houses on base, taught him the meaning of their motto: *De oppresso liber.* To free the oppressed. For Slade, the idea that there was a world outside of himself and his bad attitude was totally foreign, but the more time he spent with the men, the more he wanted to belong. In fact, he was actually thinking about joining the military, seeing if he had what it took to become a Green Beret himself, when Boone got him thrown out.

Even now, so many years later, remembering the disapproval he'd seen in Grant's eyes nearly brought him to his knees.

Fuck him.

Shoving free of the past, Slade turned just as Buck came jogging up the steps with the medical bag. "Shit, this kit isn't going to do anything for him. We've got to get him outside."

"I know. Help me move him."

Wiping his bloodstained hands across his pants, Slade got to his feet and grabbed Boone under the shoulders, waiting until Buck had his legs before picking him up. They lifted him from the floor and carried him outside, the jostle of the steps eliciting only a low moan.

"How long on that helo?" Slade asked.

"It's coming now."

He could hear the beat of the rotors in the distance, but one look at Boone's face, and Slade had the sinking feeling that it was already too late.

CHAPTER 27

Even with the warning from his source, Tito hadn't heard the beat of the helicopter until it was nearly on top of them. Luckily the Marines were well trained, and before he could tell them to get down, they were already diving for cover. Tito was quick to follow and unslung his rifle before quickly wedging himself into a spot of scrub next to a lopsided boulder.

Professionally he was annoyed that he hadn't heard the helicopter's return, but considering the way the sound bounced off the ragged peaks, he knew it wasn't fair to blame himself. Tito recognized the Black Hawk from his time with the army, and he watched as the pilot settled into a hover over the fire that had been ignited by his driver's errant flash-bang. As pissed as he was about Enrique, the two bullets he'd taken to the chest were more than enough to pay for his stupidity, and while Matt and Johnny had done their best to patch him up, Tito knew he wasn't long for this world.

What he didn't know was who was inside the helicopter, which was why he had Ringo and Nash pulling security.

The answer came a second later, when two men leaped from the cargo hold. From the way they handled the chutes, Tito's first thought was they had to be military. But instead of the assault rifles he was expecting them to remove from their bags when they hit the ground, the men pulled out yellow hard hats and quickly got to work putting out the brush fire.

What is going on?

"They're smokejumpers," Johnny hissed. "Firefighters."

It was too absurd to believe, but there was no denying what was in front of him. Not that it mattered. Boone was dead, and all that was left was getting out of the mountains and back to their safe house in Eureka. Then it was off to a nonextradition country for a much-needed break.

Let them waste their energy trying to put the fire out.

"Boss," Johnny hissed.

Tito looked up to see that the fire was out and one of the men was now moving quickly toward the cabin. His instinct was to kill the man, but hearing the echo of the helicopter somewhere to his rear, he was loath to give away their position unless it was absolutely necessary. Besides, the smokejumpers weren't a threat, and the only thing waiting for them inside was Boone's dead body.

He'd been tough, Tito had to give him that, but in the end, there was only so much punishment a body could take. Tito was an expert on dispensing pain. An artist who treated each victim like a potential masterpiece. In a perfect world, he liked to take his time—introduce his victims to levels of agony they hadn't known even existed—which was exactly what he'd wanted to do with Boone.

Unfortunately, time was not on his side, and Tito had been forced to beat on the man until his heart stopped. He'd checked his pulse before leaving and knew he'd done his job, which was why Tito was floored when he heard the shout from inside the cabin demanding a medical kit.

That rat bastard is still alive? How?

Tito didn't know, but seeing one of the smokejumpers dart from the side of the cabin and race down the hill, of one thing he was certain. Helicopter or not, he was going to end this right here and now.

"Johnny, I want you and Matt to get ready to hit the cabin. Ringo and Nash, I want you pulling security in the trees in case that helo comes back," Tito said, pointing out the position. "Do *not* start shooting until everyone is inside the cabin."

"Roger that."

"Good, then move," Tito said.

Johnny and Matt eased back down the trail that would take them to the cabin while the other two moved left into the trees.

While they slipped into position, Tito settled behind the rifle and waited for the man to come running back up the hill. *C'mon. Where are you?* Finally, the smokejumper came jogging back up the slope, his footfalls kicking up ash from the fire he'd helped extinguish, and Tito took a breath to prepare himself for the shot. A quick range estimation told him his target was less than fifty yards away, and while he could have dropped him where he stood, Tito held his fire.

Slowing his breathing, he used his toes to push his body weight into the rifle, loading the bipod until man and rifle were one. He made a tiny adjustment to the focus knob until the man's chest filled the glass big as a billboard, and then Tito flicked off the safety. But before he had a chance to pull the trigger, the Black Hawk came roaring overhead, men with rifles leaning out the open doors.

If the helo had come straight in, the shooters would have caught Matt and Johnny in the open, but Tito got lucky, and instead of landing, the pilot yanked the Black Hawk into a high orbit. Taking advantage of the reprieve, the two Marines scrambled behind a pair of boulders on the left side of the cabin, but though the rocks offered cover, they provided zero concealment from the air.

Tito wanted to tell them to move to the trees, but with Ringo and Nash still struggling to get into position, he had no one to cover their withdrawal.

"We've got our asses hanging out here," Johnny advised over the radio. "What do you want us to do?"

Stay or move? That was the question, but before Tito could make a decision, the two smokejumpers came shuffling out onto the porch carrying a limp Boone between them. No sooner had they started down the stairs than the pilot pulled the Black Hawk out of its orbit in preparation to land.

Out of time and options, Tito keyed up on the radio and made the only call he had left. "Get ready to fight."

CHAPTER 28

THE CITADEL
SIX RIVERS NATIONAL FOREST
Humboldt County, California

True to his word, Keller kept the Black Hawk well south of the wildfire, and while the pilots fought the thermals coming off the mountain, he struggled to keep his mind calm. As much as he wanted to agree with Buck that the smoke they'd spotted coming out of the trees was just a coincidence, he'd been around long enough to know that in *his* line of work there was no such thing.

No, something was wrong. He could feel it in his bones.

A glance at his watch showed that it had been less than five minutes since Slade's last update. He was about to key up and ask for a status report when the smokejumper's voice came booming through his headset.

"I found Boone. He's hurt bad."

Bad, how bad?

Shaking off his shock, Keller turned to the SWAT team leader. "If the guys who did this are still on the ground, they aren't going to let us land and extract Boone and the smokejumpers without a fight."

"Roger that. Let's lock and load," he ordered, before keying up on the radio. "Variable Six is now in command. What's our fuel?"

"Fifteen minutes until we need to head back."

"Then let's turn and burn."

The pilot responded by shoving the throttle forward and jamming the stick to the right. The force of the maneuver sent Keller sliding toward the open door, and while he was belted and in no danger of falling out, one look out of the aircraft brought his thoughts into sharp focus.

This was not his first time dealing with a lost source or an amped-up team leader intent on getting his men into the fight. No, it had happened before in Veracruz, and even now, sitting there in the helicopter, Keller could vividly remember the terror in his source's voice when the man called, begging for someone to get him out.

The flashback unfolded in real time, and in the blink of an eye, Keller was back in Mexico, his source pleading for him to come and save him while members of the Jalisco Cartel worked to beat down his door.

"They're here, and they are going to kill me. You've got to get me out."

In retrospect, the signs were all there: the intel Keller and the members of the DEA-trained Sensitive Investigative Unit had been given was too clean. The snitches on the street had been too helpful, and gaining access to the middlemen running the show had been way too easy. Looking back on it, Keller realized they'd played him, fooled him into showing all of his cards, and by the time he understood that it was a trap, all he could do was call in the Mexican commandos and beg them to get his man out alive.

The commander they summoned had been waiting for just such an invitation—a chance to settle old scores—and with the blessing of the Americans, he'd gone in guns blazing. Killing everything that moved. By the end of the day there were fifteen sicarios dead, plus Keller's source, and five Mexican federales.

All under his watch.

When the smoke finally cleared, he'd lost both his reputation and his one shot at moving up the ladder. At landing one of those cushy office jobs back in DC.

The similarities of the two operations were impossible to ignore, and with Buck back on the radio yelling at them to "hurry the hell up," Keller could feel a panic attack clouding his mind.

No. Not now.

It took all he had to pull free from the memories, but he made it happen and turned to focus on the SWAT team leader, who was barking orders to his men.

"We are going to do a flyover before we touch down. I want heads on a fucking swivel, and make sure you get positive ID on a target before you take a shot."

The men nodded and moved into their firing positions on both sides of the open doors.

Once they were settled, the pilot brought the Black Hawk in a tight circle over the clearing, and while the assaulters concentrated on covering their sectors of fire, Keller did his best to be an extra set of eyes. The temptation was to stay focused on the smokejumpers kneeling over the bloodied figure laid out in the dirt in front of the cabin, but Keller was too experienced to get sucked in, and he kept his eyes moving. Scanning the boulders and trees that lined the clearing in search of any hidden threats.

The team leader was just calling it clear when Keller spied the dirt bikes parked beneath a stand of trees on the west side of the ridge that overlooked the cabin. He tried to shout a warning, but before he had a chance, the pilot was muscling the Black Hawk toward the ground. He brought it in low and fast, the sudden descent sending Keller stumbling against the bulkhead and ripping his radio cord from its jack.

Fighting the shove of the helicopter, he went to grab the end of the cord, but by the time he got it, the pilot was flaring for landing. Giving up on the radio, Keller was trying to slap the team leader on the shoulder when he saw the glint of sun off a scope from the boulders on the east edge of the clearing.

"Shooter," he yelled.

The team leader was quick to react and snapped his rifle onto target to fire, but before he could identify the threat, a line of tracers came snapping from the shadow. The burst sliced across the skin of the aircraft like a flail, the impacts sparking off the metal before finding the team leader's flesh. He fell backward in a spray of blood at the same instant the crew chief screamed that they were taking fire. Then the pilot was twisting on the throttle and pulling back on the stick, Keller holding on for dear life as the Black Hawk banked hard to port and thundered clear of the mountain.

CHAPTER 29

Humboldt County, California

Time slowed, and Slade watched in horror as a machine gun opened up from the wood line to his right and the Black Hawk veered out of view. Shoving Buck out of the line of fire, he ran for the porch just as the first rounds came chewing across the front of the cabin like a leaden flail.

Ducking beneath the spray of wood chips and siding, Slade dove through the open doorway and landed on his side. He caught a glimpse of Boone's body lying in the dirt where they'd left it, but knowing there was nothing else he could do for the man, Slade kicked the door shut.

He rolled right, and a second burst from the machine gun shredded the door and wall behind him. Slade wanted to get behind the fireplace, but the spark of a bullet off the stones changed his mind, and he settled for the couch instead.

After slithering behind it, he lay flat, the punch of the bullets through the wall and door filling the air with dust. The primitive part of Slade's brain screamed at him to run—to get the hell out of there while he still had a chance—but he knew it was the wrong move. Knew that if he wanted to survive, he needed a plan.

Think, dammit.

Remembering the rifle he'd left by the upturned table, Slade waited for the shooter to reload and then darted from cover. He snatched the gun from the floor and moved to the window for a quick look outside. Seeing the man working his rifle, Slade scrambled back into the kitchen and ducked behind the refrigerator.

Looking down at the weapon, Slade took a second to consider his life. He'd done his share of dirt, lied, stolen, and cheated when it benefited him, yet through it all, there was one line Slade had never crossed. But staring at the rifle in his hands, he knew that was about to change.

For a moment he wasn't sure he could do it, but then he remembered the sight of Boone's battered face, his plea for help.

The rage started in the pit of his stomach—ice cold and all-consuming. He and Boone had never been *that* close, but the man deserved better than what he got, and if it was up to Slade to collect the butcher's bill, then so be it.

With his mind set on what he knew he had to do, Slade waited, senses straining to understand what was going on outside the cabin. At first there was nothing but the distant hiss of the wind through the trees; then he heard movement on the front steps, followed by the light scratch of boots across the porch. Slade closed his eyes and flicked off the safety, listening to the rattle of the knob and creak of the door as it swung open.

Here we go.

Slade shifted into a crouch and crept forward, the cold steel of the rifle in his hand reassuring. He took a breath and eased an eye around the couch in time to see a short, muscular man with a dusty AR-15 and a military-style chest rig step into the cabin.

The man swung left, barrel snapping to the hard corner. Finding it clear, the shooter relaxed, the weapon dipping to the floor as he panned back to the center of the room. Slade waited another second and then stepped from cover, the squeal of the floorboards beneath his feet alerting the shooter to his presence.

The man turned to face him, nonplussed at the sight of the rifle leveled at his chest. "Drop it," Slade ordered.

Instead of complying, the man just stared at him, his hollow eyes dark as two piss holes in the snow. There was something unnerving in the man's gaze, as if he could see right through Slade and somehow sense that he wasn't a killer.

"Don't make me kill—"

Before the words were off his lips, the man was moving, the rifle coming up to fire.

Slade had no memory of pulling the trigger, but the rifle bucked against his shoulder, and he worked the lever, firing a second shot that hit the man high in the chest. But his target shook it off and stomped forward. He threw himself at Slade, the momentum of his body slamming Slade backward.

Slade reached out, snagging the handle of the Pulaski he'd left leaning against the wall, and then he was falling, the man holding on to his shirt as they tumbled out the window. He landed flat on his back, the impact blasting the air from his lungs and tearing the Pulaski from his grip.

Sucking wind, he hammered an elbow into the man's face and rolled onto his feet, thankful for all the painful hours Buck had kept him and the rest of the rookies in the sawdust pit practicing their parachute-landing falls.

A look to his left showed the Pulaski lying in the dirt five feet from the weathered propane tank, but before he could go for it, his opponent was on his feet, reaching for the Glock holstered at his waist. Seeing the pistol come up, Slade ducked under it, buried a fist into the man's stomach, and then snapped his head up and into his opponent's chin.

It was a staggering blow, one that resulted in a spray of blood and shattered teeth, but the man was quick to recover and raised a knee to Slade's groin that broke his grip. Biting down on the pain and trying not to puke on himself, Slade countered by shoving the man to the side and lunging for the haft of his Pulaski.

He grabbed it and lifted it smoothly from the ground, his face a bloody mask as he turned toward his attacker, but he had shifted away, diving for the Glock that lay in the dirt. Just as the man rolled up to a knee, the barrel of the pistol snapping up to fire, Slade brought the Pulaski up and over his head, his muscles taut as a bowstring as he tomahawked it at the man. The axe blade sank into the man's chest with a hollow thunk and a spray of blood—the impact spinning him to the right.

It was a killing blow, but the man's brain didn't know it yet, and his finger spasmed reflexively on the trigger. He fired three times, the first shot snapping past Slade's face, the second hitting the ground, and the third finding the propane tank. Even with his ears ringing from the gunshots, the metallic ting of the bullet finding steel was all too clear.

Then the world went red.

The propane tank erupted with a resounding boom. The overpressure that followed the blast lifted Slade off his feet and cartwheeled him through the air. Unable to control his body position, all he could do was brace for impact as the ground rushed up to meet him. He hit hard and skipped like a stone, the bounce of his body across the hard earth blasting the breath from his lungs.

Slade came to a skidding stop at the top of a slope, flaming debris and lengths of wood from the shattered cabin raining down on him. The biting pain in his side warned him of a cracked rib, but before he had a chance to check, he was sliding backward. He tried to dig the toes of his boots into the earth, but the ground gave way, clods of dirt and trickle of shale trickling over the edge and down into a jagged crevasse. Slade reached out and managed to snag the edge of a boulder, the sudden halt stretching his shoulder ligaments to their limit. A second later he came to a jarring stop, his singed hiking boots dangling over the edge.

Reaching up with his left hand, Slade hauled himself away from the precipice and collapsed in a heap of dust, but the relief was short lived and replaced by panic when he saw Buck lying crumpled beneath the smoldering porch.

He shouted the man's name, but instead of a response, a crackle of gunfire erupted from the front of the cabin, the slap of bullets all around him shoving him into action. Slade scrambled to his feet. *You need to get the hell out of here before you join him.* With an unknown number of shooters still hunting him from the shadows, Slade knew it wasn't just the right call—it was the only call. But as he stood there looking over at his jump partner, the words of the cadre back at Redding came echoing loudly through his head.

"No matter how bad it gets out there, smokejumpers never leave a man behind."

It was a sacred oath. A code born of blood and ash. But while the words had seemed so simple in the safety of the classroom, standing there in the open, lungs burning from the choke of the black smoke, skin beginning to blister from the heat of the flames starting to close in around him, all Slade could think about was *not* dying.

CHAPTER 30

Buck was dead, and for the first time since joining the smokejumpers, Slade was alone. He knew he needed to do something—anything—to get away from the gunmen trying to kill him, but with his weapons limited to the jump knife on his hip, Slade's options were limited.

"Use what you have."

They were Grant's words, not his, but they got Slade looking, and when his eyes landed on the burning deck, he knew what he had to do. Seeing a flaming two-by-four among the smoldering remains of the cabin, he grabbed the unburnt end and scrambled to his feet. The movement drew a shout from one of the armed men, followed by the crack of a rifle. Slade ran for the trees, hoping to use the flaming brand to start a fire that would cover his escape, only with most of the area around the cabin already charred over, there was nothing to light.

Shifting east, he ran for the virgin timber ten yards to his left, the shooter tracking him across the open ground. A second shooter appeared with a machine gun, and Slade zigged to the left to throw off the man's aim. The man fired a long burst, and Slade could hear the crack of the near misses as the bullets zipped past his head. A ricochet off a sequoia hit stone, and the shards of rocks sliced through his pant leg and into his flesh like a razor. He was bleeding now, the blood warm as it ran down his calf and into his boot, but he stayed on his feet and thundered into the trees.

Once into cover, he touched the end of the flaming plank to the pine straw and fallen branches that covered the ground. *Burn, baby, burn.* As dry as it was, there was no need for coaching, and within seconds he had a fire spreading across the duff. With the newborn flames covering his back trail, Slade moved deeper into the trees, and after tossing the torch into a tangle of brambles, he ducked behind a scrub oak. Suppressing a cough from the encroaching smoke, Slade pulled the grimy bandanna from around his neck and wet it down with water from the CamelBak. He tied it over his mouth to protect his lungs from the smoke and then used the rest of the water to drench his clothes.

While not as effective as the Avon respirator back in his gear bag, the makeshift filter would buy him some time. Now able to breathe, Slade took stock of his situation. With the terrain blocking any escape to the north and the fire closing in fast from the south, he had two options: He could head west. Brave the clearing and try to make it to the outcropping of rocks that would take him higher into the mountains and presumably toward Grant. Or he could forget about his promise to Boone and head east. Try to make it down the mountain to the safety of the valley below.

Not wanting to expose himself to the shooters in the trees and risk getting shot in the back, Slade decided the best course of action was to head back the way he'd come. But before he had a chance to move, a dry cough came echoing through the trees to his left, followed by one of his attackers stepping into view.

Unprepared for the heat and the smoke, the man was keeping his distance from the fire. Slade knew that if he could just wait him out—stay still until he passed by—he might be able to slip behind him.

Confident in his plan, Slade settled back in his position and was trying to work out his next move when a high-pitched buzzing drew his attention skyward. Squinting against the smoke and the glare of the sun, Slade scanned the treetops, searching for the source of the noise, but he saw nothing. Any other time and he would have been content to let it go, but there was a disquieting familiarity about the sound, something about it that put him instantly on edge.

But what the hell is *it?*

He was about to give up, chalk up the unseen noise to the blow to the head he'd taken after the explosion, when the quadcopter slipped out from behind the crown of a pine. The instant he saw the drone, Slade knew he was screwed—a fact confirmed when the gunman whirled in his direction.

"Matt, he's over here," the man shouted before opening fire.

Surrounded by the trees, each gunshot reverberated loud as an artillery shell. But besides the sound there was the realization that it was only a matter of time before the gunman closed in on his position, and when that happened, Slade knew he was as good as dead.

He thought about trying to surrender but knew that after all he'd seen, there was no way this enemy would let him live. No, the only way he was going to keep breathing was by getting the hell off the mountain. *But how?*

Then he remembered the parachute he'd left on the drop zone.

Designed exclusively for the rigors of smokejumping, the seven-cell CR-360 ram-air parachute was as tough as it was durable. It was capable of safely delivering a jumper to the ground from both high- and low-altitude jumps. But would it carry him off the mountain? Slade didn't know, but considering his options, he knew it was either roll the dice and escape or stay and take a bullet.

His decision made, Slade waited for the man to reload, then took off, sprinting hard for the drop zone twenty yards down the hill to his right. He made the first ten yards in Olympic time, but there was no outrunning the bullets that came snapping up his back trail. Seeing the edge of the hill ahead, Slade threw himself forward, diving for the slope. He landed on his stomach and tumbled head over heels, shedding gear and supplies as he cannonballed down the slope that led to the drop zone.

By the time he skidded to a halt, Slade was battered and bruised, bleeding from the hundreds of small cuts that lacerated his body, but he pushed the pain away and scampered for the aviator's kit he'd left in the center of the clearing. He reached it just as one of his attackers made it to the top of the hill and shouted to his partner, "I've got him."

Knowing what was coming next, Slade grabbed the kit bag and dragged it behind a large boulder, getting into cover just as the man opened fire. Ignoring the slap of bullets off the stone, he fumbled the zipper open, yanked his parachute harness from the bag, and shrugged it onto his shoulders. He buckled the chest and leg straps and pulled out the slack, making sure everything was as tight as possible, before gathering the balled-up chute into both hands and sprinting for the ledge.

Slade ran across the open ground, the bullets impacting around him like a leaden hailstorm. A geyser of dirt and razor shale tore through his pant leg and into his flesh, but Slade kept running.

It was five feet to the edge of the cliff, but it might as well have been a mile. A quick glance over his right shoulder showed the man with the sniper rifle running through the trees. Not wanting to take a bullet in the back, Slade was tempted to go to ground, but knowing the only way he was ever going to get justice for his dead friends was by getting the hell off the mountain, he kept running.

Summoning the rage he'd felt inside the cabin as fuel to propel his tired legs the final feet, he threw himself off the ledge. His momentum carried him clear of the mountain, and for a moment he hung there weightless—at one with the infinite blue sky. Then gravity took over and he was falling, his unopened chute trailing behind him as he plummeted toward the Volkswagen-sized boulders that littered the shoulder below.

Not good.

Locked in a free fall, he had no time for panic or fear, just the cold realization that if he didn't get his chute open soon, they would be cleaning up his remains with a mop. Then his training kicked in and his hands rose unbidden to the riser straps, fingers fumbling for the toggles. Somehow, he found them, and once he had a firm grip, Slade pulled them down to his chest.

At first nothing happened; then slowly the canopy unfurled, its cells expanding like a pair of lungs catching their first breath of air. But before the chute could unfurl all the way, one of the canopy lines found its way over the nose of the chute, and Slade watched in horror as it snapped taut—the friction of the line clamping the canopy into an oversized bow tie.

Then he was spinning.

With the ground rushing up to meet him, Slade didn't have long to clear the malfunction. Remembering the training he'd received at Redding, Slade gave the risers three hard pulls. According to the manual, if that didn't fix the problem, the jumper was supposed to jettison the chute and pull his reserve. Unfortunately for Slade, he'd left his reserve up on the mountain.

His vision began to blur as he spun. The centrifugal force shoved the blood from his brain. Realizing he was on the verge of passing out, Slade gripped down hard on the toggles and gave them a final pull. *C'mon, you bastard, open.* Then, just as suddenly as the spin had begun, it was over. Slade released the tension and brought the chute level, the gust of the thermals off the rock face sending him sailing into the sky.

Slade let out a whoop of triumph and was banking east when a streak of orange came snapping past his head. He was searching for the source when he heard the *pop pop pop* of the gunshots. The sound combined with the finger of flame told him exactly what was happening.

Those assholes are still shooting at me.

CHAPTER 31

Tito knew that he'd missed the shot the moment he pulled the trigger, but before he could work the bolt and get another round into the chamber, his target was gone. For a moment all he could do was stand there and stare, his mind struggling to process what it had just seen.

There is no way that just happened.

As a sicario Tito was well acquainted with desperation and the lengths a person would go to save their own life. He'd had targets beg and cry, and one had even tried to sprint across a congested highway to get away, but never in his wildest dreams would he have imagined someone BASE jumping off a mountain.

Lowering the rifle, Tito started toward the cliff, the two Marines who'd been shooting at their target from the top of the hill jogging to meet him. "Looks like that problem just took care of itself," Matt said. "No way anyone could survive—"

The unfurling of the man's parachute cut him off midsentence, and his eyes bulged as the smokejumper worked to get control of his chute. "Damn, that is one ballsy son of a bitch," Ringo said. While the Marines seemed content to watch, Tito had a job to do, and he quickly traded out his bolt gun for one of the extra M4s and then centered the EOTech reticle on his rapidly diminishing target.

Hitting a static target at distance was one thing, but trying to hit a man swinging back and forth in a parachute harness while the parachute itself was moving on a different axis proved well out of his skill set. After his second missed shot, Tito had an idea. "Do you have any tracers?" he asked Matt.

"Yeah, right here," he said, tapping a magazine marked with red tape on his kit. "Why?"

Not bothering to explain, Tito snatched the magazine from its pouch and switched it out with the one already in the rifle. "Watch and learn."

Unlike the ball ammo he'd used on his first attempt, the tracer round had the added benefit of a magnesium and strontium nitrate mix packed into the base that left a burning orange trail behind it. In the military Tito had used them to mark targets he wanted a gunship or the rest of the team to shoot at, but this time he was hoping to use it to ignite the man's chute.

Here goes nothing.

Thumbing the selector to full auto, he pulled the trigger to the rear and mashed his shoulder into the buttstock. Muscling the rifle to keep it on target, he worked the tracers back and forth across the multicolored chute. When nothing happened, he was beginning to think the canopy was fireproof, and then he saw a wisp of black smoke followed by a shimmer of orange.

He kept firing until the man was out of sight, and then he flipped the selector to safe. "Let's go," he said, starting up the rise that would take him to the cabin.

"Go where?" Ringo asked.

"We need to ensure this guy doesn't make it out of this forest alive." Tito moved through the charred trees up to the flat ground. As a result of the propane explosion, the cabin looked like it had been hit with a bomb, with a ragged hole in the roof and the three remaining walls on the verge of collapsing. Turning to his right, Tito crossed the blackened earth and moved to the unburnt island of trees where they'd dropped their gear before taking on the helicopter.

He stepped over what he thought was Enrique's dead body, but when he bent to pick up his pack, his driver let out a pained groan. "H-help me."

Before Tito could respond, Ringo came stomping up behind him. "Hey, we aren't going *anywhere*."

"And why is that?"

"Well, for one thing, we don't leave our wounded behind."

"He's not gonna make it," Tito said simply.

"So you're just going to let him die?" Ringo asked, spinning to Matt and Nash, who had just arrived. "And what about Johnny—are we going to leave him too? Let the wolves eat his body?"

Tito understood the man's concern. He'd been a soldier once and had lived by the same code, but now he followed his own rules. "Get your gear. We need to move."

"Go where? Johnny was the one who knew the area. I've never been here before. Have you?" he asked Matt. "What about you, Nash?"

"Hell no, this is my first time back to Cali since I got out of the Corps," Nash replied.

"That's what I thought," Ringo said. "Now that Johnny's gone, I say we do this by rank, which means, Matt—you're the one in charge."

Leaving the Marines to bicker, Tito eased the pack off Enrique's back and pulled the Glock 17 from his holster. He centered the reticle on his forehead and said, "*Vaya con Dios.*"

Then he pulled the trigger.

The gunshot echoed loud over the clearing, and the other men whirled their weapons up and ready to scan the scene. Then, seeing Tito standing there with a smoking pistol, they realized what had happened.

Ringo was the first to react, and he turned his rifle on Tito, the barrel locked on his chest. "What the hell did you do that for?"

"You'd rather I let him suffer?"

"No, you fucking psycho," Ringo said through gritted teeth, "I'd rather you'd taken him to a doctor."

"Do you see an emergency room around here?" Tito demanded.

"No, but . . ."

"You knew what kind of mission this was when you signed on. Now it's time to finish it."

"And if I refuse?" Ringo asked, fingers flexing on the grip of the rifle.

"Then you've got a decision to make," Tito said, tossing the bag at his feet. "You can take the *plata* or *plomo*."

"What the hell does that mean?"

"It means you can have the silver in the bag or the lead," he said, bringing his Glock to bear. "The choice is yours."

Ringo studied Tito for a moment; then his gaze shifted to the bag, and he dropped to a knee, eyes widening when he unzipped the zipper and looked inside. "Holy shit. That's a lot of money."

"Enough," Matt said. "You two stand down."

Ringo nodded his head and zipped up the pack. As he stood up, he said, "All right, I'm in, but if you *ever* point another gun at me, I'll kill you."

Tito shot him a wink and holstered the Glock, already thinking of his next move when Nash's voice came cracking through the trees. "Hey, while you assholes were arguing, I found one of those smokejumpers, and he's alive."

CHAPTER 32

Richard Cole stood in the middle of the ops center at the Six Rivers National Forest, the already shitty day getting worse by the second. It had started with a call from the forest supervisor, his boss's usually placid voice shaking with barely controlled anger.

"What the fuck is going on out there?" he demanded.

"Sir, I can explain—"

"No, you listen! I authorized you to conduct a rescue mission, not to turn my forest into a war zone. And if that isn't bad enough, now I've got every news station on the West Coast asking me about Hannah Fowler's murder?"

"Fowler's murder?" Cole asked.

"I take it you haven't seen the news," his boss shot back.

"No sir . . . I've been a little busy."

"Well, let me break it down for you then, *Director* Cole. This is a PR nightmare, and when the brass back in Washington hears about it, they are going to be looking for someone's ass to nail to the wall," he said. "If you don't want that to be you, I *suggest* you find out what the hell is going on and who is responsible, or I can guarantee that you will be looking for another job."

Then he hung up.

Cole stared at the screen until it went black, a dark rage building in the pit of his stomach. The blood rushed hot to his face, and he gripped down hard on the phone. He imagined his fingers around his boss's fleshy throat, and he squeezed until his knuckles turned white.

He had half a mind to call the man back and tell him where he could stick his job *and* his threats. But Cole was no martyr, and he forced a calming breath and returned the phone to his pocket.

Flexing his fingers, Cole grabbed a Styrofoam cup from the nearby table and filled it to the brim with coffee before snagging a day-old cheese Danish from the box in the corner. For someone used to a clean bed and healthy food, the conditions in the operations tent had taken some getting used to. He wanted to go home, take a shower, and change into clean clothes, but Cole knew he wasn't going anywhere until he figured out what to do about the debacle on the mountain.

Even now he found himself unable to comprehend how Keller had managed to turn what was supposed to be a straightforward operation into an epic clusterfuck. But here it was, not even four hours after they'd left, and Cole had two smokejumpers missing and a Forest Service SWAT team leader in critical condition at Saint Joseph Hospital.

Considering everything that had gone wrong in the past two days— the fire at Fowler's trailer and the subsequent discovery of her body, the failed rescue mission and wounded SWAT captain, plus whatever news story his boss was talking about now circulating in the media—it seemed an impossible mess.

If they'd had a TV inside the operations center, Cole would have been able to watch the news and understand the media ramifications, but everything inside the tent was mission specific. And with the spotty internet this far out in the sticks, he was effectively cut off from the outside world.

Feeling the walls closing in around him, Cole dumped the coffee and Danish in the trash can and headed for the door. He stepped outside, hoping a walk around the tent would help clear his head. But this time there was no breaking free.

Furious he'd gotten himself into this situation, Cole lashed out and slammed a fist into one of the generators. The pain cleared his mind like a shot of epinephrine, and for the first time that morning, he could actually think.

What the hell do I do?

His usual tactic was to try and control the narrative, but with the forest supervisors already on his ass and Tito running wild in the mountains, Cole knew he wasn't talking his way out of this one. No, if he wanted to keep his job—and his freedom—he needed to stop the bleeding. Put an end to this fiasco before it spun further out of his control. And to make that happen, Cole knew he needed a scapegoat.

There was a skill to covering one's ass, and it all came down to controlling the narrative. Walking the fine line between what was said and what could be proved, and with Captain Dyer in critical care and the two smokejumpers either dead or missing in the mountains, Cole knew that it would be his word against Keller's.

If he'd been a Forest Service employee, Cole could have had him relieved of duty. Sent home without pay or any contact with the department while *he* took his time convincing the command staff that it had been Keller's negligence that had caused the loss of life on the mountain. Unfortunately, Keller didn't work for him, and no matter how big of a fuckup he was, Cole was confident the DEA wouldn't stand by and watch while he railroaded one of their special agents.

Which meant the only way to keep Keller quiet was to put him in the ground.

Dead men tell no tales.

But how?

The obvious choice was to pay Tito to kill him. The only hiccup was that while the cartel had no problem killing Mexican federales, they had strict rules about killing American cops. Rules etched in stone after the Guadalajara Cartel was nearly wiped out by the DEA following the abduction and murder of an undercover operative in 1985.

Looks like I'm going to have to do it myself.

The only question left was, could he pull it off? Could he pull the trigger on the man he'd once considered a friend? Knowing there was only one way to find out, Cole walked over to his pickup and climbed in. He started the engine and used his phone to bring up the directions to Saint Joseph Hospital, then bent down and retrieved the unregistered Glock from beneath his seat.

Holding the pistol, he felt a pinprick of conscience. Heard the tiny voice in the back of his head begging him to reconsider. *There has to be a better way.* He wished it were true, but he wasn't willing to risk it all to find out. His mind made up, Cole silenced the voice and racked the slide. The metallic thunk of the round into the chamber was reassuring, and he shoved the now-loaded Glock into his pocket before glancing up at the rearview.

"It's either him or me."

CHAPTER 33

SIX RIVERS NATIONAL FOREST

Humboldt County, California

Jake Slade sailed into the trees, the snap of the gunfire receding as he veered out of the line of fire. The unmistakable scent of burning nylon drew his attention to the canopy, but before he could evaluate the damage, he was pulling hard on his right toggle to avoid slamming into a large branch jutting out from one of the pines.

While he'd been under fire, getting to the timber had seemed like his only escape, but now that he was in the trees, Slade's survival was far from assured. Mainly because traveling at thirty miles an hour without a helmet or any protective gear, Slade knew that even a glancing blow from one of the baseball-bat-sized branches would be enough to snap his neck.

Determined not to have "death by tree" carved on his tombstone, he gave the forest his full attention. Gritting his teeth, he sawed the toggles from right to left, slaloming the chute around the pines like a professional skier.

Fifteen yards to his right, Slade saw a narrow opening and, through the break in the timber, the valley beyond. But seeing it was one thing; maneuvering his chute into position without snapping one of his burning risers was another. Praying the chute would hold together long enough for him to make it to the clearing, Slade continued working the toggles, but with every pull he felt the resounding pop of a suspension line. He glanced overhead and saw a hole burnt through the center of the canopy, the responsible flame already licking at his left risers.

Trailing smoke and already losing altitude, Slade realized there was no way he was going to make it to his goal. Needing a closer and more forgiving landing zone, Slade knew his only choice was to try for the river. He eased the crippled chute into a gentle right-hand turn, his eyes locked on the sliver of gray water snaking west across the landscape.

With no time to line up for a proper landing, Slade swung wide and put the chute into the wind, settling in on the base leg of his emergency landing pattern. Just then, a crosswind came gusting in from the east, shoving him out of position, and by the time Slade recovered and turned into the wind, he was running out of both time and airspeed. He lifted his legs to clear the line of trees that shielded the bank, and then he was over the water.

With the rocks and sharp edges of the far bank ripe with the promise of a broken back or leg, Slade knew it was now or never, and he yanked the toggles down to his waist. The chute reared into a stall, its transition from forward flight to a vertical drop instantaneous. He crashed into the river, the chill of the glacier-fed water seizing the breath from his lungs.

Slade fumbled with the canopy release, trying to jettison the chute before it filled with water and dragged him down like an anchor, but his fingers were numb.

He tried to break free, but the undertow held him down while the relentless churn of the current sent him bouncing across the riverbed. Trapped in a demonic spin cycle, all Slade could think of was which would kill him first: the relentless cold or the lack of air.

Knowing that his only chance of escape was to dump his gear, Slade tried again to release the canopy, but his numbed fingers were still useless. Giving up on the loop, he attacked the buckles, clawing at them like a rabid animal trying to escape a snare.

Finally, Slade broke free of the chute and, pushing off the bottom, propelled himself to the surface. He took a greedy breath and kicked hard, trying for the bank, but he'd never been a strong swimmer, and he couldn't pull free from the current. Urgently seeking a way out, Slade spun his body in a tight circle, searching for anything that would float, but he hadn't scanned more than a section of the river before he was dragged under.

Slade sank quickly, the mounting pressure in his already tight lungs sending a spark of fear arcing through his body. He knew that he needed to stay calm, keep his mind focused on how he was going to get out of here, but as his back scraped against yet another unseen obstruction, all Slade could think about was drowning.

Like most smokejumpers, Slade had always considered water an ally—a tool that protected him from the heat and dehydration that came with the job. It was a helper and, compared to the blazing heat and smoke of a wildfire, relatively tame. But fighting to get free of the bone-chilling grip of the river, Slade realized his mistake, understood that water was every bit as callous and lethal as any flame.

A killer.

But just as that thought hit him, another came through even more clearly.

No, I'm not dying here.

CHAPTER 34

Slade tore free of the undertow and pushed off the riverbed. He breached the surface and managed a choking breath before the river tried to drag him back under. Kicking hard to keep his head above water, Slade spied a spit of land in the middle of the rushing current with a section of log he thought big enough to hold him.

If he could make it.

As a smokejumper, Slade was required to maintain peak physical fitness. Their ability to outwork and outlast *any* team on the fire line was the reason smokejumpers were in high demand. Which was why it came as such a shock that he couldn't outmuscle the river. But here he was, and with his legs beginning to cramp, Slade knew it was time to adjust his tactics.

Having identified his target, Slade forced himself to relax and give in to the water, allowing it to pull him back under. Though it was crystal clear from the air, beneath the surface the broiling mix of bubbles and silt made it hard to see, and Slade had to navigate by feel. Using the river stones as handholds, he crawled across the bottom, trying to maneuver himself into position to utilize the current when he came up for breath.

When Slade thought that he was in line with the spit, he curled his legs in and once again pushed off, rising fast to the surface. A quick look showed that he was somehow still too far right of his target, and once again he went under. Diving deep, he fumbled blindly for the rocks, the scrape of a sharp edge against his outstretched palm adding a crimson cloud to the already murky depths. Ignoring the pain, Slade began pulling himself laterally across the riverbed, the algae-slicked stones making him struggle for each precious inch.

Even with the lactic burn of his muscles heating him from the inside, there was no escaping the cold. It closed around him like a leaden hand, the unrelenting squeeze of icy fingers chilling Slade down to the marrow. He was shaking now.

Just a little bit farther.

Slade managed to claw out a few more inches, and then the primitive part of his brain took over, and fueled by the need to breathe, he went racing for the surface. He came up exactly in line with the spit, just at the point where the banks began to come together and the river picked up speed.

With the current pushing him faster and the log only a handsbreadth in front of his face, Slade had just enough time to wriggle his upper body out of the water before impact. He threw his arms over the limb an instant before his chest slammed into the log, the impact sending it twisting on its moorings. For a moment Slade thought it would hold, but then it was pulled away, the fan of branches on the end dipping into the river.

He fought to hold on, but the bark was slick, and soon the current was pulling it out of his grip. Refusing to give up, he kicked after it, choking on the river water that filled his mouth. He chased the limb for ten yards and was on the verge of giving up when he snagged one of the branches. It cracked beneath his weight, but Slade knew this was his last chance. *I'm getting on this log.*

Levering his torso out of the water, he dragged a sodden boot over the trunk and hauled himself on top. Straddling his makeshift raft, Slade let out a triumphant shout and turned to raise a middle finger to the men he knew were likely still watching him from the mountaintop.

"*Ha!* I made it, you bastards."

Drunk off the euphoria that came with cheating death, Slade turned back to face the river, the grin he'd worn seconds before falling from his lips when the log rounded the bend and he saw the raging white water of the waterfall ahead. "No. No. *No!*" Out of sheer desperation he threw himself flat and tried to paddle for shore, but no matter how hard he stroked, the log stayed on course.

Too tired to swim toward land and too weak to hold, Slade quickly realized his only option was to tie himself to the log. Not giving himself time to overthink what he was about to do, he reached into his pocket for his lowering line and quickly lashed himself to the log.

Adding an extra knot for good measure, Slade wrapped his arms around the trunk and closed his eyes. The water became even more turbulent as he neared the edge of the rapids, and the log pitched beneath him like a Dornier circling a fire. Even with the rope, Slade was sure he was going to be thrown off, but he was committed now, and all he could do was close his eyes and offer a silent prayer.

The crash of the water reached a crescendo as he neared the crest and the pool shallowed, the scrape of the log on the riverbed slowing its forward progress. For an instant Slade thought that he'd run aground, and sensing his salvation, he cracked open an eyelid. But then the log ripped free of the snag and went sliding over the edge.

"This is bullshiiiiiit . . ."

The pool below rushed up to meet him, the crash of his body through the water leaving Slade feeling like he'd just tried to high dive through freshly poured concrete. Knowing he had to move quickly, he shook off the impact and tugged at the lowering line, trying to get an arm free. The rope tore into his wrists, and the blood trickling from his sliced palm went from red to black as the weight of the log carried it deep.

Slade finally jerked a hand free just as the nose of the log hit bottom and sank into the silt. The burst of adrenaline cut through the numbness in his hands. Desperate, he grabbed for the hilt of his knife and pulled it from its sheath, careful not to cut off a finger as he sawed through the lowering line. Heart hammering in his ears, Slade sliced through the last strand, and then he was finally free. Shucking off the rope, he was tempted to let go of the knife in preparation for his mad swim to the surface, but a long-forgotten voice stopped him.

"Take care of your gear and your gear will take care of you."

They were Grant's words, and for once Slade found himself listening.

Clamping the spine of the knife between his teeth, Slade swam upward. He didn't know how long he'd been under, but with his vision throbbing at the edges and his lungs aching in his chest, Slade was afraid he wasn't going to make it before he ran out of air.

Shoving the thought away, he kept going, following the slope of the river bottom, until his feet touched stone, and then he stood up, mouth gaping as he sucked in much-needed oxygen. He was alive, but the endorphin rush that followed his survival was short lived, and soon Slade was shivering hard enough to pop his joints.

With muscles so stiff it was hard to walk, he forced his legs to move, and as he sloshed through the water, he prayed he had enough energy to get to shore and make a fire before he froze to death.

CHAPTER 35

SAINT JOSEPH HOSPITAL

Eureka, California

Keller stood at the sink, the dried blood of the SWAT team leader stain-
ing his hands like an old henna tattoo. He turned on the water, and while
he waited for it to warm, he focused his attention on the soap dispenser
mounted on the wall. Keller worked the pump, filling the palm of his
hand with squirts of the hot-pink liquid, then rubbed it into a lather.

According to the label stuck to the front of the dispenser, the indus-
trial-grade soap was rated to kill 99 percent of germs known to man.
Keller found himself wondering if somewhere in the hospital there was
a doctor who could give him a pill to do the same for his conscience.

The scenes from the cabin came rushing back. Slade's frantic voice
on the radio and the sudden rush of testosterone and fear that filled the
cargo hold of the cabin when the team leader took over. *Variable Six is
now in command.*

In the moment, the man had seemed so sure of himself—so damn
cocky. Then five minutes later he was laid out on the filthy floor of the
Black Hawk, gasping for air while Keller held pressure to the hole that
had been blown into his chest.

He and the SWAT team medic had done what they could to save
him, but despite the speed of the helicopter, he was fading fast. The pilot
had radioed ahead, and by the time they landed at the hospital, nurses

and doctors were gathered at the landing pad with the gurney, ready to rush him into surgery.

That was two hours ago, and since then Keller had heard nothing.

Eager to free himself from his emotional free fall, he plunged his soapy hands beneath the faucet. The pain of the scalding water over his flesh electrified his nerve endings like battery acid, but Keller held them there as if seeking atonement for his sins. Waiting until his hands were clean before turning off the water, he glanced up at the fog-filled mirror. The face that looked back at him was a caricature of his own—hard and haunted.

That the armed men on the mountain had known they were coming was obvious, but who'd tipped them off? Keller didn't know. Frustrated, he walked over to the paper towel dispenser and yanked down hard on the lever, but nothing happened. He repeated the process again and got the same result. There was paper in the dispenser—Keller could see that by peering through the opaque plastic. *Then where the hell is my paper towel?*

Frustration turned to anger, and he slammed a fist into the machine, hitting it hard enough to crack the plastic. Wiping his hands dry on the front of his filthy pants, Keller stomped out of the bathroom and stepped into the hall, the wash of fluorescent lights and the antiseptic bite of the industrial cleaners leaving him momentarily queasy.

Keller's hatred for hospitals stemmed from his childhood and the weeks spent in the ICU watching cancer quickly destroy his father. Prior to the mass the doctors found on the MRI, his father had seemed invincible. The man was a war hero who'd survived two tours in 'Nam and a .38 from a drug dealer in South Florida, only to be brought low by an insidious disease that ate him alive from the inside out.

Shoving the thoughts away, Keller went and grabbed a Styrofoam cup of hospital coffee from the machine at the end of the hall and then started back to the waiting room. He took a sip of the coffee, then set it on the end table and pulled out his phone. The alerts on the screen showed a handful of missed calls from David Rollins, the special agent in charge of the Sacramento office, and a text that read *CALL ME ASAP!*

As much as Keller wanted to ignore the text, he knew that wasn't an option. Not if he wanted to make it to retirement.

Best to get it over with.

Bracing himself for the storm he knew was to come, Keller dialed the number and offered a silent prayer to whoever was listening before lifting the phone to his ear. It hadn't rung twice before Rollins picked up, the resignation Keller heard in his voice turning his insides cold.

"Pete, how are you doing?"

"I've been better, sir."

"Yeah, I bet you have," he said. "Look, there's no easy way to say this, but the forest supervisor is pissed. I mean, he's losing his mind."

"Sir, I can understand that, but Cole and I briefed him on the risk of the operation. Hell, we even took a SWAT team up there with us."

"I know, Pete, I know. But this is the Forest Service we're talking about, not the DEA, and they've had enough."

"What does that mean?"

David was silent for a moment, then said, "They are disbanding the task force. It's over."

"Over? How can it be over? We've still got people up there—hell, *they've* still got people up there."

"I agree, and if it were up to me, we'd go up there and get them out," David explained. "But this is a Forest Service initiative, and without their assets or authority to go back up the mountain, we are dead in the water. I'm sorry, Pete, but my hands are tied."

Keller felt like he'd been gutted, and it was all he could do to manage the "yes sirs" required to get off the phone.

With the call ended, he moved to the window and looked out over the cityscape, the distant glimmer of the Pacific Ocean reminding him of Mexico.

It's happening again. Everything falling apart right in front of me.

That the Forest Service wouldn't just let this go with disbanding the task force had been left unspoken, but Keller knew it to be true. They would need a scapegoat, someone to hang the blame on, and he knew that he'd be their obvious target.

What was worse: since he was due for retirement, Keller knew the DEA wouldn't bother putting up a fight.

Shit.

Not sure what else to do, he dropped into a chair, his eyes drifting to the TV mounted to the wall in time to catch the *Breaking News* banner spilling across the screen.

The picture flashed to a silver-haired reporter in a blue windbreaker standing in front of Fowler's burnt-out trailer. With the volume low, Keller's first thought was that the segment was just another update on the Willow Creek fire, but then the closed captioning caught up with what the reporter was saying. The words that scrolled across the bottom of the screen, *former forest ranger brutally murdered*, instantly grabbed his attention.

Forgetting the coffee, Keller leaped to his feet and moved closer to the TV in time to catch the picture of Fowler in forest greens popping up in the upper right corner. Though he was now close enough to hear the sound coming from the speaker, the low murmur of conversation from those gathered in the waiting room made it difficult to comprehend.

Keller reached for the volume button and turned it up in time to hear the reporter say, "According to a source close to Channel Five, Hannah Fowler was reported to have been working with the *LA Times* to expose cartel activity in the Six Rivers National Forest."

Keller stood rooted in front of the screen, waiting for more, but besides the reporter promising to keep the public updated on the rapidly evolving story, there was nothing else. Feeling the tug of a lead, Keller pulled his phone from his back pocket, a look at the screen showing two missed calls from Cole as well as a text that he was on his way to the hospital.

Since the man was coming to see him, Keller felt no need to call him back. Instead, he opened the phone's web browser and typed Fowler's name into the search bar. The results came back slow but steady, and a cursory scroll showed most were headlines from other affiliates.

But buried near the bottom was a link to Fowler's web page.

Keller clicked on the link and was redirected, but as the page began to download, a drop of his bars caused it to slow to a crawl. Cursing the hospital's thick concrete walls, he moved to the window in search of a better signal.

He paced back and forth in front of the glass until he was back to four bars and then hit the refresh button, begging the signal to hold. *C'mon . . . C'mon.* It did, and when the page finally loaded, he tapped the navigation menu, not exactly sure what he was looking for.

The *My Blog* tab seemed like the best place to start, and he clicked on it, knowing he'd struck gold when the first subject line he read was *Red Cap Exposé Update.* Keller tapped the hyperlink, and the low murmur of the voices inside the waiting room vanished as he began to read.

CHAPTER 36

Tito stomped over to the collapsed porch just as Nash dragged the singed smokejumper from his hiding place and hauled him to his feet. The propane explosion had left him dazed and the man wavered, but before he could go down, Tito had him by the front of his shirt.

"Who are you and what are you doing here?"

"I'm a smokejumper." The man winced. "I saw the fire—"

"Bullshit," Tito snarled, backhanding him across the face.

The blow buckled the smokejumper's legs, and Tito let the man fall, watching as he spit a mouthful of blood into the dirt. In Tito's experience, pain was usually the quickest way to the truth, but when the man looked up, his eyes were defiant behind the mask of dirt and soot that covered his face.

"Is that all you've got?" he taunted. "I've got a niece who hits harder than that."

"A tough guy?" Tito asked, his hand dropping to the Glock at his hip.

"That's right, and you don't scare—"

Before he could finish, Tito had the Glock out and the barrel pressed into the center of the smokejumper's forehead. He watched the man pale over the pistol sights and flashed him a cold smile. "Not so tough now, are you?"

"You're not going to shoot me."

"And why is that?" Tito asked.

"Because right now I'm the only one who can get you off this mountain alive."

"He's right, boss," Matt said, stepping into view. "Just think about it for a second."

With his finger already on the trigger, it took everything Tito had *not* to kill the smokejumper, but knowing Matt was right, he took a deep breath and holstered the Glock. "Check his pockets. See if he has anything on him."

The smokejumper cursed and tried to get to his feet, but Nash shoved him face first into the dirt and dropped a knee into his back to hold him down while Matt began ripping through his pockets. "I've found a map, a wallet, and some dusty old protein bars," he said.

Tito dropped to a crouch beside the man and picked up his wallet. He fished out his driver's license and read the name printed on the front of the card. *Buck Granger.*

Shoving the license into his back pocket, Tito reached down and grabbed a handful of the smokejumper's hair. He twisted the man's head to face him and leaned in close. "You saw what I did to Boone, so you know what kind of man I am."

Buck managed a strangled nod. "Y-yeah."

"That's good, because if I even *think* that you're trying to screw me, I will make you suffer in ways you can't possibly imagine."

"Even if I get you out of here, you are still going to kill me."

"Probably," Tito said, shrugging, "but if you do what I want, I'll make it quick—otherwise, I'm going to introduce you to a world of pain you never even knew existed. I'll give you a few minutes to think it over."

Leaving the man in the dirt, Tito got to his feet and dusted off his pant legs. "I need to make a call. While I'm doing that, Matt, get the drone up and see if you can find our missing friend."

"On it," the Marine said.

Leaving the other two men to watch Buck, Tito retrieved his sat phone from his pack and dialed his source's number from memory.

The line connected on the third ring, and when the man answered, his voice was shaky.

"What in the hell is going on up there? I've got a Forest Service officer in critical condition and the news media on my boss's ass. Do you have *any* idea how much shit I'm in?"

"You never said anything about a tactical team when you alerted me to the helicopter," Tito said, his voice cold as ice. "If that cop dies, his blood is on your hands, not mine."

There was a moment of silence on the other line, and when the man finally spoke, there was desperation in his voice. "This has gotten out of control. *You're* out of control. I'm calling Hale; I can't—"

"You call Hale, and I will kill everyone you love," Tito warned. "The *only* way you get out of this alive is by doing *exactly* what I tell you."

"OK. OK. I'm listening."

"Good. Now I don't want any more surprises. No more cops, no more helicopters, no more smokejumpers. You keep everyone off this fucking mountain until I clean up your mess."

"I've made the fires down south a priority, so you don't have to worry about any more aircraft."

"That's a good start," Tito said. "I'm also going to need everything on the smokejumper you sent up here. Not Buck; I've already taken care of him. The other one."

"Oh God, you killed another—"

"You need to stay focused, Director Cole, do you hear me?"

"Yeah, I—I hear you."

"Good, now get me what I need. I'll be in touch."

Tito ended the call and was shoving the sat phone back into his pack when Matt came over. "I found him. He's on the east side of the river."

Nodding, Tito pulled out his map and walked over to Buck. "Well, have you made up your mind?"

The man glared at him for a moment but finally offered a slight nod. "Show me where you need to go."

"You're a smart man."

When he nodded to the Marines, they hauled Buck to his feet, and

Tito spread the map on the ground. "Your friend is on the east side of the river. How do we get there?"

Buck looked up from the map and studied Tito's face, and then with a sag of his shoulders he pointed to a narrow spot a mile northeast of their position. "The river narrows after the falls, and it's shallow enough for you to cross."

"Are you sure?"

"Yeah, I'm sure," Buck sighed in defeat.

"Then let's get moving."

CHAPTER 37

Humboldt County, California

Slade dragged himself onto shore, his body waterlogged, his skin criss-crossed by a lattice of bruises and cuts. That he was alive gave him the strength he needed to stumble across the stone-lined bank but no far-ther. His legs gave out just short of the pool of orange sunlight, and he crawled the rest of the way, hands bleeding as he reached the circled glow and collapsed.

Slade flipped onto his back and closed his eyes, savoring the warmth of the sun on his body. He'd made it. But no sooner had the thought crossed his mind than a cloud slipped across the golden face of his savior. Enveloped by the sudden shade, his muscles seized beneath his skin, tightening until they were taut as iron hawsers as his body waged a losing battle against the cold.

Gripped in the early stages of hypothermia, all Slade could think of was going to sleep—closing his eyes and giving in to the endless creep of the cold spreading through his core like a sheet of unseen ice. Dimly aware that he was drifting closer to the point of no return, Slade had two options: give in and die right there on the riverbank, or get moving and try to find a way to ward off the encroaching darkness.

A fire. I need a fire.

If he'd had his pack, building a fire would have been as easy as pulling out a lighter, but all Slade had was the sodden clothes on his back. Then he remembered the emergency survival kit—the box Grant had taught them all to make during his time at New Horizons. It was the one item Slade carried on his person at all times.

Praying it had survived the fall, Slade ran a trembling hand over his pant leg, and the reassuring feel of the square box beneath the zipper breathed new life into his beaten mind. Slapping his hand against his leg to get the blood flowing, he managed to undo the zipper and dig out the weathered box secured by a nearly rotted rubber band. Survival kit in hand, Slade pushed farther up the bank, collecting every stick and sliver of dried wood in his path. By the time he made it onto level ground, he had enough kindling for a small blaze, and after digging out a small bowl in the earth with the heel of his boot, he set about making the fire.

Slade grabbed a handful of dried marsh grasses and twisted them together before placing them at the bottom of the hole. He tried to build a tepee of sticks around it, but his fingers were just too cold, and with his dexterity nonexistent, it was like playing a perverse game of jackstraws.

Dammit. C'mon.

While blowing on his fingers and slapping his hands against his arms managed to get the blood moving again for a short period of time, it did nothing for the shakes. Still, he kept at it, and after five minutes of work he had managed to construct a passable tepee. Kindling in place, Slade opened the tin and pulled out a bundle of waterproof matches. He struck one off a rock and cupped it in his hand, the rush of sulfur into his lungs choking him when he leaned down to set the match to the kindling.

Holding his breath, he nursed the flame to life, feeding bits of wood and pieces of grass to the glowing ember until it finally caught. Though the fire was small, the heat against his outstretched palms brought a semblance of control back to what had been a hopeless situation. Fingers loosening, Slade continued to nurture the fire until it was crackling merrily in its pit. The temptation was to let it grow until its heat rivaled the now-absent sun, but he couldn't forget the fact that there were still men out there who'd tried to kill him.

Not wanting to give them a second chance and give away his location, he kept the blaze small and turned his attention back to the Altoid tin. The sight of the small compass nestled inside reminded him of Boone, and he reached into his pocket for the ziplock bag containing the map they'd given him during the briefing. When he took the bag from his pocket, Slade found that the seal had failed and the paper inside was soaking wet. Careful not to tear it, he pulled it out and spread it carefully on the ground.

Using the compass and the map, Slade found his position, but knowing where he was mattered little. What he really needed was food, dry clothes, and a place to lie up. As luck would have it, Slade knew exactly where to go.

Face hovering inches over the map, he scanned the terrain features, searching for the little spit of land that contained the hunting shack used by some of the survivalists who frequented the area. Though a secret to most, the network of way stations was well known to anyone who'd been at New Horizons, because keeping them stocked was part of their monthly chores.

With his destination set, Slade shot a quick azimuth toward the distant peak, then slowly folded up the map and returned it to his pocket. Kicking dirt on the fire, he forced himself to his feet and then stepped off.

The first hundred yards weren't bad, and Slade took advantage of the gentle incline to try and make up some time, but he hadn't made it halfway up the side of the ridge before his legs felt as if they were going to give out.

Just keep pushing, he told himself, *one foot in front of the other.*

His mind slipped back to smokejumper training and the final week in the mountains, when Buck and the rest of the cadre had tried to break the rookies. Slade had landed wrong on the jump in, and by the time they finished the first day's work, his ankle was so swollen he'd been afraid to take his boot off lest he couldn't get it back on.

The next morning was even worse, and for the first time since training began, Slade was struggling just to keep up. *You're hurt; there's no shame in tapping out.* Like a tape on an endless loop, the voice in his head was incessant, and by the end of the third day, it had begun to wear him down. That night over a cold MRE dinner, Slade was feeling sorry for himself and on the verge of packing it in when one of the other recruits beat him to it.

"Your back hurts, does it?" Buck asked the other rookie.

"Yes sir. It's killing me. The pain is—"

Buck had been quick to cut him off. "Let me tell you something about pain. It's all in the mind," he said, tapping the side of his head. "And if you don't mind, then it don't matter."

The other recruit hadn't gotten the message, but Slade did. He heard it loud and clear. His mind was his enemy, not a friend, and as long as his ankle would support his weight, he was determined to go on.

It was this mindset that fueled him now. Still, it wasn't easy, and by the time he reached the top of the rise, Slade was sucking air like a lawnmower with a bad carburetor. He sagged against the nearest tree, wincing at the headache forming at his temples. Slade had pushed hard, knowing the men were following him, and while he should have been soaked with sweat, instead his skin was clammy and dry.

For most people, dehydration was something you worried about in the summer when the sun was out and the temperatures high, but though it was cool in the mountains, the lack of water could kill you just as fast as a bullet. Spurred by the thought, Slade fished the sodden map from his pocket and carefully laid it across the rock. The ink was fading and the contour lines were smudged, but the thin blue line of the intermittent stream on the far side of his current position was clear to see.

Water.

Slade pushed himself to his feet and started off, weaving through the thick curtain of trees. He forced himself to stop every twenty yards, check his back trail, and listen for any signs of his pursuers, but even then, there was no escaping the constant burn of his thirst. Though the terrain was flat, traversing the spiny ridge was anything but easy, and the distance seemed to crawl by, leaving his mind filled with doubt.

What if it's not there? Or it's dried up?

Knowing he had to be getting close, Slade pushed the fear away and kept moving. Eventually, the babble of water drew him to the edge of the hill, and he looked down, relieved to find a creek at the bottom of the gorge. But the reprieve was short lived, vanquished by the nightmare of loose shale and razor-sharp boulders that marked the descent.

"Nothing to it but to do it," he mumbled.

Grabbing hold of a sapling, he eased his way downslope, taking it slow, testing each step before bringing his full weight to bear. Whenever possible, Slade kept his boots parallel to the rock face in case he lost his footing and started to slide. Near the bottom, the ground leveled out and the sharp rocks gave way to moss-slicked stones. With the water so close that he could almost taste it, the extra time it took to clear the stones without breaking an ankle seemed cruel and unusual. By the time he made it to the edge of the stream, Slade was panting, and he lowered himself to his stomach and stuck his face beneath the surface.

Nothing had ever tasted as good.

He gulped down the ice-cold water until his belly felt stretched as an old wineskin. Thirst quenched, he sat back on his haunches and was contemplating his next move when the distant hum of voices followed by the unmistakable buzzing he'd heard earlier filled his ears.

CHAPTER 38

SIX RIVERS NATIONAL FOREST

Humboldt County, California

Slade scanned the sky, not sure if the sound was real or if it was the dehydration playing tricks on him. Figuring it better to play it safe, he moved away from the stream and sought the shelter of the trees. Dropping flat, he wiggled beneath the low limbs of a juniper and pressed his back to the trunk. He waited, his hand curled around his jump knife, eyes scanning through the breaks in the limbs.

The silence was deafening, the only sound the hammering of his heart in his ears. *Am I* that *messed up?* Considering how many times he'd hit his head during his escape, Slade couldn't discount a concussion, but he was sure that he'd heard something. Just as he was beginning to think that maybe he'd made it all up, a pair of crows leaped from a pine. The rustle of wings and the metallic caw that followed drew his eyes left in time to catch the glint of sun off plastic.

Well, shit, the drone is back.

That the enemy had an eye in the sky changed everything, and suddenly the voices that Slade had *thought* he'd heard became a very real threat.

What would Grant do?

It was a question Slade hadn't asked himself in over a decade, but hiding beneath the tree, he instinctively knew that the *only* way he was getting off the mountains alive was by remembering the skills the ill-tempered Green Beret had forced him to master when he was a teenager. There had been a time when Slade was a better tracker and survivalist than most professionals, but he was rusty, and even if he could remember what to do, he was limited with only the knife and the tiny survival kit in his pocket.

It's not enough.

Assuming the drone had already seen him and that whoever was controlling it was vectoring the men from the mountains toward his position, Slade knew that hiding was no longer viable. He needed to get moving, preferably in the *opposite* direction of his actual destination. Though no expert on drones, he had to assume there was only so much juice left in the battery, and so his goal was to keep it moving. Wait until whoever was operating the drone was forced to recall it before making his final push to his destination.

Wanting to speed up the process, Slade pushed himself into a jog, but with a gut full of water and the skin of his feet feeling as if they were peeling off with each step, it soon proved too painful to continue. Slowing to a brisk walk, he forced himself to think back on his time at New Horizons and all the annoying little tips Grant used to offer when they were out in the field.

What was that thing he always used to say? Something about understanding your enemy?

Slade knew it was deeper than that, but it was enough to get his mind thinking in the right direction, and he stopped to take stock of his surroundings. The men chasing him were well armed, and the fact that one of them had a scoped rifle meant that Slade needed to stay away from the high ground and open areas where a sniper could take him out.

A look to the west showed nothing but stunted scrub and ankle-high grasses with rolling foothills in the distance. Perfect terrain for a sniper. Turning east, he stared down a draw that would take him into the timber. In addition to everything else, there was no escaping the rub of his waterlogged socks against his heel and the hot spots forming on his instep. Ducking into the trees, Slade thought wistfully of the personal gear bag he'd lost during the firefight on the mountain. He could have used the dry socks and precious foot powder now to save his rapidly deteriorating feet. But worse than the pain that came with each step was the hollow rumble in his stomach. Damn, he was hungry.

A normal man burned three thousand calories a day, and that was just surviving. On a fire, Slade and the rest of his crew burned twice that amount. In fact, it wasn't uncommon for a smokejumper to return from a fire five or even ten pounds lighter than when they'd deployed. Which was why Slade, like the rest of his team, never missed a chance to stuff his face when back at base. But out here the only sustenance to be had was that offered by Mother Nature.

Staying at the edge of the timber, he scanned the brush until he finally stumbled upon a blackberry bush growing among the trees. The berries were ripe and their juices sweeter than any candy, but there were not enough, and even after picking the bush clean, Slade was still starving when he heard the distant scrabble of boots over rocks.

When a cursory search of the sky failed to show any signs of the drone, Slade thought he was in luck. *They can't track what they can't see.* With that thought in mind, he was ready to move out, but then he looked down and saw the prints of his boots circling the blackberry bush. Damn, he was sloppy. Quick to rectify the problem, Slade slipped into the timber, cut a limb from a pine tree, and then used it to brush away his tracks.

Now what?

A flitter of movement drew his attention to his back trail, and he eased back into the timber, careful to stick to the rocky soil at the edge so as not to leave any tracks. Moving at a crouch, he slipped behind the trunk of a redwood and dropped to a knee. His breathing came faster than he liked, and he was aware of the slight tremble in his hands when the first armed man stepped into view. Slade was sweating, and he could smell his own fear oozing off him. There were two of them now, one tall and wide shouldered, the second short and built like a fireplug, and both were armed to the teeth. But it was the way they moved, eyes shifting from ground to blackberry bush, that confirmed his worst fears.

They were definitely tracking him.

Slade watched, trying to gauge their skill, knowing that if they were good, they wouldn't be fooled by his hastily brushed-away tracks. Sure enough, they moved straight as an arrow to his last position and then began circling the dirt.

"He was just here," one of the men said, his voice barely above a whisper. "Couldn't have gone far."

Slade's hand closed around the hilt of the knife, but he stopped just short of pulling it from his sheath. They were out of contact range, and even if they weren't, there was no way the blade was punching through their body armor. No, if he was going to fight these men, he would have to do it on his own terms. On his own ground. Even then, he wasn't sure if he could win.

Better to keep moving. Try to lose them in the rocks.

With that in mind, Slade waited until their backs were to him, and then he turned and slipped silently to the next tree. Ducking behind it, he waited for a second to make sure they still weren't looking before repeating the process. Though he was walking as lightly as possible over the dried pine needles, each step sounded impossibly loud, but he kept at it, avoiding the sticks and twigs that crisscrossed his path.

It was less than fifteen yards to the far edge of the tree line and the stretch of rocks where he planned to lose the men, but by the time he made it, Slade was soaked with sweat. Lowering himself onto all fours, he crawled the rest of the way, fully expecting to hear the rush of boots behind him at any second. But there was nothing.

Scrabbling over the rocks, he ducked behind a boulder and paused to catch his breath. A quick look back the way he'd come showed the men had left the bush and were now circling the redwood that had been his first hiding place. However, it wasn't the two trackers that held his attention but the flash of the bedraggled man in the yellow shirt being pulled along in the rear.

Buck?

No, it wasn't possible. Buck was gone. Slade had seen the man go down, seen the blood.

You need to get moving, the survival voice in his head told him.

Slade wanted to listen but knew he needed to get a better view.

Needed to know if the man he'd seen was Buck or just another figment of his imagination. The only problem was, with the trackers so close, Slade knew a closer examination would most likely end with a bullet.

Just leave it and go.

Slade closed his eyes and wrestled with his dilemma. *Do I stay or go?* He didn't know, but of one thing he was sure: staying could get him killed, which meant his only real chance of survival was getting to Grant and the Citadel as fast as possible.

Besides, what could he do to help Buck, if it actually was Buck, with only a knife? With the man in yellow now out of sight, Slade cast a final glance through the trees and then, tearing himself away, slipped into the shadows, praying that he'd made the right decision.

CHAPTER 39

Humboldt County, California

In an effort to corral the smokejumper on the run, Tito had split his remaining men into two teams, and while Ringo and Nash beat the brush, he and Matt lay flat on the edge of a rim three miles south of where their quarry had stopped to take a drink.

The crossing had been exactly where Buck had said, but he still didn't trust the man, and while Matt brought the drone in for another slow sweep of the trees, Tito studied the smokejumper out of the corner of his eye.

"You wondering if I'm going to run?" Buck asked.

"The thought crossed my mind."

"Well, it's kind of hard to go anywhere with these on," he said, nodding to the flex cuffs Ringo had pulled over his wrists.

"Let's hope so," Tito sneered.

"You got any water?" Buck asked.

"There was plenty in the river; you should have gotten a drink," Tito said, savoring the angry glare the man shot back. He was waiting for one of the smokejumper's pithy comments when Matt pulled off the goggles with a curse.

"Shit, I think he saw the drone," the former Marine intoned. "We had him, and now he's gone."

"I need you to be sure."

"Give me a second," Matt said, pushing the goggles back over his eyes. With every passing second Tito could feel the momentum shifting in the other man's favor, and after a few minutes of not reestablishing contact, he knew it was time to roll the dice.

"What was his last direction of travel?"

"West."

Exchanging the sat phone for the radio, Tito hailed the other team he was trying to vector in on their target's location and brought them up to date on the situation. "I think he's heading for the highway."

"What do you want us to do?" Ringo asked.

"I need you to head west and set up a blocking position at the following grid," Tito said, reading the coordinates from the map he had spread out on the ground. "We are going to come in from the east and try to push him toward you."

"Roger that."

With the second team on the move, Tito rolled up his map and hauled Buck to his feet, leaving Matt to retrieve the drone. Despite all of his hard work up to that point, there was no escaping the stark realization of what would happen if he let this man get away. Working for the cartel was a zero-sum game. A job where yesterday's success would never be enough to save you from today's failures, and standing there, Tito could feel the unseen noose slowly tightening around his throat.

Knowing they needed to get moving, he was about to order Matt to pack up his shit and get going when the man tugged off his goggles and shoved them angrily into his pack.

"Fucking drone ran out of juice. We're blind."

"Looks like we're going to have to do this the old-fashioned way." Returning the binos to his pocket, Tito slipped down to the low ground and alerted the second team that they were moving out.

Once at the bottom, he took point and led them west. He and Matt moved as fast as they could with Buck in tow, the only break in their pace the few seconds Tito occasionally took to check the GPS secured to his wrist. Thanks to the distinctive tread of the man's boots, he had no problem following the trail even at a jog. They followed it down the spur and through the timber, passing the blackberry bush where Matt had last seen their quarry.

Seven minutes later, the GPS alerted Tito that they were in the area of the grid he'd given to the second team, and he slowed his pace.

"Where are you?" he asked over the radio.

"About two hundred meters north of the ambush point," Ringo answered. "We were tracking him through the trees, but then old Davy Crockett here lost his trail."

"Hold what you've got. We are on our way."

The terrain was more difficult than it looked, and it took a good ten minutes to catch up with Ringo and Nash.

"What the hell happened?" Matt asked.

"He lost him," Ringo answered.

"Don't put this on me. That little fucker has skills," Nash replied.

"Skills," Ringo taunted. "This dude fights fires for a living, but all of a sudden you lose his track and he's Bear Grylls?"

"What are you saying?" Nash demanded.

"I'm saying you suck at tracking, city boy."

Tito watched as the larger Marine walked over to Ringo, his fists balled at his sides. Considering what was at stake, a fight was the last thing any of them needed. Still, there was a part of him that wondered if the man was going to finally put an end to Ringo's bitching. As he closed the gap, Tito thought he might, but then at the moment of truth, Nash balked. "If you think you can do a better job, then be my guest."

"Thought you'd never ask," Ringo replied.

Moving off by himself, he slung his rifle and began walking ever-increasing circles over the rocky ground.

"Looks like a dog chasing his tail," Nash jabbed. "Bet you ten bucks he don't find shit."

The look in Matt's eyes told Tito that he was considering taking the bet, but before he had a chance, Ringo's whistle drew their attention to the edge of the clearing. "Heading back north, exactly like I said."

Tito nodded for them to move out and then turned to Buck. "You stay close and keep your mouth fucking shut," he snapped. "If I even think you're trying to warn him, I'll cut your tongue out of your mouth. Understand me?"

CHAPTER 40

Special Agent Keller was still trying to process what he'd just read when Cole came striding into the waiting room, his face haggard beneath a five-o'clock shadow.

"I take it you've heard that they are shutting us down?" he asked.

"Yeah," Keller said, getting to his feet, his face flushed with anger. "But that's not *all* I've heard. You lied to me."

"Whoa, take it easy, man," Cole said, holding up his hands in front of him. "What are you talking about? I never lied to you."

"You never told me that Fowler was a forest ranger, either, or that she'd been investigating the Red Cap."

Cole recoiled like he'd been slapped in the face. "Pete, look, I don't know who you've been talking to, but—"

"Here, let me show you," Keller said, holding his phone in front of Cole.

Cole frowned, his eyes darting from the phone to Keller's face, then back again. "This is your source, Fowler's website? C'mon, man, this is—"

"This is what?"

"This is crazy," Cole said. "Fowler was crazy. She was always going around making these kinds of wild accusations, which is why she was fired from the Forest Service."

"No, she found something in those mountains, and they killed her for it."

"That's bullshit and so is this," Cole said, tapping the phone.

Keller glared at the man, searching his eyes for the lie, but it wasn't there. *Damn, what if I'm wrong?* The glimmer of doubt cut through his anger like a knife, and he stepped back, suddenly unsure. "Then why not tell me about Fowler and, more importantly, why the Forest Service is so damn eager to leave those men on the mountain?"

"You're right; I should have told you about Fowler," Cole said. "But that doesn't mean I had anything to do with the decision to leave those guys in the mountains."

"Does that mean you'll help me go get them?"

"That's not my call," Cole said.

"Of course it is. You're just too chickenshit to make it." Disgusted, Keller spun on his heel and, leaving Cole standing there in the waiting room, stomped out into the hall. He headed for the elevator, his hands balled into fists at his sides.

Fuck 'em—I'll do it myself.

Keller was almost to the elevator when Cole caught up with him, grabbed him by the shoulder, and spun him around. "Don't you put that on me," he barked. "If my boss says to stand down, then we stand down. That's the job."

"No, our job is to catch the bad guys, no matter who is trying to protect them," Keller said, pulling his arm free. Spoiling for a fight, it was all he could do to turn on his heel and continue down the hallway. Seething, he punched the elevator button, hoping Cole had the brains to leave him alone.

But he wasn't giving up, and a moment later Cole was standing behind Keller. "Protect them?" he demanded. "What the hell are you talking about?"

"What am I talking about?" Keller threw up his hands in exasperation. "The cartel has someone on the inside, feeding them information."

"Do you have proof?"

"Yeah, I've got proof," Keller said. "First someone spoofs my cell number to get Boone to show up at the motel, then Fowler dies in some bullshit trailer fire, then we've got shooters waiting for us in the mountains . . ."

The ding of the elevator arriving cut him off, and Keller shook his head. "You know what, forget it." Leaving Cole standing there, he turned and stepped into the car. "I'll see you when this is over," he said, reaching for the lobby button. He punched it, shoulders sagging as the doors began to close, but before they could slide all the way shut, Cole shot a hand between them.

"We don't need a helicopter to get back up to the mountain," he said.

"What are you talking about?"

"Look, I should have told you about Fowler working for the Forest Service. I fucked up and I want to make it right."

"How?" Keller asked.

"When I first became a ranger, I spent a few summers fixing the trails around Red Cap. I know the area, and I've still got some of my old maps, and if—"

Trust was a sacred commodity among cops, and as far as Keller was concerned, Cole *not* telling him about Fowler was the ultimate sin. But as much as he wanted to tell him to fuck off, he knew he needed the man's help.

"Fine."

He shifted over to the side, and Cole stepped into the elevator, nodding his thanks. "I wasn't sure you were going to let me in."

Keller waited for the doors to close before turning on the other man. His blood was up, and he had half a mind to slap the emergency stop button and give Cole a quick beatdown, but he calmed himself with a deep breath.

"No more secrets. You try to screw me again and I'll put you in the dirt, you got me?"

He half expected Cole to bring up how he was still technically his boss, but to his surprise he held Keller's gaze. "Deal."

"All right, so what's the plan?"

"I've got a ranger buddy in the Smith River district who owes me a favor. Can you ride?"

"Ride? Like, a horse?"

"Yeah."

Keller hadn't ridden a horse since his time in the Boy Scouts, and even though he'd been proficient enough to earn the skills badge, he'd never felt comfortable in the saddle. But he wasn't about to tell Cole that. "Yeah, I can ride."

"If you can ride, then I can get us up there. Of course, we're going to need some camping gear and supplies, and all my stuff is back at the office. But we've got to get going while we still have the light."

"The light? What time is it?"

"Almost three."

Keller looked at his watch in disbelief, unable to comprehend that it had only been four hours since their failed mission when it felt like a lifetime ago. But the watch didn't lie. "Can we . . ."

"Pull this off?" Cole finished for him. "Yeah. We can do it, but if we're going, we have to go *now*."

Keller had been in the game long enough to know that there was no such thing as a second chance. Sure, there were reassignments. Desk jobs in the basement of DEA headquarters or banishment to backwater posts where word of your screwups had yet to spread, yet in the end, there was no escaping the past.

No atonement for your sins.

But standing there in the elevator, seeing the conviction in Cole's eyes—hearing the confidence in his voice—Keller knew that was exactly what he was being offered. He was being handed a gift, free money in the mail. Still, as much as he wanted to take it and run, Keller knew there would be consequences for their actions.

"You realize what you're doing, right?" he asked. "I mean, even if we finish this, it's not going to end well. Not for you, not for me, and certainly not for anyone we find on that mountain. Are you ready for that?"

Cole paused, weighing his answer, and when he spoke, there was steel in his voice. "It's like you said: those are *my* guys up on the mountain."

"Well, all right then. Let's get it done."

CHAPTER 41

SIX RIVERS NATIONAL FOREST

Humboldt County, California

By the time he reached his destination, it was nearly dusk, and Slade covered the final hundred yards beneath a cotton candy sky. He'd pushed himself hard, but despite making good time, all he could think of was Buck. Logically he knew there was little chance his team leader had survived the blast, and even if he had, there was absolutely no way he'd be helping the men trying to kill him.

Still there was no denying what Slade had seen. *Or what you thought you saw*, he reminded himself. Slade knew from experience how stress and sleep deprivation could play tricks on your mind. He'd seen it happen on fires when men dead on their feet had started attacking nonexistent spot fires and flare-ups. Hell, it had even happened to him during his second season as a hotshot, when he'd woken up from a half sleep swearing that his bivy sack was on fire.

Shaking his head to clear his mind, Slade focused on the cabin half-visible through the trees. Though he called it a cabin, it was in truth a plywood lean-to with a salvaged metal door and a patinaed chimney for the wood-burning stove he knew was inside. When he got to the door, he used his knife to pop the latch and slipped inside, his wet boots squishing on the rough board flooring.

Locking the door behind him, Slade stripped out of his sodden clothes and limped over to the cast-iron stove. He built a fire using the newspaper and kindling he found in the galvanized bucket on the floor, the warmth loosening muscles still tight from the river. He could have stayed there forever, but the hollow rumble of his empty stomach was quick to send him searching for food. Leaving his clothes to dry, Slade opened the cupboard, where he found a stash of long-expired canned goods.

Can't go wrong with SpaghettiOs.

He opened the can with his knife and dug in, too hungry to bother with warming it up. As he ate, Slade began looking around the cabin, searching for anything he could use against the men he knew were still on his trail. They weren't going to stop, and if they had Buck, they would kill him too.

Unless I can kill them first.

Leaving the now-empty can on the makeshift counter, Slade walked over to the old compound bow and quiver of abused arrows by the door. Their broadheads were chipped from use, but they were still sharp and serviceable—perfect for the task at hand. Slade continued his search and found an old climbing stand and pair of steel coil-spring traps in a footlocker shoved against the far wall.

Studying the traps and the climber, Slade felt the hint of a plan forming in the back of his mind. *This could work.* Now properly armed and his hunger slightly abated, Slade stowed the traps in an old duffel bag and added two more logs to the fire before pulling on his still-damp clothes. With the fire burning merrily in the stove, he shouldered the climbing stand, grabbed the bow and quiver, and stepped outside.

It was dark now, and the sliver of the moon revealed dark hills and the distant glow of the fire still burning on the mountain. Slade watched the shadows dance while he waited for his eyes to adjust. The Citadel was to the north, but instead of heading up the slope that would take him there, Slade headed south, back toward the ambush spot he'd picked out in his mind.

The silence enveloped him, the only sounds the rush of the wind through the branches and the gentle chirp of the meadowlarks in the trees. Every step he took sounded like a gunshot, every twig that cracked beneath his feet loud as a stick of dynamite.

This is a great way to get yourself killed.

Slade shortened his steps, remembering what Grant had taught him about staying quiet in the woods. He scanned the terrain, taking his time until he found a deer trail, a scratch of bare earth that he followed down the hill. Even with the moonlight, it was slow going, but Slade made it to the bottom, where he stopped near a lodgepole pine and studied the cast of the moonlight through the branches.

This is it.

That the men chasing him were well trained was obvious from what he'd seen at the cabin, but Slade knew that they had to be tired. Plus, the landscape was unfamiliar, and even with night vision it was going to be hard going. With that in mind, Slade laid out his ambush.

He set the traps among the prints he'd left on his way to the cabin and then covered them with pine straw. Next, he found a slender oak without any low-hanging branches and shrugged out of the climbing stand.

The climber was a favorite of deer hunters because of its portability and ease of use, and after separating the platform from the seat, Slade connected both halves to the tree using the rubberized cable that fastened it to the trunk. Once it was secure, he stepped onto the platform, raised the seat a few feet up the tree, and sat down on the bar. Feeling the teeth sink into the bark, he used the loops attached to the bottom to lift it up and then repeated the process.

The bow banged against the back of the frame as he climbed, and the bark scratched his face, but Slade managed to get six feet off the ground before the larger branches blocked his way. It wasn't until he'd turned around and was facing the ground that Slade wished he'd thought to look for a strap to hold him in.

Can't have everything.

As he waited, his mind began to wander, over his past and what he hoped was his future. There were no promises for men who fought fire, no guarantees that they would live to see the dawn of another day. For some the uncertainty and danger that came with the job were an impossible burden, one that led them to search for more stable work, but for Slade it was all he'd ever wanted.

Eventually he grew tired of thinking, and resting his head back against the tree trunk, he looked up, taking in the multitude of stars spread across the heavens. While there was privation to living out in the open, there was also freedom—an opportunity to see the world as it was originally created. Free from the greed, lies, and pollution that ruled the cities. There was a purity about this place equaled only by its savagery that spoke to the hearts of men, and sitting there, staring up at the heavens, Slade could almost hear its primal call.

The snap of a branch drew his attention back to the ground, and he lifted his bow and nocked an arrow. He waited and stared into the darkness, his heart hammering in his chest. At first there was nothing; then the low limbs parted and a wolf padded into the clearing. It stopped to study Slade, its muzzle bloody from a fresh kill, and then, with a flash of bone-white teeth, it offered a deep growl. Man and beast locked eyes, and even though he was in a tree, Slade had to fight to keep the bow steady.

"This doesn't have to be your day," he said softly.

The wolf cocked its shaggy head and spent a moment taking the measure of the man before him. The growl faded, and realizing he was in the presence of a fellow predator, the shaggy beast offered a low whine before trotting toward the woods.

Slade waited until the wolf was out of sight and then released the draw, his muscles quivering from the effort. Even in the tree stand, ten feet above the ground, the sight of the wolf had been terrifying, and the adrenaline dump that followed the confrontation left him tired. Realizing he was on the verge of nodding off, he stood up in the stand to stretch. Slade savored the feel of the blood rushing back into his legs and then looked at his watch. The illuminated dial told him that he'd been sitting there for almost two hours, and Slade began to wonder if he'd made a mistake, misjudged their approach.

What if they came in from the east, circled around behind you?

The thought made the hairs on the back of his neck stand up, and suddenly Slade felt exposed. Vulnerable. *I need to get out of here.* He was on the verge of climbing down from the stand when he saw a glow of green light moving through the trees off to his right, then heard the metallic click of a selector being flicked from safe to fire.

CHAPTER 42

Slade nocked an arrow, the thrill of the oncoming action sending his heart skipping in his chest. He waited, his senses on full alert as he eyed the darkness, searching for the first signs of the men. At first there was nothing but the blowing of the wind and the distant hoot of an owl; still, Slade could feel their presence, knew that the enemy was near. Keeping his breathing measured and his eyes open, he shifted his focus from the green glow of the night vision to the darkened outlines of the traps and finally to the circle of moonlight across the forest floor that marked his kill zone.

C'mon, you bastards, keep moving.

Slowly the first man emerged from the shadows, followed by a second, their rifles up and ready as they searched for any threats. Once they were moving, Slade shifted his attention back to the shadows, his eyes narrowed as he searched for Buck.

Where the hell are you, buddy?

A third man stepped out, but still no Buck, and Slade was beginning to fear that either he had imagined seeing Buck to begin with or they'd already killed him when he heard a crash of brush followed by a muffled curse.

"Dammit, I can't fucking see shit."

There was a low curse followed by a muffled thump of fist on flesh and a pained cry, all in rapid succession. Short, but loud enough that Slade knew without a doubt that he'd heard Buck's voice. A crack of a branch and another curse drew his attention to the back of the pack, where he saw a fourth man standing over the muted outline of a figure not wearing night vision. Having identified Buck, Slade drew the bow and watched the first man striding toward the trap.

Here we go.

He brought the bow to full draw and waited, the seconds seeming to stretch into hours before he heard the snap of the metal trap and the bloodcurdling scream that followed. With the first man caught in the steel, Slade settled the aiming pin on the green glow that washed across the face of the second man and let go of the string.

The arrow leaped from the bow with a hiss, its one-hundred-grain broadhead tearing through the man's throat. He dropped with a gurgle, and Slade nocked a second arrow, aiming low at the figure still standing in the shadows. He fired, screaming for Buck to run before the arrow left the string.

Before he could grab another arrow, the man caught in the trap spun toward him, flame spitting from his rifle. "He's in the trees."

Fumbling the bow, he had just enough time to see Buck bull through the undergrowth, and then he threw himself clear of the climbing stand. He landed on his back, the impact blasting the air from his lungs and ripping the bow from his hand.

Gasping for breath, Slade rolled to his right, hands scrabbling across the ground in search of a weapon. He found a branch and darted behind the oak, angling for the man in the trap. Brandishing the branch like a club, he slammed it hard across the back of the man's neck.

The shooter dropped, and Slade grabbed his fallen night vision goggles, jamming them over his head. Now able to see, he tried to grab the man's pistol but, finding it pinned, went for one of the grenades attached to his kit. Pulling it free, he ripped out the pin and tossed it toward the remaining shooters, and then he was running.

It was Slade's first time with night vision, and while the emerald glow peeled back the darkened veil of the night, the lack of depth perception left him reeling like a drunken sailor. He stumbled through the trees, searching for the escape trail he'd picked out earlier, but his boot snagged a root, and before he could catch his balance, he pitched forward into the dirt. He landed on his side and looked back to see one of the shooters bounding toward him, the infrared laser attached to his rifle slicing through the darkness. Slade closed his eyes, waiting for the gunshot that he knew would follow, but then the grenade went off. The roll of flame and surging heat quickly brought him to his feet.

Ignoring the pain in his side and back, Slade pushed himself into a jog. He ran north, sprinting past the cabin and the emerald-cast mountains. He kept going, the ground rising beneath his feet—running until his legs and lungs were on fire. When he didn't think he could manage another step, Slade stopped next to an outcropping of rocks and, after catching his breath, fished out the long-expired energy gel pack he'd taken from the cache site. Slade had planned on saving it for the last leg of the journey, when he knew he'd need it most. But the comedown from the adrenaline rush that followed the ambush had left him shaky and on the verge of a crash.

Needing to put some distance between himself and his pursuers, Slade ripped the top of the pack and sucked its contents down. His tired body begged him to sit down and take a rest, but knowing there was a good chance he wouldn't be able to get up again, Slade stayed on his feet. Needing to think about anything but sleep, he let his mind wander like a dog off a leash and soon found himself thinking about Grant and what he would say when he arrived at the Citadel.

His journey took him north, away from the timber and higher up into the mountains. He measured his progress in inches rather than feet, each step leaving him feeling like he was slogging through quicksand, but Slade had come too far to give up now.

As he plodded up the slope, his exhausted mind weaved fanciful hallucinations, every shadow hiding a threat, every gust of wind a prelude to another attack. Nerves frayed and muscles on the verge of failure, Slade pushed through the pain and the exhaustion and kept climbing.

It was nearly dawn when he scrambled over the last ridge and caught his first glimpse of the house perched in the rocks. He stumbled over to a ponderosa pine and sagged against it, his fevered senses struggling to figure out if what he was seeing was real or just another dehydrated hallucination. Knowing there was only one way to find out, he staggered forward, managing a few shuffled steps before his body finally gave out and he dropped to his knees.

Keep going—you're almost there.

But his body had finally reached its limit.

Unable to move, Slade tried to call for help, to scream Grant's name, but all that came out was a ragged croak. Throat burning from the effort, he fell silent, the realization that he'd come so far only to fail at the end enveloping him like a leaden blanket. The weight of the moment pressed him into the dirt, and he lowered his head, a whispered apology spilling from his cracked lips.

I tried, Boone. God knows I tried.

CHAPTER 43

Humboldt County, California

Keller opened his eyes and watched his crystallized breath rising toward the slate-gray sky. He lay there for a moment, trying to remember where he was and why his body felt like he'd just gone nine rounds with Mike Tyson. Then it came rushing back: the reporter on the television, Fowler's blog, and Cole showing up at the hospital offering to help him get back into the mountains.

Rubbing the sleep from his eyes, he climbed out of the Gore-Tex sleeping bag he'd borrowed from Cole. He shoved his feet into his hiking boots and tied the laces, then got to his feet, the dry pop of his joints and the pang of the recently formed saddle sores eliciting a pained groan.

Keller stretched, working the stiffness out of his back, and then looked around, searching for Cole. Bladder full, he shuffled away from their camp and into the scrub to take a piss. He stopped next to a young spruce and unzipped. The relief was immediate, and Keller let out a contented sigh.

He finished his business and was about to head back to the camp when he heard a voice filter through the trees. "Cole, is that you?" When there was no answer, Keller moved around the spruce and was about to call out again when he saw a flitter of movement to his left.

Not sure if it was animal or man, he reached for the Glock holstered at his waist, only to realize that he'd left it back at his sleeping bag.

Stupid.

He was thinking about running to get it when Cole stepped into view, his sat phone pressed to his ear. Relieved, Keller felt his muscles relax and was about to step from cover when his curiosity got the better of him.

Who is he talking to at this hour?

Keller didn't know, but it was clear from his tone and the angry way he walked back and forth that he wasn't happy. He strained to hear what Cole was saying, but with the man constantly on the move, Keller could only pick up snatches.

Finally, he stopped close enough that Keller could hear his first clear sentence. "How many times do I have to tell you that I'm handling it? Stop worrying about me and do your fucking job."

Then he was moving again, circling out of earshot.

Not wanting to be discovered, Keller waited until Cole was facing the other direction, then slipped back the way he'd come, the same questions echoing in his mind. *Who is Cole talking to, and more importantly, what is he going to handle?*

The unanswered questions put him on edge, and the first thing he did upon returning to the camp was retrieve his Glock. He checked to make sure it was loaded and was belting on his holster when the snap of branches announced Cole's return.

"Well, look who's up," he said, heading over to their saddlebags. "How'd you sleep?"

Keller feigned a yawn and another stretch. "Good, but I'm going to need some coffee."

"That's a good idea. You handle that and I'll get the horse fed," Cole said, grabbing the feed bags and carrying them over.

Keller crammed the sleeping bag into its stuff sack and deflated his air mattress, then carried both to the saddlebags, his eyes never leaving Cole. "How long have you been up?" he asked, grabbing the Jetboil stove and a pack of freeze-dried coffee from his pack.

"About thirty minutes. That stew we made last night didn't agree with me," he said, patting his stomach.

"Yeah, those freeze-dried meals can be rough."

Keller didn't know if that was true or not, because last night was the first time he'd ever tried one, but Cole's response confirmed one thing: something was up, and he didn't want Keller to know about it. Preoccupied with his thoughts, he fumbled with the backpacking stove, but after a few tries he managed to get the fuel canister secured to the burner before attaching the coffee press to the top.

Once he had it snug, Keller filled it with water from his canteen, added three scoops of the freeze-dried coffee, then hit the button on the front of the burner. The stove hissed to life with a spout of blue flame, and Keller pulled the map from his pack and spread it on the ground.

He traced the neatly penciled line from their current campsite back to the parking lot at the trailhead where they'd left the truck. The bay Cole had saddled for him bore little resemblance to the docile ranch horse he'd ridden during his time in the Boy Scouts. It was taller and, from the looks of the muscles rippling beneath its coat, incredibly powerful.

Sensing his hesitation, Cole had been quick to dismiss his worries. "It's a trail horse, not a mustang, Pete. Just get on and stay calm. He'll handle the rest."

"I sure hope you're right," Keller said, putting his foot into the stirrup.

True to Cole's word, the bay hadn't offered any problems as they trotted along. Still, Keller had spent the first mile stiff in the saddle until he finally began to relax. The first two hours of the trip had been relatively easy, as they stuck to the horse trails, but it wasn't to last, and soon they were breaking brush across the backcountry.

The rolling hills and valleys had slowly given way to the treacherous terrain he'd seen from the helicopter on the flight in. Sitting there now, watching the water boil, Keller could feel every rock, every slash of the tree limbs across his face. He reached into his saddlebag for the bottle of ibuprofen he'd been smart enough to pack. Deftly shaking four of the pills into his hand, he chased them with a drink from his canteen and then tore into a Clif Bar while he waited for the coffee to finish.

By the time Cole finished feeding the horses, the coffee was steaming in two enamel mugs, and Keller was rinsing out the pot. Cole walked over and took the offered mug with a grim nod.

"How you feeling?"

Keller shrugged and sipped at his coffee. "My ass hurts, but I'll live."

"Good, because we've got a hard ride ahead of us."

Keller studied the man over the rim of his mug, searching his eyes for any sense of what he was thinking. While Cole wasn't as gabby as some of the special agents Keller had worked with in the DEA, he wasn't exactly the strong, silent type either. No, Cole liked to talk, or more accurately he liked to hear himself speak, but something in the man had changed following the failed rescue operation.

Keller had been too angry to notice in the hospital, but out here in the wild the man's reticence had been impossible to ignore. At first, he'd assumed that Cole was still struggling with his decision to go against his bosses' orders and accompany Keller back to the mountains, but after hearing Cole on his sat phone, Keller began to suspect there was something more sinister at work.

"I think we should change our route," Cole said, reaching for the map. "There's an old trail that runs right along this pass. It's rough going, but if we can make it through, it will cut a few hours off the trip."

Keller looked where he was pointing, the tightly bunched contour lines telling him that it was indeed steep. "Looks dangerous. Are you sure it's worth the detour?"

"Our guys have been out in the elements with no food or water going on twelve hours now. You saw how cold it got last night, didn't you?"

"I did," Keller said.

"Well, would *you* like to stay out here longer than you had to?"

It was a good point and, despite Keller's misgivings, one he couldn't argue with. "Then let's do it."

"All right then," Cole said, tossing out the dregs of his coffee and getting to his feet. "Let's get moving. We're burning daylight."

They rode north through the timber, the early-morning sun filtering through the trees. At first it was silent as the grave, but as the chill receded and the dew melted away, the forest came back to life, the chirp of the songbirds in the trees and the skittering of the squirrels through the undergrowth competing with the measured tread of the horses.

Cole took lead, and Keller fell in behind him. He tried to get him talking, hoping to find a natural opportunity to bring up the phone call, but Cole parried his every attempt, not offering more than a grunt or a nod until they stopped for a lunch of freeze-dried chicken and rice. When they were finished, Cole pulled out the map. "We've got five more miles to go," he said, pointing to the red *X* that marked the pass.

Keller swung into the saddle and followed Cole up the trail. The meadow grasses that marked their lunch spot gave way to stone as their horses carried them higher into the mountains. The first two miles passed easily, and even though the trail was wide enough for them to ride two abreast, Keller stayed behind Cole, his right hand never straying from the butt of the Glock.

There was a tension in the air that reminded him of Mexico. An eerie stillness that preceded everything going to shit. As if sensing his trepidation, the bay shortened her stride and lifted her head, and Keller leaned forward to give her neck a reassuring pat.

Ever so slowly, the trail began to narrow, and while there was still flat ground to the left, a glance to the right showed nothing but air. Looking ahead, Keller could see the mouth of the pass, the ragged craters and rock above giving the opening the look of a yawning skull.

It was the perfect spot for an ambush or at the very least an unhappy accident, and the moment he saw it, Keller knew that if he followed Cole in, there would be no coming out.

CHAPTER 44

THE CITADEL
SIX RIVERS NATIONAL FOREST
Humboldt County, California

Three hundred yards to the east of the cleared property line, Tito slithered through the scrub, his eyes locked on the weed-covered brush pile ten yards to his front. He took his time, ignoring the buzz of insects around his ears and the sharp pain from the arrow that had creased his side. Tito's mood turned dark when his thoughts shifted back to the ambush the night before, and even now he couldn't get his mind around how a fucking smokejumper had been able to kill Ringo and maim Nash with a bow and arrow and some antiquated bear traps.

He wanted to blame the Marines for their shoddy field craft or Buck for giving away their position and then escaping, but deep down Tito knew it had been his fault for getting sucked in. The signs were all there. The lights inside the half-assed lean-to and the woodsmoke billowing from the chimney practically screamed ambush—and still he'd walked right into it.

Now Tito was a man down, and with the added complication of Buck running free, he had to plan for the possibility that he might show up and try to warn Slade. There was a part of him that hoped Buck *would* show up, because it would save Tito the aggravation of having to hunt him down and kill him later. But he doubted the man was *that* stupid. No, Buck was long gone, and now it was time to focus on the task at hand.

Pushing all thoughts of the ambush from his mind, he thought back to what Cole had told him about the former Green Beret who owned the cabin.

"His name is Thomas Grant, and he's a tough old bastard who knows these mountains like the back of his hand. You guys need to be careful with him."

Having worked with the Green Berets during his time in the army, Tito knew them to be hard and capable men who were not to be underestimated. The two remaining Marines, on the other hand, were less than impressed.

"Don't tell me you're worried about some old-ass Green Beret," Matt sneered before downing another one of the Dexedrine tablets Tito had given them. "I say we march up there, shoot them both in the face, and be done with this shit."

Beside him Nash looked up from the fresh bandage he was wrapping around his mangled ankle. "It could be John fucking Rambo waiting for me in that damn cabin, and it's still not gonna stop me from cutting the face off that son of a bitch who killed Ringo."

That the men were out for blood was to be expected. An eye for an eye, that was their code, and as much as Tito wished they were capable of handling the task, they'd already made too many mistakes.

"No more cowboy shit. We're going to do this the right way."

"Which is?"

"I'm going to recon the area and make sure we have the men and firepower needed to finish this."

Matt frowned and spread his hands wide as he looked around. "We're in the middle of nowhere. Where are you going to get more men?"

It was a good question, one Tito was still mulling over as he crawled the final few feet to the brush pile. Once in position, he wiped the sweat from his eyes with the arm of his sodden BDU top and then gently removed some of the smaller branches. The sticks were old and brittle, and some of them snapped when he tried to pull them free, the resounding crack of the dried twigs sounding loud as a gunshot on the silent mountain.

Dammit.

After a few painstaking minutes, Tito managed to remove enough of the deadfall to create a small window, and now that he could see the target, he eased his spotting scope through the hole and scanned the area.

The cabin sat in the center of the clearing. It was a concrete-block building with a wraparound porch and a heavy iron door in the middle. To the left of the house was a small brick shed and a low wall protecting a well pump and an orange generator. Both structures had cameras and motion detectors mounted to the eaves.

As far as security features went, the cameras and lights were minor annoyances compared to the much larger problem at hand. Mainly the lack of any trees, shrubs, rocks, or blades of grass within fifty yards of the buildings. Most people would have attributed the clearing to an overzealous landscaping technique. Tito, on the other hand, recognized it for what it was.

A kill zone.

His original plan was to wait for dark, then head in under night vision and take out the men inside, but with no cover or concealment to use on the approach, even the darkness wouldn't be able to protect them from the men in the cabin.

Shit.

Realizing there was only one way he was going to get anywhere close to the house, Tito carefully backed out of the brush pile and crawled back the way he'd come. When he reached the safety of the trees, he pulled out his sat phone and dialed a number from memory.

The line connected on the third ring, and a man answered in Spanish. "Yes?"

"Jorge, it's me."

"Tito, are you OK? Where is my brother?"

"Enrique's fine," he lied. "But I need a favor. How many men do you have with you at the grow site?"

"I have three guards and seven farmers, but—"

"I need all of them—anyone who can carry a rifle."

"All of them? But Tito, what about the harvest? The boss said everything has to be loaded up and ready to go by—"

"I'll handle the boss. You just get them armed and up here to my position. Do you understand?"

There was a moment of silence, and Tito was about to repeat the question when the man finally answered.

"Yes. I understand."

"Good, now grab a pen, and I'll give you the coordinates." Tito gave him the nine-digit grid from the GPS, and after the man had read them back without error, he said, "And Jorge, there is one more thing I need you to bring."

"What is it?"

"There is a wooden crate in the drying shed, the one with the Russian markings. Do you know it?"

"Yes, Tito, I know it."

"Good. I need you to bring it, and I need you to hurry. We don't have much time."

CHAPTER 45

Slade woke up in another world, the warmth of the sunlight across his face and the softness of the sheets that surrounded his battered body making him assume that he'd died and gone to heaven. Then he tried to move, and the pain came rushing back. The agony of his blistered feet and rock-torn hands was quick to convince him that he was still in the land of the living. Stifling a groan, Slade took in the room, his eyes drifting left and settling on the half-empty 500 ml IV bag hanging from the stand at the head of the bed. He followed the clear tubing down to the catheter inserted in his right arm and was reaching over to pull it out when the scrape of a chair across the floor stopped him cold.

Braving the pain that came with the movement, Slade turned his head to follow the sound to its source and found Grant sitting on the other side of the room in a rocking chair, a weathered CAR-15 resting across his lap. They studied each other for almost a minute, neither man uttering a word; then finally Grant broke the silence.

"You're the *last* person I expected to see when I woke up this morning."

Slade tried to speak, but despite the fluids being pumped into his body, his voice was gone, and all he could manage was a noncommittal grunt. Grant got to his feet and, after leaning the rifle in the corner, crossed over to Slade and lifted a cup of water from the bedside table. He adjusted the straw hanging over the rim and then lowered it to Slade's lips with a warning. "Not too much. I don't want you to get sick."

Slade ignored him and took a long gulp, the rush of the cold water down his parched throat a welcome relief. While he drank, Grant looked him over, a wry smile creasing the corner of his lips.

"Still as headstrong as ever, I see."

Slade drained the cup, and when he finally spoke, his voice was rough as thirty-grit sandpaper. "That makes two of us, old man."

Grant rolled his eyes and set the cup on the table. "So, what brings you way up here looking like you just got in a fight with a grizzly?"

"Boone," Slade said, pulling the IV line free.

"What about him?"

The words unleashed a dam of pent-up emotion, and Slade bit down on a sob, the rush of tears that welled in his eyes burning hot as battery acid. Unable to speak, all he could do was look up at Grant, watch the concerned frown crease the corner of his weathered face like lines on a topo map.

"Jake, *what* happened to Boone?"

Slade wiped a hand across his face and took a breath, a part of him embarrassed for the tears. He swallowed hard to clear the lump in the back of his throat before speaking. "Boone's dead."

Grant stepped back, the blood draining from his tanned face, leaving him white as a corpse. "He's dead? How?"

"The cartel killed him, and they won't stop until they've killed us too."

Grant stood still, then left the room and returned a few moments later with a bottle of Johnnie Walker Red and two glasses. He filled each with a healthy pour and slid one toward the edge of the table. "Here."

Slade carefully pushed himself up into a sitting position, but before he could reach for the glass, Grant had gulped his own down and carried his glass and the bottle back to the rocking chair. He dropped heavily into the seat and, after fortifying himself with another drink, set the bottle and empty glass on the floor.

"Tell me what happened."

Not sure where to start, Slade lifted the glass and took a drink. After nothing but water to drink for the last three days, the booze went down hot and settled in his empty stomach like a ball of fire. He winced and returned the glass to the table, feeling Grant eyeing him from across the room.

Figuring it best to start from the beginning, Slade cleared his throat and brought him up to speed, telling him about the frantic call from Boone, the trailer fire where he'd first met Special Agent Keller, and the plan that sent them up to the mountain.

"We were just supposed to go in and get him out, but . . ."

As he spoke, the raw emotions of that day came rushing back, the horror of finding Boone's battered body inside the cabin and the roller-coaster ride of death and destruction that followed. He tried to find the words, but when he opened his mouth, nothing came out.

"Take your time," Grant said.

Slade nodded and swallowed the rest of the booze. With the alcohol in his system, the words flowed freely, and he walked Grant through the jump and what he'd seen when he entered the cabin. Told him about Boone's last words and the promise he'd made before coming under fire by the men who'd shot Buck.

From beginning to end it took less than ten minutes for Slade to tell the entire story, but by the time he was done, it felt as if he'd been talking for hours. He fell silent and reached for the glass of Johnnie Walker, not realizing it was already empty until he tried to take a drink.

The flash of the booze had worn off, and now Slade was shaking. The guilt that came with admitting he'd left his jump partner on the mountain without knowing if he was actually dead left him feeling raw as an open wound.

"There was nothing more you could have done for your friend," Grant said, standing up and grabbing the bottle to refill his glass.

Slade wanted to believe him—hell, he *needed* to believe him—but sitting there on the bed, all he could do was drain the glass and wait for the booze to numb his gut-churning guilt.

"As for Boone," Grant sighed, "I warned him about working for the cartel."

The words were like a bolt of lightning, and Slade looked up, his guilt flashing to anger in the blink of an eye. He pushed off the bed and got to his feet, voice hard when he stepped toward Grant. "What did you just say?"

Grant stepped back, his words stumbling in the face of Slade's rage. "I—I said there was nothing you could have done—"

"No, you said that you warned Boone, which means you knew about the cartel. Knew about this fucking illegal grow they are trying to protect." Slade was shouting now, but he didn't care. "How? How did you know?"

Grant shifted from retreat to attack in an instant, the veins in his neck bulging when he stepped forward and jabbed a finger into Slade's chest. "Just who the hell do you think you are, coming in here and barking at *me* like a junkyard dog?"

If Slade had been the same scared young punk who'd first come to New Horizons all those years ago, the bass in the man's voice and the fire in his eyes would have sucked the air from his lungs. Sent him cowering to the corner. But whatever fear and weakness had defied prison had not survived the blazing heat of the fire line, and after standing toe to toe with a blazing inferno, it was going to take a hell of a lot more than words to get Slade to back down.

Still, Grant kept jabbing him in the chest, trying to impose his will. "Now, if you will just take a breath—"

Slade reached forward and slapped the bottle of Johnnie Walker from Grant's hand, sending it cartwheeling across the room. It hit the ground next to the old rocker and shattered, the spray of glass and booze splashing out into the hall. The old Green Beret looked at the mess, then back at Slade, his fist curling at his waist. "All right, if that's how you want to play it."

"Bring it on, old man."

CHAPTER 46

Grant moved with a vigor that belied his age and fired a straight right hand that put Slade immediately on the defensive. He slipped the first jab, but Grant's quick follow-up caught him on the chin. The blow starred his vision, but he shook it off and circled left, Grant taunting him as he closed the distance.

"Still dropping your guard. Guess they didn't teach you how to fight in prison." He punctuated the comment with another snapping left hand, but Slade saw it coming. He brushed it off and stepped inside Grant's guard, shoulder down and aiming for his chest.

Slade drove him into the wall and then hit him with a light jab followed by a wicked hook to the liver that dropped Grant to his knees. Standing over him, it was all Slade could do not to hit him again, but he was quick to stifle the urge and stepped back.

"I don't want to hurt you, but if you don't answer my question, I've got no problem fucking you up."

Grant held up a hand in surrender. "J-just lemme . . . c-catch my breath."

Feeling pity for the older man, Slade helped him sit up, and once his back was against the wall, he lowered himself into a crouch. Again, there was silence, and they stared at each other, Slade's leaching anger leaving him suddenly sheepish. Wondering if he'd hit him too hard.

"Are you going to make it?"

"Yeah," Grant grunted.

"Good," Slade said, hauling the man to his feet. "Now why don't you tell me what the hell is going on."

"We can talk about that over lunch," Grant said. "You hungry?"

"Yeah . . . I could eat."

"I've got some steaks that I've been marinating. Might as well eat well if the cartel is coming to kill us."

"You think that's smart? I mean, shouldn't we be watching?"

"That's what the cameras are for."

Out of all the man's considerable talents—his tracking skills and his preternatural ability to live off the land with nothing more than a knife and a flint—none compared to Grant's culinary expertise. The man was a savant in the kitchen—a true master of the grill—and after two days of eating nothing but protein bars and canned goods, the mere thought of one of Grant's steaks had Slade salivating.

His fatigue instantly forgotten, Slade followed the man down the hall and into the den. "Make yourself at home," Grant told him before ducking into the kitchen.

The room was smaller than he remembered but every bit as spartan, the old couch and sagging leather chair in front of the TV he'd never seen turned on the same ones that had been there during his time at New Horizons. While Grant pulled a pair of steaks from the fridge and tossed them on the indoor Viking grill, Slade moved to the handcrafted shelves and scanned the titles of the books they contained.

It was a warrior's library. Grant's copies of Thucydides, Herodotus, and Miyamoto Musashi's *The Book of Five Rings*, encompassing the best and worst of mankind's violent history. For his part, Slade had tried to listen and understand when Grant read these books aloud during their nightly lectures, but after spending most of the day outside sweating in the mountains, he could barely stay awake, and most of what he'd heard had gone over his head.

Back then his focus had been on forgetting his past, pretending that it no longer existed, but it wasn't until Slade found himself in prison, wondering what he was going to do with the rest of his life, that he began to understand the truth. See that life itself was a struggle. A war that had to be first fought and won in the mind before a person could break free of his past and create a new future.

After lingering at the bookcase, Slade crossed the room and studied the rows of neatly framed pictures that adorned the far wall. Besides the cabin itself, the photos were all that was left of Grant's original vision for New Horizons. The pictures were taken at the end of the *agoge*—the seventy-two-hour endurance challenge each boy who attended New Horizons had to complete prior to graduation—and like its Spartan namesake, it was designed to test everything the troubled youths had learned.

It was a battle of wills, a contest between man and nature, and for a troubled boy on the verge of manhood, it was the hardest thing Slade had ever attempted. There was no sleep. No food. Just him and the mountain. At the time it had seemed harsh, almost abusive, and he wanted to quit, but something inside of him had refused to give in. It was the same struggle he'd faced during smokejumper training, and though Slade didn't want to admit it, it was hard to ignore that stamp Grant had put on his life.

Standing there he felt a softening inside of him, an easing of the resentment he'd been harboring against the older man. But then he came to Boone's picture, and his reason for being there came rushing back.

Not this time.

Disgusted with himself, Slade whirled back to the kitchen, his voice hard when he spoke. "Tell me about Red Cap."

Grant stiffened at the stove, pausing to pull the steaks off the grill before answering. "What do you want to know?"

"Let's start with how long you've known that the cartel was running an illegal grow site right under your nose."

Grant plated the steaks and carried them into the living room, setting them on the same hand-carved table where they'd shared countless meals. "People showed up last spring with some machinery and began clearing a few acres of burnt timber around Red Cap," he began. "Since most of what they were clearing was all dead, I figured they'd been contracted by the Forest Service, and seeing as it wasn't any of my business, I didn't give it another thought."

While Grant talked, Slade gathered his knife and fork and cut into the steak, the rush of flavor that assailed him when he began to chew making it difficult to pay attention. He followed the first bite with a second, then a third, feeling the strength returning to his body.

"That's great, but what I really want to know is when you learned about the grow."

"About the time Hannah Fowler reached out to me."

The name caught him off guard, and he almost choked on the mouthful of steak. Coughing, he held up his hand and reached for the glass of water, taking a deep gulp.

"Are you OK?"

"Yeah, went down the wrong way," Slade answered, "but I'm fine now. Go ahead."

"I'd just started doing some backcountry guiding when I got a call from Fowler. She said she was working on a piece for the *LA Times* about illegal logging and asked if I'd take her to Red Cap."

"Did you take her?"

"Not at first, but then she called back and offered to pay double my usual rate."

Now it was Slade's turn to stare. "Double your rate, and you didn't think that was strange?"

"Look, this place might be small, but it's not cheap," Grant said, waving his fork in an encompassing arc. "The land taxes alone are eating me alive, and last year I had to drill a new well, so when someone offers that much cash, I'm not thinking about strange. I'm thinking about paying my bills."

"Fair enough," Slade conceded. "Then what happened?"

Grant finished the last of his steak, then leaned back in his seat. "I took her to Red Cap and let her snap some pictures . . ."

"And that's when you saw the grow?"

Grant was silent for a moment, then finally managed a nod. "Yeah . . . among other things."

"What other things?"

"Easier if I show you," Grant said, pushing away from the table. "C'mon."

Slade got to his feet and followed him down the hall to his office. They went inside, and he watched while Grant pulled one of the pictures off his wall of plaques and army memorabilia and peeled the backing free to reveal a brown envelope. Setting the picture on the desk, he squeezed the metal clasp together, opened the flap, and was about to reach inside when he stopped and handed it over to Slade.

"Here. I don't even want to look at them."

Slade took the envelope and reached inside to find a stack of glossy photos. He pulled them out and began flipping through the pictures. The first few were taken from a distance, wide-angled shots that showed figures in straw hats tending an endless field of what he assumed was marijuana, as well as a large truck and three more men standing off to the side. Slade tried to make out their faces, but they were too blurry, and he continued sorting through the photos.

"Did you take these?" he asked without looking up.

"No, that was all Fowler."

Not sure of the point, Slade kept flipping through the pictures, scanning each one before tossing it on the desk. He was almost through the stack when the photographer finally returned to the men standing in the rear of the clearing. These pictures were up close and personal, and this time he had no problem recognizing the first man in the shot.

"Boone was . . ."

"Working for the cartel," Grant finished for him.

"How could he be so stupid as to get mixed up with the Mexicans? He's lucky he survived his first brush with them back when you kicked both of us out. Why would he risk his life, and why do you have these?"

"Insurance. Turns out Boone has been living in Eureka since getting out from his last stint in prison. I knew he'd lie to me, so I asked Fowler for copies and then went to confront him."

"What did he say?"

"You know Boone—what do you think he said?" Grant demanded.

"He gave me some bullshit about him working undercover. Informing on the cartel for the DEA," he scoffed. "Do you believe that crap? The balls that kid has on him?"

Slade could because he knew it was true. He was tempted to tell Grant as much, but he held his tongue, feeling the pieces slip into place, as the other man continued.

"Anyway, I told Boone that I'd give him twenty-four hours to get the hell out of town, or I was going to turn him in."

"Turn a suspected informant in to the cops? Well, I guess that's one way to figure out if he was lying," Slade said. "Did you do it? Did you turn him in?"

"You're damn right I did, but not to the cops."

"Huh?"

Grant shook his head and began talking slow, like he was explaining something to a child. "Son, this is federal land; the cops don't have jurisdiction here."

"O-K. Then who did you call?"

"I called a buddy of mine at the Forest Service, an old Green Beret who came to the unit right before I got out."

"The Forest Service . . . shit," Slade groaned.

"What's wrong?"

"The whole reason Keller sent me and Buck in to find Boone was because he thought there was a leak in the DEA," Slade explained. "But it wasn't the DEA; it was you. You started all of this."

CHAPTER 47

Humboldt County, California

Keller tugged back on the reins and brought the bay to a halt, his eyes snapping left to the sliver of a meadow visible through the break in the rocks. His escape route identified, he waited for Cole to realize that he was no longer right behind him.

It took a second, but finally the man whirled his mustang and guided it back the way he'd come. "What's up?" Cole asked. "Is there something wrong with the horse?"

"Who were you talking to this morning?"

"You must have been dreaming," Cole said, stopping his mustang a foot from the bay, "because I've got no idea what you're talking about."

"Then let me see your sat phone."

Cole ran his tongue across his lips, thinking it over. Then he laughed. "Man, you are one paranoid dude," he said.

"Then prove me wrong and show me your phone."

The smile vanished and Keller moved to draw the Glock, but before he had a chance, Cole spurred his horse forward. The mustang slammed into his mount and drove it back toward the edge. Keller grabbed the reins and tried to turn, but the bay reared in protest, and he was left holding on for dear life.

A glance over his shoulder showed they were a mere foot from going over the edge. Keller was sure they were going over when the bay came down on all fours. There was a second of relief; then Cole pulled a pistol, and Keller was driving his heels into the horse's flanks.

The bay took off, running for the gap in the rocks just as Cole broke his first shot. The bullet snapped past his head, and Keller laid himself flat on the animal's neck as he reached back for his Glock. He managed to yank it from the holster and fire two blind shots before the bay thundered into the trees.

The first branch slapped him hard across the arm and sent the Glock spinning to the pine straw; the second caught the side of his head and nearly took it off. Bleeding now, Keller hauled back on the reins and yanked the bay to a skidding halt.

The moment it stopped, Keller was out of the saddle and yanking a Remington 870 from the scabbard. He racked the pump and was searching for a target when bullets came snapping through the trees. Keller threw himself to the ground and rolled left, desperate for cover.

Cole taunted him from the shadows, his voice echoing off the trees. "You should have retired when you had a chance, you stupid fuck, but you just couldn't help yourself, could you?"

Keep talking, asshole.

Keller scrambled behind a medium-sized pine and wiped the blood from his face, then brought the shotgun to his shoulder. Hearing a snap of a branch to his left, Keller spun, only to find the mustang walking riderless through the trees.

Where the hell is he?

The answer came from the right, a single shot that splashed against the tree and sent bark spraying into his eyes. Keeping the tree between them, Keller rolled left, wincing with every round that slapped into the trunk. In training they'd been taught to try and count the shots so they would know when a shooter was reloading, but he'd forgotten all of that when the first bullet just missed his head.

Looking south, Keller was thinking about making a run for it when he saw the flash of a man in a yellow shirt running through the undergrowth. Though he was only out in the open for a second, the man's shirt must have caught Cole's attention, because he opened fire.

The bang of the Glock off to Keller's left alerted him to Cole's position, and he continued around the tree until he could see his target standing in the open. Part of him wanted to take him down right there. No warning. No Miranda. Just pull the trigger and let the load of double-aught buckshot be the judge, jury, and executioner.

But that had never been Keller's way.

Taking a breath, he stepped out and leveled the shotgun on Cole's unprotected back. "Drop the pistol—it's over!"

Cole glanced over his shoulder and seemed unimpressed to find Keller standing there with the shotgun. "Are you going to shoot me in the back?"

"If I have to."

"That's not very noble of you, Keller," he said, slowly turning around.

"Don't make me kill you."

Cole was facing him now, the Glock held at his side. His hand was trembling, but his voice was strong and sincere when he spoke. "It doesn't have to be this way, Keller. I've got plenty of cash stashed away. I can share it with you . . . Just let me go."

"That's not happening."

The facade fell away and Cole sneered. "You always were a fucking Boy Scout."

The pistol came up fast, but Keller was already on target. He pulled the trigger and the shotgun boomed—the blast of double-aught buckshot bowling Cole off his feet.

He landed flat on his back, the massive crater where his chest used to be leaving no question that he was dead. Still, Keller moved to check the body before suddenly remembering the man in the yellow shirt.

Whirling on his heel, he took a bead on the cluster of bushes where he'd last seen the figure and called out, "I'm a DEA special agent, and unless you want to get shot, I suggest you come out. Hands in the air."

His voice echoed loudly across the clearing, but besides the flutter of wings from the startled birds, there was no response.

There was someone in there, of that he was sure, but damned if he could see him. "This is your *last* chance," he said, racking a fresh round into the shotgun.

Where his words had failed, the heavy *cha-chunk* of the 12-gauge had the desired effect, and slowly a pair of filthy hands appeared from behind a squat juniper. "Keller, it's me . . . Don't shoot."

The flow of adrenaline that had been coursing through his veins vanished at the sound of the man's voice, and he lowered the shotgun, not believing his eyes when the bedraggled man in a filthy yellow shirt and torn pants stepped into view.

"Buck? Is that you?"

"Yeah." He grimaced, his raspy voice edged with pain.

Seeing the smokejumper alive provided instant relief, and Keller lowered the shotgun and stepped forward. "Why didn't you come out when I announced myself?"

"Are you serious?" Buck snarled. "Do you have *any* idea how many people have tried to kill me since you dropped us off? And what the fuck was going on here? I wasn't going to be part of some shoot-out."

Though justified, the smokejumper's anger caught Keller off guard, and he held up his left hand in mock surrender. "Now, hold on. I know you've been through a hell of a lot, but you need to take it easy."

"Take it easy?" Buck demanded.

Keller knew it was the wrong thing to say the moment the words were off his lips, but before he could take them back, Buck had him by the throat. "You left us to die up here, you son of a bitch!"

Keller tried to shove him away, but still holding the shotgun in his right hand, he was at a distinct disadvantage. Afraid it might accidentally go off in the struggle, he tossed it away and grabbed hold of Buck's wrists, trying to break free. But the smokejumper was strong and pissed, and he held him fast.

"L-let go," Keller gasped. He didn't want to hurt the man, not after everything he'd put him through already, but with his vision beginning to blur at the edges, he didn't have a choice. Letting go of Buck's wrists, Keller slammed a fist into his gut. It was a hard blow. One that should have doubled him over, but the smokejumper merely grunted.

The hell with this.

Keller leaned back, gathered the last of his strength, and then snapped his head forward. The headbutt dropped the smokejumper to his knees, and Keller stepped back and grabbed his throat. Panting, he retrieved the shotgun and held it on the man. "Y-you try that again and I'll kill you."

Buck looked up at him with dazed eyes. "I . . . I'm sorry . . . I don't . . ."

Keller glared at him, part of him pissed, part of him feeling sorry for getting Buck into the mess. "Are you done?"

"Yeah, I'm done."

Keller offered his hand. "Here, let me help you up."

Once on his feet, Buck brushed himself off, his eyes drifting to Cole's body. "I saw what happened—he didn't give you much of a choice."

"No, he didn't."

"What are you going to do with the body?"

"I'm going to leave it for the animals," Keller said, turning and heading back the way he'd come.

"Where are you going?" Buck asked.

"I need to find my pistol *and* the horses so we can get the hell out of here."

Keller found the Glock where he'd dropped it and then went looking for their mounts. The mustang was nowhere to be seen, but he found the bay munching on the grass at the edge of the meadow and walked over slow, careful not to spook it. "It's all right. Everything's fine." The horse let him take its bridle, and Keller shoved the shotgun into its scabbard and then led the bay back to where Buck stood waiting.

He tied the reins off to a tree and then, not sure what else to do, dug into his saddlebags for the extra canteen and two meal-replacement bars.

"You hungry?" he asked.

Buck nodded, and he handed them over.

"You want to tell me what happened up there?"

"I don't remember much after the shooting started." Buck shrugged. "One minute I was running for cover; the next thing I know some asshole in a plate carrier is pulling me out from beneath a porch and shoving a gun in my face."

"Sounds like you met Tito Zavalia," Keller said. "You're lucky to be alive. He's a very dangerous man who works for the cartel."

"If he works for the cartel, then why aren't there like five SWAT teams up here ready to smoke this guy? Where's your backup?"

"I thought Cole was my backup," Keller said. "But it turns out he was a piece of shit. Worse than that, I've got no idea where Slade is or *if* he's still alive."

"He's alive, and he's gone full Chuck Norris on these guys," Buck said. "Killed one of Tito's goons with a bow and arrow."

"Wait, what? He's alive? Are you sure?" Keller asked.

"Yep, and I overheard Tito on the phone saying he was going to someplace called the Citadel."

"I need you to stay here," Keller said, moving back to his horse for his DEA-issued sat phone and map. "You can use this to call in a helicopter to pick you up."

"Yeah. That's not happening," Buck said, getting to his feet. "Slade is my jump partner, and that makes him *my* responsibility. So if you're going after him, then I'm coming too."

"You're willing to help me? You could get killed."

"Hell, I was already shot once and should have died. What do I have to lose? Killing this cartel son of a bitch will be the icing on the cake. But to do that, I'm going to need a gun."

"You think you can control yourself this time?" Keller asked.

CHAPTER 48

An hour later, Tito stood at the top of the trail, watching the bedraggled line of reinforcements trudge up the hill that led to their makeshift camp. He could smell the fear on the seven farmers, see the terror in their eyes, and knew if it hadn't been for the armed guards bringing up the rear of the sorry procession, they would have long since bolted.

Beside him Matt spat in the dirt, his voice disgusted when he spoke. "Dude, these guys are farmers, not fighters."

"They're bodies, and that's what I need them for."

Nash looked at him, not understanding. "Bodies? What the hell are you talking about?"

Tito was about to reply when the two guards lugging the rectangular wooden crate made it up the hill. "Where do you want this heavy bastard?" one of them asked.

"Over there," he said, pointing to where Nash sat cleaning his rifle.

The men nodded and carried it over. Tito waited until everyone else was up the hill and safely hidden beneath the timber before moving over to the guards. "Where is Jorge?" he asked.

"It would take a stick of dynamite to get that *cabrón* out of his trailer, but he gave me this to give to Enrique," the bigger one said, producing a bottle of tequila from his pocket and handing it over to Tito.

He took it and studied the label. "Patrón—Jorge has good taste."

Considering everything he'd been through in the last few days, Tito figured he deserved a drink, and he cracked the top. Closing his eyes, he took a long pull, savoring the taste and reminding himself how much was riding on this mission.

"So where *is* Enrique? I don't see him," the guard asked.

"He's on the other side of the target, keeping watch," Tito lied. "We'll meet up with him later. Right now, everyone needs to rest so they are ready to move."

The guard nodded and was about to walk away when Tito slapped the top back onto the bottle and pressed it into his hands. "Give this to the men."

"The men, are you sure?"

"Yes, just don't let them get too drunk."

Nash waited until the guard was out of earshot and then said, "Giving booze to the troops before a mission? If I didn't know you better, I might start thinking this was a one-way trip. And who is Jorge, by the way?"

"Enrique's brother."

"Damn, and you didn't tell the guy that he got smoked? That's cold as shit," Matt said.

Tito shrugged and moved to the crate, where he cut the packing wires with his knife and opened the lid, revealing an RPG-7. He lifted the launcher from the case and checked it over before turning his attention to the thermobaric grenades packed neatly inside.

"Looks like playtime's over, boys," Matt said with a grin. Then, growing serious, he moved closer to Tito. "But you still haven't told us about this plan of yours."

"It's like I explained—there's no cover or concealment at the top of the hill. No way to get close enough to the house to breach the door without getting picked off," Tito replied, hefting one of the 40 mm grenades from the case and sliding it into the launcher.

"So we use the RPG to breach the door from the trees," Nash said. "I get that part, but why don't we go at night?"

"Because they don't have night vision," Tito said, nodding to the farmers passing around the bottle of booze. "And they can't make it to the house if they can't see it. So we attack while it's still light, and *if* Grant and Slade survive the initial blast, they are going to be way too busy trying to hold off the human wave rushing their house to even know that we're there. Well, at least not until it's too late."

"Damn, you are one devious son of a bitch."

"I prefer *tactical*," Tito said. "Now get them ready."

He glanced at his watch, then back at the farmers, who were checking the rifles they'd brought with them. *It's almost time.*

Beside him, Nash shoved a fresh magazine into his rifle and dropped the bolt, the metallic thunk of the round being shoved into the chamber causing one of the farmers to flinch. "They're scared shitless. No way they are going to fight."

"That's why I'll put the guards behind them," Tito said, nodding to the two men with loaded AKs posted up behind the scrum. "Self-preservation is the ultimate motivator."

Nash squirmed. "This plan—using those dudes like human shields—it's the same kind of shit ISIS did in Mosul."

"What's your point?"

"I don't know. It just feels . . . wrong." Nash shrugged.

"A little late for morality, don't you think?"

The former Marine opened his mouth to speak but then thought better of it and whistled at Nash. "Let's go."

Tito watched them move up to the crest of the hill, and once they breached the top and slipped out of sight, he motioned over one of the guards. "Do you understand the plan?"

"Yes, boss," he said. "We are to keep them moving toward the *casa*. No one stops."

"That's right. Now get them ready."

While the guards got the farmers rounded up, Tito grabbed the RPG and started up the hill, his BDUs blending in with the foliage of the sparse trees he'd selected as their line of departure. Matt was already in position behind his SAW, and Nash lay beside him, pulling an extra belt of 5.56 from an olive-green ammo can.

Tito took a knee to the left of the men and lifted his binos for one last look at the battlefield. Their position was twenty yards south of the brush pile he'd used for his recon, and while it didn't share the same unobstructed field of view, he could still see the cabin. A quick scan showed everything as he'd left it.

It's time.

He gave the RPG a final check, making sure the grenade was secure in the launcher, before pulling the safety wire free. He could just hear the guards giving the farmers their final orders.

"Remember to take your safeties off, and don't start shooting until you are close enough to actually hit something. Understand?"

One or two managed a dazed nod, but most just stood there, hands shaking on the pistol grips as they stared at the open ground before them. All were silent until a broad-shouldered man on the end finally spoke up.

"This is suicide. I'm not going out there."

A second man was quick to join in, then a third—this one going so far as to throw his rifle on the ground.

"Pick it up," the guard growled. But the man wasn't having it.

"Last chance," the guard warned, drawing his suppressed pistol from its holster. "Pick it up and get back in line."

"Fuck you."

With a shrug, the guard lifted the pistol to the man's face and pulled the trigger. The bullet hit the farmer in the center of his forehead and sent the contents of his brains blasting from the back of his shattered skull. Death was instantaneous, and before his body hit the ground, the guard turned to the rest of the farmers, gun smoke trailing from the end of the suppressor.

"You can stay here and die, or you can go out there and have a chance to live. Your choice."

At first no one moved; then one of the men offered a low curse and stepped out of the trees. Like lemmings, the rest of the farmers fell into line, jaws set as they filtered from the forest and started toward the cabin. They moved slowly, hesitantly, but then one of the guards sent a burst from his AK snapping low over their heads, and they were running.

Sprinting for the cabin.

The men were halfway across the open ground and closing in fast when there was the flash of a muzzle blast from the window near the door, followed by one of the farmers pitching forward in the dirt. Instead of breaking as Nash had feared, the rest of the men kept running, their earlier fears forgotten as they gave in to the bloodlust.

They ran for another ten yards, and then just as they'd been instructed, they dropped to their stomachs and opened up. The men fired more to pull the trigger and feel the bang of the rifle than to hit their target, and back in the trees, Tito watched the proceedings through the optic mounted to the RPG. As expected, there were more misses than hits, but Tito didn't need them to kill anybody. No, he just needed them to hold the defenders in place long enough for him to finish them.

CHAPTER 49

Slade stood silent in Grant's office, his head spinning as he tried to make sense of what he'd just heard. "How could you do that to Boone, turn him in to the Forest Service while the cartel was running an active grow site in your backyard?"

"Jake, there was no way I could know what would happen," Grant said. "Believe me, if I'd had *any* idea how things would turn out, I would have *never* made that call."

Slade wanted to believe him—needed to even—but standing there in the office, all he could think about was Boone's mangled body. He'd come to the Citadel for answers, and now that he had them, Slade wished he'd never asked. In that instant he knew his world had fundamentally changed.

He stared at Grant, searching his eyes for some semblance of the man who'd taken him in—the one who'd preached personal responsibility and duty over self. But that man was gone, and in his place was a caricature of the warrior Slade had once known.

"What the hell happened to you?"

"You're going to judge me now? Is that it?" Grant demanded. "You sure as hell weren't judging me when I took you in all those years ago. Fed you and clothed you after the rest of the world had kicked you out."

Slade sneered at him. "Kicked me out—that's rich coming from you."

"Hey, you knew the rules."

"And which of your rules did I break?" Slade glowered. "Tell me—oh, that's right, you can't, because you never gave me a chance to tell you what happened."

Grant let out a pained hiss, his anger deflating like a punctured inner tube. Unable to hold Slade's gaze, he dropped his eyes to the floor and walked over to the chair by the safe. He dropped into it with a heavy sigh and took a deep breath before looking up. With his rage spent, Grant looked tired and gaunt. Beaten.

"All my life I tried to do the right thing, but you're right—I failed you. I failed you both."

Slade was about to respond when the burp of an automatic rifle cut him off, the rolling echo yanking Grant from the chair. He was up in a flash and crossing to the desk to retrieve the ruggedized tablet balanced on the edge.

Grant shook the tablet awake and began swiping through the camera feeds, his face grim when he saw the line of men rushing from the trees. "They're here." Tossing the tablet back on the desk, Grant retrieved his CAR-15 from the corner and pushed it into Slade's chest. "You remember how to shoot one of these?" he asked as he moved over to the safe and opened it.

Slade nodded, thoughts of the gunfight in the cabin rushing back into his head. "Yeah. I remember."

"Good," Grant said, handing him two loaded magazines and a holstered Beretta.

Slade clipped the pistol to his waist and then shoved one of the magazines into the rifle and pulled the charging handle to the rear. With the rifle loaded, he put the spare magazine into his back pocket and watched while Grant grabbed a scoped M14 and a bandolier of ammo from the safe.

"Let's go, son," he said, heading for the door. "We've got work to do."

Son.

There had been a time when being called *son* had meant the world to Slade. It was a sign that he finally belonged—that he'd finally been accepted. Now it was just another word. After what Grant had done to Boone, it was another lie to be piled atop all the rest.

A betrayal.

In that moment Slade had a decision to make: Would he stand and possibly die with Grant, or had he done his part? The survivor in him told Slade that he'd done his part, kept the promise he'd made to Boone, and now it was time to get the hell out of here.

You're a smokejumper, not a Green Beret.

He knew it was the right call, the smart call, but there was something inside that just wouldn't let him cut and run. He would be abandoning the man who'd been the closest thing to a father he'd ever had.

"Slade, hurry up—they're coming."

The shout followed by the bang of the rifle in the other room made him flinch, but it was the overwhelming roar of return fire that made up his mind. Realizing that Grant was as good as dead without him, Slade knew he didn't have a choice. Not anymore.

Lifting the rifle, he started down the hall, the slam of the incoming bullets into the exterior wall ringing like hail against a tin roof. A few of the rounds punched through the concrete blocks, leaving a line of neat holes inside, but it was the sudden explosion of glass from the window that sent Slade dropping to a knee.

"How many of them are out there?" Grant called out.

Staying low, Slade inched toward the window and looked out. But instead of the men in body armor he'd expected to see, the attackers were dressed in work clothes and lay in a ragged line twenty yards from the front door. They were obviously untrained, but they were well armed and firing fast, most not even bothering to aim. However, considering the size of their target and the amount of lead they were pumping out, it was hard to miss.

As much as Slade didn't want to kill these men, it was obvious they didn't share his concern, and so he dutifully lifted the rifle to his shoulder and took aim. Cursing his attackers for what they were making him do, Slade squeezed the slack from the trigger. He fired twice, the first shot high, the second low—the slap of the near miss sending a shower of dirt over his chosen target.

From the next room he could hear Grant yelling at him over the bang of his rifle. "Stop trying to scare the son of a bitch and kill him."

Taking a deep breath to calm his nerves, Slade was getting ready to take the shot when his target wiped the dirt from his eyes and swung to engage him. The man fired fast, walking the string of bullets up the wall toward the window, Slade feeling each impact.

In that instant time slowed, and it finally dawned on him that these men were there to kill him. *Well, fuck that.*

Armed with his new resolve, Slade let go of his inhibitions, and just as the incoming round found glass, he put a bullet through the center of the man's forehead.

He collapsed over his dropped rifle, and Slade was hunting for his next target when from somewhere in the distance a machine gun opened up. The operator worked the gun in short but effective bursts, alternating between the two windows. "Get down," Grant screamed from the other room. "This one has talent."

Ducking beneath the hail of lead that came spraying through the shattered window, Slade low crawled down the hall, ignoring the glass slicing across his forearms. Once past the front door and out of the immediate line of fire, he leaped to his feet and charged into the den, where he found Grant using the back of a chair as a rifle rest.

"Stay where you are until I take out this machine gun," the older man ordered, his cheek pressed tight to the buttstock. He fired once and cursed the miss; then, taking a deep breath, he lined up for another shot. "I've got you now, you son of a bi—"

But before he could pull the trigger, another burst came blasting through the window. The first two rounds hit Grant in the chest and sent him sprawling backward in a spray of glass and blood. The sight of it shocked Slade to the core, and he stood there open mouthed, unable to move until a screaming sound from somewhere outside jerked him from his trance.

What the hell is that?

Slade didn't know, but like the urgency of the fire siren back at base, the increased pitch and ear-shattering volume of whatever the sound was drew his attention to the window. A quick glance outside showed a white contrail slicing in from the far tree line, and then Slade was running toward Grant. He shouted his name, instinctively knowing that he had to get the wounded man out of the cabin, but before he could reach him, there was a massive explosion at the door, and his world disappeared beneath a rush of flame and smoke.

CHAPTER 50

Slade lay in the center of the den beneath a pile of drywall and blackened concrete that pinned him to the floor. His body felt like a continuous bruise, and his ears rang from the explosion. However, it wasn't the pain that had his attention but the weight of the debris covering his face and chest. That and the rapidly diminishing oxygen that came with each labored breath.

Breathing. It was the only thing that mattered, and to that end, Slade moved like a caged animal to free himself from the rubble of his prison. He kicked, clawed, and twisted his way out, only to find himself in an even more precarious situation.

The den was bathed in smoke, and weak flames fed on the books spilled out from the overturned shelf. Slade's first thought was of Grant, and he shouted the man's name, his voice weak compared to the continuing gunfight outside. Seeing a leg jutting out from behind the couch, he stumbled to his feet and staggered over.

He was almost there when a man came rushing in through the gaping hole that had once been the front door. Slade had just enough time to roll to his left before the man opened fire, the bullets eviscerating the books scattered on the ground. Slade scrambled into the living room and dove beneath the table, his right hand feeling for the Beretta holstered at his hip.

Slade pulled the pistol free and fired two wild shots before remembering to aim. Hunkered behind a chair, he lined up the sights on his attacker's leg and pulled the trigger. The pistol bucked in his hand, and the bullet blasted through the man's shin. The man howled and stumbled backward, his left foot sliding off one of the books.

He went down, and Slade scrambled to his knees, bracing his shoulder against the edge of the table. Pushing hard with his legs, he flipped the table onto its side and laid the pistol across the edge of the makeshift barricade as he engaged the second man who came running through the door. The pistol drills Grant had taught him came rushing back, and he quickly fired three shots—two to the body and one to the head. Earlier Slade had seen the farmers as men, but that time had passed. Now they were targets, and if they stayed to fight, he sought to see them dead.

He kept the pistol trained on the opening, waiting for any additional targets, and when none came, he shuffled over to Grant, who lay behind the couch in a pool of his own blood. "The p-picture," he wheezed.

"Don't worry about the pictures. They're in your office," Slade said.

"N-no . . . *the* picture. On the desk."

Slade had no idea what he was talking about, and considering the amount of blood lost and Grant's shallow breathing, he wasn't going to waste their remaining time worrying about it. He wished he could say that everything was going to be all right, but it was a lie. Grant was dying, and just like with Boone, all Slade could do was hold the man's hand and watch him fade away.

"Stand up, slow," a voice from behind him ordered.

Slade lifted his hands and got to his feet, a look over his shoulder showing the man who was clearly in charge grinning at him from across the den. "You're a hard man to kill, Jake Slade."

"How do you know my name?"

"I know lots of things," he said, shrugging. "One of the benefits of having friends in the right places. Now, where are those pictures the old man was talking about?"

"First, how about you tell me your name."

The man stared at him over the pistol, his hooded eyes narrowed as he thought it over. Then he shrugged. "It's Tito. Now, where are the pictures?"

"Why should I tell you if you're just going to kill me anyway?"

"Because your cooperation is what determines whether you die fast, like the old man, or slow, like Boone."

The mention of his friend unleashed a flooding anger, and Slade stepped forward, his eyes on Grant's fallen M14. "Yeah, I saw what you did to him, you son of a bitch."

"Easy," the man warned.

Pictures or no, the look in his eyes told Slade that he wouldn't hesitate to kill him right where he stood. There was a part of him that didn't care. He'd had enough of this game, and since the man was going to kill him anyway, Slade figured it best to go out on his own terms. But the rational part of his brain wanted answers. Wanted to know who was helping the man and who was still shooting outside, and it was this voice that stayed his hand.

"The pictures are in Grant's safe."

Tito nodded and took a step forward. "Turn around and put your hands on the wall."

Slade tensed as the man closed in, thinking he might have a chance to go for his pistol, but Tito was fast, and before he could make a move, the sicario clipped him on the side of the head with the pistol. The blow made him stagger back, and before he could react, the man grabbed him by the shoulders and shoved him face first into the wall.

Tito jammed the pistol into the small of Slade's back and kicked his legs wide, his free hand closing around the butt of the Beretta. He tugged the pistol from its holster with a practiced ease. Tossing the pistol across the room, he ran a hand over Slade's body and, finding him free of any additional weapons, swung him back to the door.

"Now walk."

Dripping blood from the cut on his forehead, Slade moved into the hall. He tried to get a look outside, but all he could make out through the smoke was bodies splayed out on the ground and muzzle flashes in the trees.

"In there."

He already knew the other man wasn't going to let him go anywhere near the gun safe, and once Tito guided him through the doorway and shoved him to the side, Slade made a big show of stumbling to the desk. He fell across it with a pained groan, trapping the photos from the grow site beneath his torso. Slade leaned forward, trying to reach the butt of the double-barreled shotgun hanging beneath the desk, but when he shifted his hand, it came down on the framed unit picture Grant had left on the table.

The glass cracked beneath his weight, and the sound, plus the slice of pain from the shattered glass, was quick to change his mind. Knowing he couldn't reach the shotgun, he turned his attention to the survival knife strapped beside the trauma kit on the front of Grant's pack.

Thinking him beaten, Tito continued toward the safe, and Slade watched him from the corner of his eye, waiting until he was peering inside the safe before snatching the blade from the pack and rolling off the desk.

The sudden movement caught the sicario's attention, and he spun to his left, pistol snapping up to fire. Tito managed to squeeze the trigger, but the round slammed harmlessly into the wall, and then Slade was inside his guard, grabbing him by the forearm. He shoved the man's gun hand against the jamb and shouldered the safe door shut, the well-oiled hiss of the hinges followed by the sickening crunch of bone. Tito's mouth opened in a silent scream, and he tried to jerk his hand free, but Slade held it fast.

He slashed the back of Tito's arm, severing his triceps, then reversed the blow, this time aiming to drive the blade into the killer's chest. But before the blade found flesh, Tito brought up his leg and kicked Slade hard in the stomach. The blow doubled him over and left him gasping for air, but more importantly it gave the sicario a chance to pull his mangled hand free from the door.

Cursing in Spanish, he aimed a kick at Slade's head, but he saw it coming and managed to shift left. His attacker's boot hit him in the shoulder, the radiating pain and screaming nerve endings causing his hand to open and the blade to clatter to the floor. He bent to retrieve it, but no sooner had his fingers grazed the hilt than Tito drove a knee into his face.

The impact whitewashed his vision, and Slade crumbled, the back of his head bouncing off the floor. He tried to shake it away and get to his feet, but before he had a chance, the assassin was on top of him, his hands closing tight around Slade's throat.

CHAPTER 51

Tito batted away Slade's hands and cranked down on his throat, cursing himself for being so stupid as to turn his back on the smokejumper. *What the hell were you thinking?* He knew the answer: he'd gotten sloppy, let his mind stray from the job, and his throbbing hand and the slash wound across the back of his left arm were the price.

Not that it mattered. He could already feel the man weakening beneath him.

That's right, die.

He squeezed as hard as his injured arm would let him, knowing that he was only seconds away from victory, before a shotgun boomed somewhere outside the house. The rolling thunder was followed by the rapid-fire pops of a pistol and Matt's frantic voice over the radio.

"Nash, he's on your left . . . He's—"

Then there was silence.

Tito didn't remember easing up or reaching for the radio clipped to his waist, but the next thing he knew, Slade was squirming in his grip. He managed to worm a right hand beneath the choke, the momentary ease of the grip enough to bring a rush of color back to his pallid skin. Then he was reaching up for Tito's arm. In an instant Tito guessed his play, and twisting his weight onto his right leg, he began hammering the smokejumper in the face with his elbow.

He landed three solid blows, each of them powerful enough to have KO'd a lesser man, but despite the ruptured skin and the splash of blood across his face, Slade was still alive. Giving up on the elbow, Tito increased the pressure of the choke, squeezing the side of the man's neck until his fingers were bone white.

"Why won't you die, you *hijo de puta*—you son of a bitch."

The man's only reply was a strangled "fuck you" from the back of his throat, and then he began probing for the ragged gash on the back of Tito's arm. Frantic now, Tito dropped his torso across the man's face and tried to smother him—crush his face with his body weight—but there was no breaking Slade's will.

Knowing there was no way to escape the pain about to come without letting go of his victim's throat, Tito gritted his teeth, promising himself that he could take whatever the man dished out.

He was wrong.

The agony he experienced when Slade's fingers found his ruined flesh hit like a Taser shot, and his back arched, the crack of his spine followed by a rush of sweat. Tito bit down on the scream forming at the back of his throat and tried to hang on, but the pain was white hot and all-consuming.

Unable to take it any longer, he released the choke and tried to untangle himself, but the smokejumper held on with an iron grip. Squeezing his mangled hand into a caricature of a fist, Tito punched Slade in the back of the head, howling with each blow. Finally, the man let go, and Tito tore himself free, throwing himself for his fallen pistol while Slade slithered for the knife. Tito grabbed for the gun, but his shattered hand was unable to close around the grip.

Shit.

A shift of the hips brought his left arm into play, and he scooped the Glock from the floor and swung it toward his target just as Slade came into his field of view. Tito saw the knife in the other man's hand through the Trijicon mounted atop the Glock, but he ignored it, waiting until the dot was on Slade's chest.

"Now you die."

He pulled the trigger and the pistol bucked in his hand, the flash of blood and the grunt from the smokejumper telling him he'd hit his target. For most men one shot would have been enough, but clearly not for Slade. He had shown himself a hard man to kill, and as the blade came slashing past his face, Tito rolled right and came up on one knee, ready to dump the rest of the magazine into his target. But when he lifted his arm to fire, both the pistol and the hand that had been holding it were gone.

His mind clouded by the onset of shock, there was no pain, only confusion as Tito studied the stump where his hand had been. Frowning, he followed the blood trail across the room, his faltering vision lingering on the severed hand still holding the Glock in the center of the room before shifting to Slade.

The smokejumper sat on the far side of the room, his head down as he studied the blood spreading from the neat hole punched in his shirt. Then he looked up, his eyes cold as he lifted the knife. "Grant always used to talk about how this thing was sharp enough to give a man a close shave—guess he wasn't kidding."

"L-lots of good it did him," Tito coughed, his body growing colder by the second, "or *you* for that matter."

"You mean *this* little scratch?" Slade said, fingering the hole on the left side of his shirt. "Well, it might keep me off the jump list for a few weeks, but it won't stop me from delivering these pictures to the right people."

Tito couldn't help but smile. "You really have no idea what you've gotten yourself into. No clue what is really going on, do you?"

"Why don't you enlighten me."

"The cartel has people everywhere, eyes and ears in *every* department. We own cops, politicians, and judges. We even . . ." He paused, momentarily overcome by the pain of his severed hand, but he kept on, determined to let this man know what he was still up against. "We even have men in the Forest Service."

"Who? Who do you have in the Forest Service?" Slade demanded.

The anger he saw in the man's eyes warmed him from the inside, and Tito let out a mocking laugh. "I'd rather keep you guessing. Wondering who the man next to you on the fire line is *really* working for."

"You're a liar."

"Am I, or are you just that naive?" Tito chuckled.

He could see the uncertainty in Slade's eyes and hear it in his voice when he spoke. "They wouldn't do that. Not for drugs."

"You think this is about drugs?" Tito shook his head. "This is about money, you fool. Greed. That is America's drug of choice and the reason you will never beat us."

Tito could feel himself fading now, his body as cold as if he were lying on a block of ice, but it didn't matter. He might be dying, but he could tell by the look on Slade's face that he was taking the man's idealism with him. "You may have killed me, but you've still lost. I'd suggest you get used to it because it's never going to change."

"That's where you're wrong," Slade said, the steel returning to his eyes. "Those pictures Fowler took might not be enough to win the war, but I can't imagine your bosses back in Mexico are going to be happy to see them in the media. Either way, you're dead, and I doubt they give consolation prizes in hell."

CHAPTER 52

THE CITADEL
SIX RIVERS NATIONAL FOREST
Humboldt County, California

Outside the cabin, Keller shoved the last of his shells into the Remington and took a deep breath. He brought the shotgun up to the high ready and scanned the bodies littering the ground around the front of the house, searching for Buck.

The last he'd seen of the man was just after the GPS strapped to Keller's wrist had alerted him to their proximity to the cabin. After the long climb up the trail, the bay had been smoked, its flanks heaving from having carried the two men up the ridge. Keller knew it needed water, but the ground was dry and scrub ridden, and with no time to look for a creek, all he could do was give the animal an apologetic pat. "Sorry, fella."

Beside him, Buck studied the Glock 26 Keller had given him. The pistol was his backup and much smaller than the Glock 17 on his hip, a fact Buck was quick to notice. "You're shitting me, right?"

"Hey, it's better than nothing," Keller said, filling his pockets from the mixed bag of double-aught buckshot and rifle slugs Cole had given him before setting out. Once loaded up, he slung the shotgun over his shoulder and started up the rocky incline that would take them to the Citadel.

They were halfway up when they heard the first shots and shouts from the trees. The gunfight unfolded like a conversation between lost lovers, the first shots tentative—almost shy. Then the shooters found their voice, and the intensity of the firefight rose to a feverish pitch—the roar of hate reminding Keller of his time in Mexico, hunting the cartel. Fueled by the angry bark of the rifles and the wall of sound rolling through the trees, Keller dug deep and with a final pull managed to drag Buck over the edge. Then he was on his feet, the shotgun up and ready.

"Try to keep up."

He hadn't realized how close they were to the action until Keller heard the RPG go off, the resulting concussion shaking the needles from the pines. "This is a bad idea," Buck yelled.

Not bothering with a response, Keller burst from cover. His first target was the man lugging the machine gun, and Keller fired on the move, the heavy slug slamming into the man's back. The impact shoved him forward, yet he kept to his feet, his face a pain-filled mask as he twisted and tried to bring the SAW to bear.

But Keller was already pressing the trigger for the second shot, and this one caught him in the side. The slug had no problem punching through the unprotected part of the vest, and the man went down, belted ammo spilling across the ground.

Alerted by the boom of the shotgun, one of the guards turned to see what was going on, his eyes wide when he saw Keller running up their back trail. He shouted a warning and tried to engage him but died without ever pulling the trigger. Slinging the shotgun over his chest, Keller scooped up the dead man's SAW, the crack of Buck's pistol behind telling him the man was well in the fight.

Good.

Hefting the machine gun, Keller ran toward the cabin just as the first men slipped through the door. While they breached the house, the rest of the ragtag army tried to move away, but a shout from the remaining guard kept them in place.

"You move, you die."

Keller had other ideas, and he brought the SAW up to his hip and mashed down on the trigger. The machine gun writhed like a snake in his hand, but he held it steady, and after the first burst he paused to shout a warning: "Get the hell out of here if you want to live."

"Stay where you are," the guard shouted as he turned to face Keller. *Well, can't say I didn't try.*

He held down the trigger and watched the tracers sail high of his target. Adjusting the muzzle until the burn of the tracers found flesh, he worked it across the men like a scythe. The wall of lead cut two of the men down, but before he could engage the third, a man in faded body armor began shooting at him from the shed. Swinging the barrel toward him, Keller fired off the rest of the belt, then tossed the empty machine gun to the ground and grabbed his shotgun.

Flanking right, he angled for the side of the cabin, blasting the final man off his feet. He slid into cover and fired his last shot just as the man behind the shed sent half a magazine snapping over his head. Darting out of the line of fire, Keller dug a handful of shells from his pocket and fumbled them into the breech, the rattle of gunfire getting closer as the man moved in on his position.

Realizing two were all he had time to load, Keller took a deep breath and waited for the other gun to go silent before stepping out. Shotgun up, he raced toward the low wall, hoping to catch the shooter in a reload, but he quickly came under fire.

Shit.

He fired blind, the spray of double-aught buckshot against the side of the shed pushing the shooter back. *I've got you now.* Keller worked the pump to chamber another shell, but the husk jammed in the ejection port. Throwing the shotgun to the ground, he reached for the Glock at his hip, but no sooner had his hand closed around the grip than his target stepped out from cover.

After the hell Keller had survived in Mexico, he'd been sure that he'd earned the right to die in bed. Old and long since forgotten by everyone at the DEA but having had enough time to make it up to Emily and, if he was lucky, maybe spend his golden years bouncing a few grandkids on his knee. Dying on some godforsaken mountain in California had never been part of the plan, but the confident smile he saw spreading across the man's face told a different story—one that ended with a flag-draped coffin and a twenty-one-gun salute. Still, if

Keller was going down, he wanted his family to know that he'd gone out in a hail of lead.

He snarled a curse at the man, fully expecting to feel the burn of the big 7.62 tearing into his flesh, but instead of the roar of the AK, it was the dry snap of a Glock that came echoing from behind. Keller looked around in time to see Buck step out from behind the shed, the tiny Glock smoking in his hands.

"I guess size really doesn't matter," the smokejumper said.

Keller let out the breath he hadn't realized he'd been holding and felt his muscles sag. The relief was overwhelming, but before he had a chance to enjoy it, there was the muted bang of a pistol from inside the cabin. The single shot was followed by an icy silence and the cold realization that Keller had failed yet again.

CHAPTER 53

Slade shuffled over to the desk and bent down to retrieve Grant's hiking bag. He tried to pick it up, but his left arm refused to work. The lack of mobility combined with the rapidly spreading bloodstain across the front of his shirt made Slade wonder about the severity of his wound.

It hadn't hurt when Tito shot him, and when he'd gotten to his feet, his primary concern had been how he was going to get off the mountain. But with the pain now pumping full bore through his body, Slade knew that was the least of his worries. Giving up on lifting the bag, he tugged the trauma kit free and dumped everything out onto the table. He tried to undo his shirt, but the blood-slicked buttons proved hard to work with only one hand, and Slade was forced to rip it open.

Though the cloth of his shirt had shown a clean hole, the wound he found below was *anything* but neat. He'd been hit high in the chest, about an inch and a half above his left nipple, and though Slade wasn't a doctor, he knew enough about human anatomy to realize that it should have killed him. In fact, the *only* reason he wasn't splayed out next to Tito on the floor was because the sicario had shot him at an angle.

Already feeling shaky from the blood loss, Slade pawed through the medical supplies until he found an olive-green packet of combat gauze. He ripped it open with his teeth and packed it into the ragged exit wound beneath his armpit. The hemostatic agent went to work with a chemical burn that made him weak in the knees, and fearing he was going to pass out, Slade dropped into the desk chair.

The QuikClot slowed the bleeding, but it took another roll of gauze and the pressure of an ACE bandage wrapped over the wound to get it all the way stopped, and by the time he was done, all he wanted to do was sleep. Recognizing the early signs of shock, he fought the urge and was trying to figure out his next move when he heard a voice come booming down that hall.

"Slade . . . are you alive? Where are you, man?"

Keller?

"I'm in here," he shouted.

Even raising his voice hurt like hell, but the slap of footsteps down the hallway and the sight of Keller stepping through the door were quick to ease his pain.

"Buck, he's in here," Keller shouted, the relief on his face shifting to worry when he saw the bloody shirt on the ground and the bandage wrapped around Slade's chest.

"I'd like to say it looks worse than it is, but I'd be lying." Slade grimaced. "Still, considering the circumstances, it's good to see you guys," he said as Buck appeared in the doorway. "Please tell me you've got a medevac on the way."

"I'm sure that can be arranged," Keller said, pulling his sat phone from his pocket. "Probably should advise them about Cole while I'm at it."

"What happened to Cole?" Slade asked.

"Keller killed him," Buck said.

Slade stared at him, not sure if it was a joke. "Wait . . . what?"

"He was working with the cartel," Keller said, his fingers flying over the keys. "Just to be clear, I didn't want to shoot him. I was hoping we could flip him and get him to turn on the cartel. Now with Boone dead, we've got nothing for the grand jury on Monday."

"That's what you think," Slade said. With a grunt, he leaned forward and shoved the manila envelope toward the DEA agent, a jagged bit of glass from the shattered picture frame below jabbing into his finger.

Keller grabbed the envelope and opened the flap, then began flipping through the photos. "That's Daniel Cortez and Boone at the grow site. Where did you get these?"

"Fowler took them," Slade said. "There's your proof that Cortez knows about the grow site. That, combined with Fowler's murder and everything that happened here, should give you something to work with."

"You're right—this is good," Keller said, returning the photos to the envelope. "There's a chance we may be able to salvage something from this shitshow after all. But first we need to get out of here. I've got to go outside; all this concrete is blocking my signal."

"Afraid I can't let that happen," Buck said, stepping forward, the small pistol in his hands leveled at Keller's chest.

"Buck, what the hell are you—"

"Shut the hell up, Slade," he snapped, his eyes never leaving Keller. "I'm going to need those pictures *and* your phone."

"That's not going to happen," Keller replied with steel in his voice.

Slade stared at his team leader, the scene before him unfolding like a fever dream. He tried to get to his feet, put a stop to whatever madness had gripped the man. "Buck, put the gun down, man," he said, struggling to stand. "You don't want to do this."

"He's right," Keller said. "Whatever you *think* you're doing, there's a better way."

"This is your fault, Slade," Buck sneered.

"My fault? How in the hell is—"

"Shut the hell up!" he snapped, swinging the pistol toward Slade. "If you hadn't come back here with your pathetic Little Orphan Annie spiel, Grant would have kept his mouth shut and let me handle this. It would all be taken care of, and he'd still be alive. But you had to be the hero."

Slade had no idea what he was talking about, but a flick of his eyes showed Keller slowly reaching for his Glock. *I've got to keep him talking.*

"Buck . . . none of this makes any sense. Why are you doing this?"

"Don't play stupid with me. You know *exactly* what's going on. I knew it the moment I stepped in here and saw that fucking picture on the desk," Buck accused, jabbing the Glock at the shattered picture frame on the desk.

The picture.

Suddenly Grant's words came crashing home, and Slade tugged the photograph from the frame. The penciled inscription on the back read *Jungle Training: Mexico 1997*—Grant's last year of service—and when he flipped it over, he found himself staring at six gaunt men in camo fatigues and sweat-stained boonie caps. It was hard to make out their faces beneath the smeared masks of greasepaint, but after a moment of searching, Slade picked out Grant standing tall in the back row. Then his eyes dropped to the front and saw a younger version of Buck staring back at him.

He looked up, his mind spinning, the rush of rage choking his words. "You . . . you did this?"

Before Buck could reply, the plastic snap of a pistol clearing Kydex cut the words short, and he pivoted right. He caught Keller middraw and dropped him with a double tap to the chest that sent the special agent crumpling forward on his face. Buck studied him for a moment, making sure he was staying down, before moving to retrieve the envelope that had fallen to the floor.

"You would have thought he'd have learned after that dumbass Marine almost burned him down outside," he muttered to himself. "Guess you just can't fix stupid."

Then he turned the pistol on Slade. "Sorry, I got distracted. What were we talking about?"

CHAPTER 54

THE CITADEL

SIX RIVERS NATIONAL FOREST

Humboldt County, California

From behind the desk Slade glared at Buck, his ears ringing from the sound of gunshots off the concrete wall. "You didn't have to kill him, you piece of shit."

"Yeah, I'm sure he would have just let me walk out of here with these," he said, shaking the envelope containing the photos. "Tell me something, Slade. Do you ever get tired of being so damn self-righteous?"

"At least I stand for something. You're no better than him," Slade said, nodding toward Tito's body. "You disgust me."

"Careful now," Buck said, waggling the gun at him. "You are coming dangerously close to hurting my feelings, and here I was thinking we were friends."

As much as he wished that he could deny it, Slade had begun to think of Buck as a friend, or at the very least someone he could trust. Which was why he'd put his own life on the line to save the man's ass from Tito and his bloodthirsty Marines. Sitting there staring at the man, Slade found himself wondering if there was anyone in this world who wouldn't lie or betray him. Considering all the lies and manipulation that marked his relationships with Boone and Grant, it shouldn't have come as a surprise that Buck would betray him too, but it had.

And it hurt, but he'd deal with the pain if he survived. Right now, all Slade wanted was the truth. "Just tell me why?"

"Well, that's a complicated question, and right now I'm kind of short on time," Buck said. "Even in the mountains you can't go around shooting off RPGs and expect no one is going to notice."

"Give me the CliffsNotes version," Slade demanded.

Buck studied him over the pistol sights and then looked down at his watch. "I've been working this deal for a year now, so I guess a few more minutes isn't going to hurt. Before the war on terror, the army was using Special Forces to train our allies, which is how I ended up spending so much time south of the border. We'd heard rumors that the cartel was recruiting men with a certain skill set—"

"What kind of skill set?" Slade interrupted.

"They were looking for guys who knew how to operate behind enemy lines. Silent professionals who were used to working alone and trained to keep things compartmentalized."

"Like Green Berets."

"Well, they sure as hell weren't looking for SEALs," Buck said, grinning. "Those dudes would have taken the cash and then turned around and written a book about it."

Slade didn't get the joke but laughed anyway, knowing that he had to keep Buck talking. "So then what happened?"

"At the time I didn't think much of it, but a few years after I started with the Forest Service, one of their lawyers reached out and asked if I wanted to make some easy money."

"One phone call, that's all it took?" Slade asked, unable to keep the skepticism out of his voice.

"Well, it was a lot of money, and I didn't have to do anything but keep my eyes and ears open, let him know if anyone started talking about a grow site."

"So you were working for Cole?"

"Working for that asshole?" Buck laughed. "No, man, Cole was working for me. So was Boone before Keller busted him moving a load."

"Wait, how is that possible?"

"Because I never let my right hand know what the left was doing."

"Compartmentalization," Slade said.

"That's right, but you want to know what the real kicker is?" Buck asked, leaning in conspiratorially. "None of this shit would have happened if Walt had just left me in ops."

"I don't understand."

"When the cartel found out that Boone was snitching, they said they'd give me two hundred grand to take him out. I had everything planned. I even managed to clone Keller's phone to get him to meet me at the Laguna Inn, but the day before the hit, Walt put me back on the jump list. Those local clowns screwed things up, and the rest is history." Buck finished the story with a shake of his head.

"Man, you had it *all* figured out," Slade said, dropping his hand down to his lap. "And you almost got away with it."

"What the hell do you mean, *almost*?" Buck frowned. "The *only* thing between me and the thirty-five footer waiting for me down in Puerto Vallarta is this bullet I'm about to put through your forehead."

"Since we're friends, I'll give you one chance to give up," Slade said, his fingers closing around the butt of the sawed-off shotgun mounted beneath the desk. "Put the pistol on the floor. Last chance."

"I think I'll pass," Buck snorted, the Glock already coming up to fire.

Slade considered giving the man a final warning, but knowing it wouldn't matter, he twisted the shotgun to the left and squeezed the trigger. The sawed-off roared like a howitzer, the wall of lead shot slamming into Buck's chest with enough force to shove him out the door and into the far wall—dead before his body even touched the ground.

Waving away the smoke, Slade pushed himself out of the chair and knelt beside Keller. He gave the man a shake, the feel of the Kevlar beneath his hand and the pained groan that came when Keller rolled onto his back providing instant relief.

"What in the hell was that? A grenade?" Keller asked.

"Grant's burglar alarm," Slade said.

Keller took his time getting to his feet, his eyes locked on Buck's body. "You didn't have a choice. You know that, right?"

"Yeah," Slade said. "But damn, it makes me sick."

"I hear you," Keller said, retrieving his sat phone from the floor. "You need me to carry you out?"

"I think I can make it to the porch," Slade said.

"Then let's get the hell out of here."

EPILOGUE

Two Months Later

Jake Slade jogged through the scrub, his lungs burning in the crisp morning air. The trail led him south, across the dry foothills, before dipping down into a shallow, gravel-filled wash. Tito's bullet had done more damage than he'd known, and according to the trauma surgeon at Saint Joseph, if it hadn't been for the medics aboard the Forest Service helicopter Keller had called in, Slade probably would have lost the arm.

It had taken two surgeries to repair the ligament and tissue damage, and even then, the doctors weren't sure if he'd ever regain full mobility. But worse than the pain that came with the physical therapy was the agony that came with being taken off the jump list.

For someone used to being active, being forced to sit on the sidelines while the rest of the team was out jumping fire had been tantamount to torture. Determined to regain his place on the team, Slade had spent most of the time lifting weights or out running. But as he was quick to learn, there were only so many hours you could waste in the gym.

The rest were spent thinking.

Relieving his near-death experience in the mountains and the path that had led him there.

Having spent most of his adult life chasing a dream and the hopes of a better future, Slade had never taken the time to deal with his past.

Now he had no choice, and while his body was quick to come around, it took a lot longer to heal the soul.

Pushing the thoughts from his mind, Slade charged up the hill, ignoring the lactic burn in his legs. From the apex he could see the jump tower and the huddled outlines of the hangars a quarter mile away. A glance at his watch showed that he was on pace to meet the time standard for getting back on the jump list, and he thundered down the back side of the hill.

Running hard, he raced across the flats and sailed through the gates, where Walt stood holding a clipboard and stopwatch. Slade slowed to a walk and worked on catching his breath before circling back.

"Well?"

"Ten minutes flat," Walt said. "Welcome back."

Hell yeah.

While Walt headed inside to add him to the jump list, Slade finished his cooldown and was thinking about a shower when Keller's black Impala came sliding through the gate. Grinning, Slade walked over, and when the man got out, he offered his hand.

"So much for retirement."

"The DEA just couldn't let me go," Keller said.

"I take it you got the promotion?"

"That's right. You're talking to the newly appointed special agent in charge of the San Francisco office," Keller said.

"Well, it's about time."

"Yeah, thanks to you," Keller said as he pulled an envelope from his jacket pocket and handed it over to Slade.

He opened it, his eyes going wide when he saw the California state seal embossed on the top. "What in the hell is this?"

"A full pardon, fresh from the governor's desk," Keller said. "Think of it as his way of saying thank you for kicking the Jalisco Cartel out of Northern California."

Slade looked up at him. "So they got the grow? It's over?"

"That's right. And now you've got options if you decide to leave this dangerous-ass job behind."

"Actually, I've been thinking about that."

"Really?"

"Yeah, a few weeks ago I got a letter from Grant's lawyer. Turns out he had an insurance policy on the Citadel and named me the sole beneficiary."

Keller whistled. "I bet that's a nice chunk of change. What are you going to do with the dough?"

"I was thinking that once fire season is over, I might use the money to rebuild the place. You know, carry on Grant's legacy. Maybe help some knucklehead kids avoid the mistakes that I made."

"And here I was thinking all you cared about was clearing your record," Keller said.

The look Slade saw in the older man's eyes made him suddenly uncomfortable, and Slade felt the blood rushing to his face. Embarrassed, he was searching for a way to change the subject when the wail of the fire siren over the airfield came to his rescue.

"Duty calls," he said, extending his hand to Keller for a final shake.

"Yeah, take care of yourself, kid."

"You too."

Leaving Keller at the car, Slade turned and ran toward the pack shed. He was the first to arrive, and after stowing the envelope in his locker, he was pulling on his jumpsuit when Walt walked in.

"What do we have?" he asked.

"A lightning strike started a big burn in the Willamette National Forest," Walt said. "Dispatch says she's a nasty one—*not* exactly the kind of fire you want on your first day back."

"I'm ready," Slade said, zipping up his suit.

"Are you sure?"

"Yeah. I was born ready."

ACKNOWLEDGMENTS

First and foremost, I would like to thank Jesus Christ, my Lord and Savior, for his grace and unfailing love. I would also like to thank the amazing Jennifer Fisher and everyone at Blackstone. From a research point of view, *Burn Out* has been my most challenging book to date. It was also a labor of love—one I hope highlights the dangers and sacrifices made by the brave men and women of the wildland firefighting community. That said, you guys aren't exactly a talkative bunch, so please forgive any creative license on my part. This is, after all, fiction.